Table of Contents

Monster Road Trip

EDITED BY DEANNA KNIPPLING AND JAMIE FERGUSON

Featuring stories by:

RON COLLINS • SHANNON LAWRENCE • MARK LESLIE
JEFF WOOD • REBECCA HODGKINS • MEYARI MCFARLAND • JASON DIAS
SHARON KAE REAMER • JAMIE FERGUSON • DEANNA KNIPPLING

BOROGROVE PRESS · COLORADO

Monster Road Trip

Introduction

The Editors

In which editors DeAnna Knippling and Jamie Ferguson embark on a journey to bring you more monsters!

Welcome to the second issue of Amazing Monster Tales, *Monster Road Trip*!

This issue's theme is, unsurprisingly, monsters and road trips! There's a monster rampaging up the Atlantic seaboard, and a group of intrepid bigfoot hunters on the usual quest—but with a twist. We've got a werewolf on a train, an assortment of werewolves who aren't on trains, and a bunch of disturbingly creepy human-like critters with haint blue eyes. Medusa, the Norse dwarf Andvari, and a few other ancients make an appearance. There are monsters chasing cars, monsters driving cars, and a dragon who enjoys riding in convertibles while extending his wings to feel the air rush by—because who wouldn't? Some of the monsters are friendly, some are cranky, and some just plain want to eat you—or step on you, as they proceed toward mysterious goals only a monster could understand.

Our Cover Artist

Paul Roman Martinez designed another fantastic cover for us, with nothing but the series theme and the title of this issue to go by. We wanted to give him room to come up with something cool and creative, and boy, did he ever! We recommend both his art, at *PaulRomanMartinez.tumblr.com*, and his board game *Adventures of the 19XX*, for which he also writes and illustrates graphic novels.

Our Stories

Our collection begins with "Tailgating," by Shannon Lawrence. Sarah and her friend Layla are driving north on the Pacific Coast Highway when Sarah sees an animal leaping through the trees on the side of the road…and it's clearly following them. To make matters worse, whoever is driving the car behind them *also* appears to be following them, the car driving so close that its headlights shine into their rear window. And on top of all that, they're running out of gas…

Sibling werewolves Mimi, Cece, and their adopted baby brother—a runt of a dragon—sneak out and take the family convertible for an evening spin along I-5 in Meyari McFarland's "Dandelion Rider." Mimi is still trying to recover from a horrible, and false, accusation that everyone—even their *parents*—believe. Who else shows up at the party, but her accuser?

Jeff Wood's "Exit Ramp" takes us to a world that used to be happy and fun, until Jimmy's dad lost his job. Now the family is on their way to Mesa, Arizona, where—if all goes well—Jimmy's dad will once again be gainfully employed. But when their car's tire blows out, they pull off on an exit ramp and find themselves stuck for the night in a place full of small, oddly shaped factories, where the mechanics at the garage have weird, underwater-blue eyes…

A trucker driving through the Nevada desert picks up a hitchhiker in "Wiggle-Wiggle, Shake-Shake," by Rebecca Hodgkins. Something about the kid seems a bit off, so the trucker stops at a diner he knows, thinking at least the kid would be safe if left there. But there's a lot more going on out in the desert than he ever could have imagined.

In Mark Leslie's "Stowe Away," Michael needs to get to Stowe, Vermont, to help his dearest friend—and it's imperative that he arrive before sunset, when the full moon will turn him into a wolf. He boards a train and meets someone else who desperately needs his help as well. But the day is growing long, and Michael is running out of time...

Ron Collins takes us on a winding path of destruction by a wonderfully vile beast in "Trail of Fears." A beast born from the foulness created by humanity, the beast would say, if it could. And some things, once birthed, cannot be killed.

Bean, a goblin who's spent most of his life below ground, agrees to drive his brilliant but transportationally-challenged cousin Heinrich across the country in Jamie Ferguson's "Goblin Road Trip." Heinrich plans to propose to his estranged girlfriend, who moved to Colorado after she got frustrated with his inability to remember, well, anything. Will she say yes to Heinrich's proposal? Will he remember where the ring is? Will the cousins even make it to their destination at all?

This collection wouldn't be complete without people searching for Bigfoot! Or is that bigfeet? "The Squatchers," by Jason Dias, takes us to the mountains with a team of YouTubers who make their living searching for sasquatch—in spite of the fact that they never seem to actually find any.

"The Plague Comet," by editor DeAnna Knippling, is set in 1957, when a comet carrying a zombie plague struck, and everything went to hell. But worse things can happen to you in the Nevada desert than getting infected by zombie plague rays...

Roland Eckstein, a couple of his friends, and a group of ancient monsters embark on a road trip across Europe in Sharon Kae Reamer's "Alexander's Gate." Their goal: a mythical, monster-populated secret hideaway, somewhere east of Turkey and north of Iran. Even Grendel agrees not to eat any humans on the trip, not even humans who happen to be Danish. Things are going well until they make a small detour to pick up Medusa and her companion—and everything gets much more complicated than Roland could have possibly imagined.

We had a lot of fun putting this collection together. There are serious stories, and funny ones...scary monsters, noble monsters, and even monsters in love! We hope you enjoy reading these stories. And the next time you're out on the highway and catch a glimpse of someone in the next car who looks a bit odd, remember that sometimes monsters take off their disguises...

—Jamie Ferguson

Tailgating

Shannon Lawrence

The car slid into the forest on the Pacific Coast Highway, occasional winks from the moon visible above the canopy.

Inside the car, the travelers grew quiet, the hush from outside contagious. This part of the highway was sheltered, with far fewer businesses open. They'd picked dinner up from a questionable gas station convenience store, which now appeared to have been the final bastion of civilization.

"Maybe we should be looking for a picnic table or rest stop," Sarah said.

"I really want to get to Newport tonight," Layla said. "I figured we'd eat in the car."

Sarah sighed, scratching her arm. Her skin felt tight and dry. "Okay." She turned up the heat.

"Besides, it's dark now that we're in the trees. In here we have music! And no bugs."

They drove on in silence, Sarah noting the shuttered old businesses they passed. The road curved here and there, making for a peaceful drive. She'd be lucky to stay awake to Newport. Good thing they'd decided not to try for Portland tonight.

Layla flexed her fingers on the steering wheel. They'd been on the road for seven hours, with her driving the last three.

"You ready for me to drive?" Sarah asked.

"No, I'm good. Just working out the stiffness."

Sarah's gaze drifted to the trees beside them, where she noticed something high in the branches. She only got a quick glance, all glowing eyes and bulky fur, but it looked to be an animal. "Did you see that? Are there wolves in Oregon? I thought I saw something in the woods as we passed, but it was in a tree. Do wolves climb trees?"

Layla laughed. "Not that I remember. Bears do."

"Could have been a bear." *Or something worse.* Sarah reached over and turned the radio up, trying to convince herself she'd imagined it. She took her seatbelt off and twisted around in her seat to fish through the bags for their dinner. When she'd arranged it all on two plates, she frowned. "How are you going to eat this?"

"Put the plate in my lap. I'll eat it from there."

Sarah carefully balanced the plate on Layla's thigh, shoving a fork into the potato salad so it wouldn't fall. She popped open a can of Coke and placed it in the cup holder for Layla. The luscious smell of fried chicken filled the car, making her mouth water. She picked up the drumstick and took a bite, savoring the salty crispness.

The trees grew closer together now, darkness smothering the road. Layla turned on the brights, which illuminated the trees nearest the road. Shadows danced as the lights moved over the trunks. One shadow in particular appeared to leap with a pattern of its own, defying the headlights.

Sarah squinted at it, heart pounding. It kept pace with the car, sometimes falling slightly behind, sometimes getting ahead, but always near. The headlights didn't reach high enough for her to see what it might be.

"Okay, there's something out there," Sarah said, squeezing Layla's arm. "In the trees. That's no bear."

"What are you talking about?" Layla leaned forward to look out past Sarah, eyes darting between the trees they passed and the road ahead. "I don't see anything."

"It's jumping through the trees!"

Layla sighed. "Maybe you were right about taking a break. We need to get out and walk around. I'll stop at the next rest stop."

"I'm not hallucinating."

"I'm not saying you are. But we're both tired and could use a rest."

Silence fell between them. Sarah looked out her window, body tense, arms crossed, jaw set. She continued to watch the shadow, irritation at her friend's disbelief battling with the trepidation she felt about giving this thing a chance to catch up to them. She sensed Layla's eyes on her and knew she was being studied, but couldn't bring herself to return the look.

Headlights appeared behind them in the distance, the first set they'd seen since entering the woods. Each time the road curved, the lights disappeared briefly, reappearing when both cars hit straightaways. The lights grew closer with every curve, creeping up on them. Seeing evidence that other people still existed made Sarah feel somehow safer.

At first, anyway.

Sarah broke her gaze away from the trees and looked back as the car rapidly approached. Within a matter of minutes, it pulled up within a car length of them and stayed close, the headlights flooding the interior of their car.

Layla looked in the rearview mirror and squinted against the eye-searing brightness reflected there. "Why are they so close? I can't see ahead of me." She adjusted the mirrors, brow furrowed.

Sarah watched the speedometer move up as her friend pressed on the gas. No matter how fast they went, the car kept the same distance, glued to them as if connected by some link. She squinted against the light, trying to see the driver, but all she could make out was the vaguely round shape of a head.

They continued in this way for twenty minutes. There were no open stores or gas stations, no passing lanes, no other cars. Sarah could feel the tension wafting off Layla, matching her own. Each time a break in the trees appeared, they both leaned forward, straining to see some other sign of humanity. The beauty and peace of the Pacific Coast Highway had become a trap of solitude. There was nothing they could do to shake the car trailing them.

Another break appeared ahead. Sarah's shoulders slumped when she saw that it was yet another abandoned, boarded-up building. A single ancient pump stood out front. There were no lights, and the parking lot had almost as much foliage in it as the woods.

The car slowed, and Sarah jerked her head around to stare at Layla. "What are you doing?"

"I'm pulling over so this guy can go around me. I can't keep this up."

"What if he doesn't pass you?"

"He will."

Layla pulled into the overgrown parking lot. The tires crunched over broken asphalt and gravel. She put it in park and took her hands off the wheel to shake them out.

The other car pulled up behind them and stopped.

"What the hell?" Layla asked. She rolled down her window and stuck a hand out, waving the other driver forward. "Pass me! What are you doing?"

The headlights continued to shine into their car. Sarah still couldn't make out the driver. What she *could* make out was the panic etched in her friend's face, forming lines around her mouth and between her brows. Her hair stood out in a golden halo.

Layla looked like Sarah felt. Somehow, knowing her friend was as frightened as she was made it all worse. More real.

Sarah's entire body felt stiff as iron, her tension pulsing through it. How could Layla just be sitting here, her window open? "Just go! He's not passing us!"

Layla put it in drive and clenched the wheel, knuckles whitening as she stomped on the gas pedal. They took off, spitting gravel behind them. They fishtailed briefly before finding purchase on the solid road and straightening out.

Sarah grasped the door handle and looked behind them. The other car grew larger in the rear window, getting closer. It sped to its former position behind them and adjusted speed to pace them once more.

"He's there again!" Sarah's chest tightened, her pulse throbbing. "What does he want?"

"Maybe he's just trying to scare us."

"It's working."

Sarah realized they'd both spoken in hushed tones, as if the driver would hear them if they spoke too loud. She swallowed against a suddenly dry mouth. It felt clunky in her throat. They both stared ahead, fixed in place. She could see Layla in her peripheral vision, eyes wide, mouth a tight line. Thoughts of everything that could happen out here on this isolated road ran through her head. For such a popular road, it was dead right now. How could they have not passed any other cars? Why were there no gas stations or rest areas? There were signs warning of being in a tsunami zone, but nothing helpful in a situation like this.

As they passed another tsunami warning, a large branch bent down just beyond the sign, weighed down by the shadow creature. For a moment, the psychotic driver had distracted her from the animal leaping through the trees.

A new sense of panic fluttered in her chest, sending another shockwave of adrenaline coursing through her. She put her face close to her window, trying to catch a detail that might tell her what it was, but it slowed, disappearing from her line of sight.

"How far to Newport?" she asked Layla, fear making her voice shake.

"Another hour, I think."

"How much longer until we're not in the trees anymore?"

Layla hesitated. "Until we reach Newport."

"Shit," Sarah whispered.

Her body buzzed. Who needed caffeine when fear did such a good job? She wondered if Layla remembered the thing in the trees, or if she had already dismissed it as nothing.

Checking behind them one more time, not sure what exactly she was looking for, Sarah stared at the shape of the driver's head. She couldn't make out the shape of a ponytail or anything, and the hair was short, from what she could tell. The car looked like a normal sedan. Not much different from their own.

Layla's tight whisper sounded. "Sarah."

She turned to Layla. "What?"

Why were they still whispering?

"The gas is getting low."

"Are you kidding?"

Layla shook her head.

"How low?"

"It's right above the red."

What the hell did Layla expect her to do about that?

"Maybe it's enough," Layla said.

"There has to be a gas station."

On other road trips, Sarah had seen signs marked "Last gas station for x miles." Did Oregon just not care if people ran out of gas in the middle of nowhere?

Sarah looked toward the driver's side of the road. The trees were even closer to the road now, no grassy bank between the pavement and the trunks.

It was then that she saw the shadow.

More than a shadow, it was a hairy beast, as big as a human, if not bigger. Dark in color, it jumped from branch to branch, astoundingly fast.

Sarah lifted a shaking finger and pointed, almost touching Layla's face with her quivering finger.

Layla looked at Sarah's finger, then Sarah.

Finally, she looked in the direction the finger pointed. Her face fell. "Holy shit!"

"Do you believe me now?"

"Yes. What is it?" Layla screeched.

"I don't know! Definitely not a wolf or a bear, though."

Layla accelerated again, but couldn't go too fast with the random, sharp curves in the road.

Sarah fumbled her cell phone out of the purse at her feet. She pushed the button, causing the phone to light up and illuminate her face. "I'm calling the police."

"I don't know what they can do."

Sarah dialed and it rang twice before someone picked up.

"Hello, 911 dispatch. What is your emergency?"

"We're on Pacific Coast Highway, maybe forty minutes south of Newport. We're not sure. There's someone following us, and…" Sarah paused. It all sounded ridiculous as she pondered what to say out loud. They would think it was a prank call if she said something was leaping through the trees. People never believed in monsters. Even when they were right in front of them. "And we can't get them to leave us alone or pass us."

"Are they doing anything other than following you?"

"No. I mean, we pulled over to let them pass, and they pulled over, too."

The other end of the line went quiet. At first, Sarah thought they'd hung up. "Hello?"

"Yes, ma'am, I'm here. Can you tell me more about the person following you? Are they doing anything threatening or dangerous?"

"Well, they're tailgating us. And like I said, they won't pass us. They're menacing us."

"Have they bumped you, honked, anything like that?"

"No."

"Do you know where you are on the highway?"

Sarah looked around for a mile marker, but didn't see any. "I don't know." Angling the phone away from her mouth, Sarah spoke louder. "Layla, have you seen a mile marker, or maybe a sign?"

Layla shook her head. "No. There's been nothing. We haven't passed any stores for a while."

Sarah moved the phone back. "We passed a closed gas station. One pump. That was half an hour ago or so. I'm not certain. And we're almost out of gas. We're not sure we'll make it to Newport."

"I'll see if there's a free unit that can head your way. I can't promise anything. With no overtly threatening acts occurring, there's not much we can do short of making our presence known. It might be enough to dissuade them. Do you have Triple A?"

"No."

"If you run out of gas, call for a tow truck."

"What if the car pulls over and they come after us?"

"Then call us back. Stay in your vehicle and keep the doors locked."

"Well, great, thanks. I'll call you if we're actively being murdered, then." Sarah hung up the phone, clenching it in her fist.

"What did they say?" asked Layla.

"They said there's nothing they can do."

"What do you mean there's nothing they can do?"

"She's going to see if there's a unit that can drive this way to check on us. Other than that she said we weren't being actively threatened."

"Why didn't you tell them about the creature?"

"Why do you think?"

Layla blew out a breath, body slumping. "What are we supposed to do?"

"Keep driving. We can make it." A glance showed Sarah the needle rested firmly in the red. They could have twenty miles left. Or two. No way to know for sure.

She asked Layla, "How long you have once it's in the red?"

"Highway miles, usually about ten miles, I think. For where it is."

"We aren't ten miles from Newport, are we?"

Layla shrugged. "I lost track. It's been years since I last traveled this road. It all looks the same."

It did all look the same. Tree after tree after dark and brooding tree. They hadn't passed any other abandoned buildings or other signs that civilization even existed. Sarah silently willed the car to keep going. She caught herself rocking slightly in her seat, as if she could rock the vehicle forward.

Up ahead, a spot of light peeked around an upcoming corner. "What is that?" Sarah asked.

"God, I hope it's a gas station or something." Layla leaned forward and accelerated, body almost touching the steering wheel.

The light grew brighter. Another few seconds and it revealed a small building, almost perfectly square. Wooden shingles slanted out from the sides, a warm light showing from windows in the front. Two gas pumps stood out front.

"Pull over!" Sarah said. A sense of hope came over her. Civilization!

"I am, I am." Layla pulled up to the front of the building. She put the car in park and reached for Sarah's hand.

Sarah took Layla's hand in hers and turned to see where the other car was. She couldn't see it. It hadn't pulled into the parking lot; it must have passed them and continued on. "They kept going. Oh my God, Layla, they're gone."

Layla twisted around in her seat to check for herself. She looked everywhere, never letting go of Sarah's hand. "I think you're right. But where's the thing from the trees?"

Sarah tightened her grip. "I wasn't watching."

They both looked around, staring intently back at the other side of the road.

Something thumped against the car, and they both shrieked, turning as one in the direction of Sarah's window.

A face peered in, and Sarah screamed again.

It was the gas station clerk. On his grey shirt a nametag hung, slightly crooked. It said "Holden." He had a hand on top of the car, and had leaned down to peer in the window at them. Late-day scruff decorated his cheeks and chin. His hair was slightly mussed, and his eyes drooped with exhaustion.

"Can I help you with something?"

A nervous laugh escaped Layla's lips, and she rolled down Sarah's window. "Hi, sorry. We need gas."

"Okay, pull on over to pump one and I'll get you some."

"Right. I'll do that." Layla rolled the window back up and pulled the car around until the tank side was aligned with the pump. "I forgot they pump the gas for you in Oregon."

"Can we leave him filling up the car? I need a pee break. Really, I need a sanity break."

"I just want to be somewhere bright."

The car shut off, Layla handed the clerk her card, and they went inside, leaving him to fill up the gas tank and clean off the windshield. The warmth made the last couple hours seem distant, unreal. Being in a gas station was so familiar and normal that thinking of psycho killers and monsters in trees made Sarah laugh. "Oh man, can you believe the night we've had?"

"It doesn't seem real, does it?"

"Not even a little bit."

They perused the shelves, grabbing sodas and candy bars, giggling and nudging each other. Sarah picked a bag of beef jerky, and Layla added sunflower seeds. Setting their snacks on the counter, they went to the bathroom, relieved to find it relatively clean. Sarah emptied her bladder, then splashed cold water on her face, still flushed from the preceding panic. She studied her face in the mirror, pulling her skin tight around her eyes to get rid of the bags.

The bell over the front door tinkled as they exited the bathroom. They rounded the corner from the hallway and found the clerk standing in the doorway. He cocked his head slightly to the side and studied them. Nervously, Sarah ran her hands over her hair, face, and clothes, tucking and straightening, wondering what had caught his attention. Finally, he spoke, jerking his head in the direction of the counter. "You guys want me to use your card for this stuff?"

"Yes, please," Layla said.

He walked around to the other side of the counter and rang up their purchases. "It's $53.27 for the gas and the food."

"Okay."

He ran the card, then held it out toward Layla. After signing for their purchase, they took one more look around at the warm normalcy of the gas station, then headed back out to the car. The darkness sucked them in like a vacuum, sealing around them more with each step they took away from the building.

"We should have asked him how far it is to Newport," Sarah said.

"We can't be far. Besides, he was acting weird. I didn't want to stick around. At least we have a full tank of gas now."

"Yeah. You want me to drive?"

"Sure. My arms are tired."

"My butt is tired."

They laughed, Layla handing her the keys and settling into the passenger seat. Sarah took another moment to stretch the kinks out. She got into the driver's side and took off, jumping when the locks automatically clamped down. She cracked her window, preferring fresh air while she drove, then turned up the heat, aiming the vents at her face and chest so she could soak up the warmth. The trees seemed to be spreading out a bit more, moving back from the road. They could see the sky now, the moon off to the side, just barely above the trees. The salty-fish scent of the ocean drifted around them in the soupy air, and fog crept toward the road from between the trees to the west. The temperature had dropped, cool air drifting in the window.

A glow in the distance indicated a good-sized town ahead. Not much longer now.

Opening her candy bar, Sarah took a bite, moaning as the sweetness of chocolate and caramel coated her tongue. "I needed this," she said, speaking around the chewy mouthful.

"Me, too," Layla mumbled, mouth equally full of food.

The sounds of their smacking and wrappers crinkling filled the car with the music of road-trip snacks. Sarah drove forward, gaze fixed on the glow in the distance, growing ever closer. She felt carefree and excited, happy to almost be to the hotel. She practically bounced in her seat. After the tension of the last few hours, she finally felt like everything would be okay.

A loud pop sounded. The wheel of the car jerked.

Sarah wrestled against its pull until coming to a stop at the side of the road.

"What was that?" Layla asked.

"I think we blew a tire."

They got out, sandals rasping over the pavement. Sure enough, the passenger side front tire hung limp and deflating.

"I'll get the jack and the spare," Layla said, taking the keys from Sarah before heading to the back of the car. After a moment she brought Sarah the cross-shaped, metal lug wrench and jack, then returned to the trunk.

Sarah positioned the jack and lifted the car up until she could spin the tire. She fitted the lug wrench to the first lug nut and put all her weight on it in an attempt to move it. It took several tries before it finally shifted. The other ones went a bit more easily and she got the tire off, reaching for the full-sized spare Layla had rested against her legs. While she put the spare on, Layla put the flat tire in the trunk.

Layla called from the trunk, "Hey, Sarah?"

"Yeah?" Sarah grunted.

"There's something weird about this tire."

"What do you mean?" She now had the tire on, and was getting the first lug nut tightened.

"Come here."

"I can't right now. Just tell me."

"Okay. There are three slashes in the tire. Almost like—"

"Claw marks?"

"Yeah. Like something scratched the tire."

"Do you think—?" The bushes behind Sarah rustled as she put the second lug nut on. She froze. "Layla?"

"I heard it."

"Get over here and help me!"

Layla slammed the trunk and ran to the front of the car. She put the next lug nut on and started spinning it manually as Sarah finished tightening the one she was working on. They took turns looking over their shoulders at the woods. Rustling continued to emit from the foliage behind them, but nothing had yet appeared.

Similar sounds came from across the street.

Layla started lowering the jack even as Sarah tightened the final lug nut.

Across the street, a creature stepped out of the trees.

It was heavy and furred like a bear, but it stood upright, long arms dangling almost to the ground. Its legs were shorter than the arms, but both were thick. The fur stopped at the neck, an oversized bald head sitting atop its broad shoulders. The face looked almost human, except for an excessively wide mouth and eyes so large Sarah could see them across the distance that separated them.

The women jumped into the car and threw the tools into the back seat. Sarah shoved the key in and turned it, slamming it into drive and taking off without putting her seatbelt on.

The creature loped after them.

In the rearview, a second one joined it. Both were visible in the rearview mirror, running faster than they had any right to move. Their eyes reflected the red of the car's taillights, making them look all the more menacing.

As Sarah sped up, the creatures broke away from each other, each going into the woods on either side. Only a moment later, they appeared in the trees, moving even faster than they had on the road. She could see now that they both swung and leaped, using those long, strong arms to maneuver from branch to branch like apes.

She clung to the steering wheel as if it were a lifeline, pressing the gas pedal to the floor. There were no curves now. She could go as fast as the car would allow. Eyes fixed on the road, she told Layla to fasten her seatbelt, using one hand to fasten her own.

The trees started to close in again, bringing the creatures closer to the road. Closer to them.

No matter how fast Sarah drove, they kept up.

A bridge appeared up ahead, the glow of lights closer. She punched it, leaning in with her speed. The needle climbed the speedometer, surpassing the last mark and twitching in place.

The trees were long gone now and the dark ocean stretched off to their left. Lack of trees didn't stop the creatures, but it did slow them. There were now houses and other buildings, plus hills covered in grass and black stone.

Once on the bridge, Sarah had to slow slightly to avoid losing control. Fearful that the creatures would catch her, she looked for them in her rearview.

They'd stopped. Standing side by side in the middle of the road, the creatures stared after the car but made no attempt to step onto the bridge.

Sarah eased to a stop in the middle of the bridge.

"What are you doing?" Layla asked, voice high.

"Look. They aren't following us anymore."

Both women looked back, watching the creatures.

"Maybe they can't cross over the water," Layla said. "They can't get us!"

Sarah put the car in gear and continued forward, calmer now, though still shooting looks into the rearview mirror. As the car went around a bend, the creatures were still standing in the road.

She made her way to the hotel. After checking in, she and Layla went to their room, dropping onto their beds in relief.

"God, I'm so tired," Layla said.

"Me, too."

"As tired as I am, I don't know if I can sleep. I'm still freaked out. Why do you think those things were following us?"

"I don't know. Do you think your parents had something to do with it?"

"My parents? No. There's no way they knew where we were going. Then again, they've used trackers before. Maybe the creatures are the newest version." Layla sighed. "Speaking of lunatics, what about that car? That was scary, too."

Sarah shrugged. The move caused discomfort, reminding her how desperately she needed to wash up and change. It had been a long day. "I think he was just a jerk out to scare us." She scratched at her neck and wrists. "Do you mind if I shower first?"

"I think I'll wait to take my shower in the morning."

"I really need it tonight. If I can get off this bed."

It took her a few minutes, but Sarah finally grunted and pulled herself up. She moved into the bathroom, taking her bag with her. Her skin felt tight and uncomfortable, like it had shrunk about two sizes. She stripped out of her clothes and climbed into the shower. The shower head was low and she scrunched down to get her head under the hot water. After thoroughly washing her hair and soaping up her body, she slipped out of the human-skin suit and hung it over the curtain rod. A groan of pleasure escaped her. All that food had made the suit too tight. She scrubbed at her scales, relieving the itching the salty air caused.

When she'd finished drying off and brushing her teeth, she turned off the light and slipped into the room. Layla had sloughed off her suit and left it hanging off the end of the bed. She'd regret it in the morning, when she had to figure out how to both clean it and get it dry enough for them to head out. The quicker they got going in the morning, the sooner they'd be in Portland, where Sarah's cousins waited to whisk them through a little-known shanghai tunnel to a boat on the Willamette River and the freedom it represented.

Climbing into bed, Sarah let out a contented sigh and snuggled under the covers.

Outside, a sedan pulled up and parked. The headlights, aimed at the room inside which Layla and Sarah now slept, shut off and the motor silenced. A shadowy figure sat inside, staring at the room. Waiting.

About the Author

A fan of all things fantastical and frightening, Shannon Lawrence writes in her dungeon when her minions allow, often accompanied by her familiars. She writes primarily horror and fantasy. Her stories can be found in several anthologies and magazines, including Space and Time Magazine and The Literary Hatchet, and her short story collection *Blue Sludge Blues & Other Abominations* is now available. When she's not writing, she's hiking through the wilds of Colorado and photographing her magnificent surroundings. Though she often misses the ocean, the majestic and rugged Rockies are a sight she could never part with. Besides, in Colorado there's always a place to hide a body or birth a monster. What more could she ask for?

Find out more about Shannon at:
thewarriormuse.blogspot.com

Dandelion Rider

Meyari McFarland

Mimi sniffed the air as she stomped down the front stairs with Cece, her twin sister, behind her. The sun had already set, leaving the evening dark and still. The pixies were in their nest out back. Even with the bulk of the old Victorian mansion between Mimi and the pixies, she could hear them muttering in their harmony of thousands of tiny voices. Past their front yard and its chalk-covered sidewalk, the asphalt changed to cobblestones in the middle of the street, legacy of the Opening that had smashed hundreds of worlds together into a mishmash a couple hundred years ago, blending every race and magic together.

The moon was up, showing the scars that criss-crossed it, as well. Another legacy. Not a full moon. A bare sliver of a moon, one like a scythe set to harvest a crop of ripe stars. The scent of lilacs hung in the air, mixing with drifting pixie dust to make Mimi's head swim. The lilacs alone were bad enough. Add pixie dust to her nose and Mimi could swear that she was already running down the road in her wolf form, clothes forgotten, their whole plan abandoned.

"Mom says we have to be back before midnight," Cece complained as she followed Mimi down the stairs, eyes flashing silver in the darkness. "I tried to argue it, but she wouldn't budge."

Stupid that they had to come home that early. Their big sister Janie never had that early of a curfew when she was in high school and she wasn't asexual like Mimi and Cece who weren't as likely to get into trouble while out on their own. Of course, Janie'd had a girlfriend whose mother was a literal terror of a fire dragon so there'd been no misbehaving at all for Janie and August. They'd settled down and gotten married right after school. Their little Baba Yaga hut up the street was cute, but not at all what Mimi wanted from life.

Mori, their adopted baby brother and a real runt of a dragon, zoomed over their back fence. "I got the convertible keys!"

He barrel-rolled, keys jingling, wings almost clipping the lilacs on one side and the hemlock trees on the other side. Then he was up into the air, shooting little jets of delighted fire that whoomped out to light the night.

"Well, toss them down," Mimi called up to him.

Mori laughed and did just that. He swooped over them, flipping mid-air. He cut it so close that the triangle tip of his tail smacked into the siding next to their third parent Giang's bedroom on the second floor. He almost crashed but kept on laughing. Mimi barely caught the keys, even with her werewolf's night vision. The scent of Mori's scales on the keys had been easier to track than the tiny flash of the keys as they tumbled through the air.

A loud growl came from the house. "Mori!"

It was Mom. Mimi and Cece ran for Giang's convertible. If they didn't hurry, all three of their parents would be out here yelling at them. Although, Giang wouldn't yell. They'd just do the sad eyes and very-disappointed-in-you speech. No way could Mimi deal with that right now.

Mimi leaped into the driver's seat. Cece took the passenger seat. Mori crooned and flew over their heads as Mimi revved the engine, then peeled out to get away before their road trip could be summarily cancelled.

It only took two blocks before Mori was falling behind. He just wasn't big enough to fly car-speed. Or hovercraft speed. Or anything else, really. Dragon runts never did get big enough to go head-to-head with anything much at all. Mimi slowed, stopped at the cul-de-sac's stop sign, and grinned as Mori perched on the back seat, his wings still spread over their heads. His tail hung over the trunk, twitching with delight. It made Mimi start laughing. Cece howled at the crescent moon while Mori crooned hard enough to rattle the convertible.

Mimi drove slowly over the patchwork streets. No one had ever paid to unify the streets, so within three miles they drove over pavement, concrete, cobblestones and a really finely done dirt road sealed by elven magic. Everett, a suburb north of Seattle that'd been hit hard by the Opening, was quiet. Only a few cars on the road, only a few flyers in the sky, including one big old Oriental dragon that made Mori crouch down, close his wings against his sides, and tuck his tail into the back seat. Once Mimi merged onto I-5 and their speed picked up, the wings came back out. Mori hung on as Mimi brought the speed up to sixty-five, then seventy. Without punching holes in Giang's seats, no less.

Cece turned on the radio. The music of The Sensory Hoard, a local band, flowed over the three of them, setting Cece's foot to tapping, Mori to crooning, and Mimi's fingers to tapping against the steering wheel.

Thankfully, I-5 was nearly abandoned. They flew past the turnoff to Mukilteo, with all its warning signs for selkie and mermaid territorial claims. Ahead of them, Lynnwood's heavy woods glimmered with the pocket dimensions created by the local elves. They passed a spot full of music and movement, shimmering lights bright enough that the pixies in the area were still up and about instead of heading to sleep.

"A rave?" Mori asked.

"Or a hunt," Cece suggested as she craned her neck and then snorted. "No, they're having a barbeque. I smell the roasting meat."

Mimi did, too. Chicken, pork, waterhorse, and what had to be snake—because even elves knew better than to go after dragon flesh. The entire population of dragons in the Puget Sound would revolt. The destruction after the Opening had showed what could happen if the dragons turned against their neighbors. Nothing like a few tons of heavily armored killing machines, sharp bits on every extremity and the ability to breathe fire, to put an end to a fight.

Which was, of course, why Mori was along on this little trip.

"You just went grim," Mori commented. He nuzzled Mimi's neck. "Still mad at Cahaya?"

Mimi breathed through the fury, lifted her chin and shrugged. "Nah, I'm over it."

Cahaya was the were who had gotten Mimi banned from all public pack activities, just for daring to insist that he couldn't force Jaiden to be his mate, especially when Jaiden said that they weren't lovers at all. It wasn't her fault Jaiden dumped Cahaya. If he hadn't been such a creep, they'd still be together and Cahaya would still be on track to being his pack's Alpha.

Both Cece and Mori stared at her, expressions going flat with disbelief. Stupid dragon and werewolf noses. But neither of them challenged the blatant lie.

Mimi wasn't going to let Cahaya ruin tonight. They were going to have fun and meet people and enjoy themselves. If anyone tried to stop them, Mimi would tear their throats out. Or have Mori toast their asses. They couldn't go to the big pack thing over in Bellevue, but the one in Seattle was free and clear. Cahaya wouldn't be there, so Mimi could go.

And where Mimi couldn't go, Cece and Mori wouldn't. Her twin and her not-twin dragon-brother had stood with Mimi even when Mom, Dad and Giang hadn't.

Mori put his head on Mimi's shoulder and kept it there until they passed Shoreline's rocky patches and dwarven tunnel openings. By the time they crossed the big bridge over Lake Washington, they'd passed through sixteen different climate and racial zones, legacy of the Opening's smashing all the planes together into one mishmash of a world.

Seattle, downtown Seattle, was human territory. It was one of the few areas left in the Puget Sound that was a nearly pure human enclave. Humans had retreated to Seattle and built walls, defenses, everything they could to stay safe from the "monsters" that had "destroyed" their world.

Didn't seem to matter to the humans back then that *they* were the monsters to the werefolk, dragons, elves, pixies and everyone else. Or that *their* worlds had been destroyed in the same way, during the Opening. At least they'd gotten over that nonsense. The Opening had been two generations ago.

Mimi took the exit into downtown Seattle, heading for the Space Needle and its many parking garages. Strange to see so many buildings that were designed only for human-sized bodies. Narrow doors, small windows, little rooms. The stairs were so small, too, barely big enough for Mimi's feet. Mimi parked the convertible in the biggest parking garage.

"Why're they holding the party in Seattle?" Mori asked, activating shields over the convertible to make sure that no one would ding or steal Giang's car.

"Cheaper than coming out to the Skagit Casino, with the Meo Clan's barn-party fees," Mimi said. She shrugged. "It's closer, anyway."

While Mimi and Cece could pass as human as long as their eyes didn't catch the light and they didn't sniff at the air too obviously, Mori was and would always be obviously a dragon. He bounced next to Mimi, standing on his hind legs so that his head was the same height as hers. Give him another hundred years and he might be as big as a normal-sized dragon his age was, right now. As it was, he looked more like he was a child than a nearly-grown teenager old enough to vote.

Especially when he went down on all fours and ran down the stairs to the ground floor. Cece laughed and followed him, leaving Mimi to trail after them more slowly. She could hear people laughing and singing by the big fountain at the center of the Space Needle's complex. That would be where everyone was.

Where the other packs were gathering for a meet-and-greet. Where most of the other young people would be looking for mates, either casual or serious. Where Mimi would have to contend with all the people who looked at her and saw only Cahaya's manipulative stories about her "abuse" and "disrespect."

Jerk. Mimi wasn't the one at fault. She wasn't. Cahaya had turned everyone against her, even her parents, but she knew one thing: it was Cahaya's own fault that Jaiden left. It was his fault she was being shunned. It was his fault top to bottom and she'd be damned if she'd let Cahaya steal everything from her. Especially getting to go out and have fun with Cece and Mori.

The party was already well under way once the three of them reached the fountain. Someone had set up fairy lights that moved in the water spraying from the fountain. Drifts and trails of more fairy lights swept across the lawn, defining light and dark patches that encouraged people to move and mingle.

Mimi stood at the edge of the gathering and breathed.

No Cahaya. No one from his pack. She was safe to go in. The worst she was going to have to deal with was some ham-handed and unwelcome flirting. It would be fine.

"We're with you," Cece murmured as she put one hand on Mimi's shoulder. "No one's getting at you without going through us first."

"Right," Mori agreed. He stood and flung his arms around Mimi, hugging her hard enough that he nearly knocked her over onto her ass.

She laughed and scratched under his wings right at the base, making Mori laugh and squirm enough that he let go. Yes. They were right. She wasn't alone. She had her siblings with her. She could do this. No lying asshole was going to take Mimi's right to mingle with other werewolves away.

Mimi raised her chin, met Cece and then Mori's eyes, and then strode out into the party.

The night shimmered with magic. Mori crooned as he ran along behind Mimi and Cece. They both sparkled with defiance, their innate shifting magic shimmering on the edge of transforming to wolves with every step. No one but a dragon would see it. Of course, it was blatant to Mori's senses, which were finally stabilizing as he neared adulthood.

Huge improvement there. The last few weeks had been painful to watch. Cahaya had all but destroyed Mimi's confidence. She'd hidden inside, refused to talk to anyone but Mori and Cece. This trip was the first that Mimi had planned since Cahaya's attack.

Mori had specifically checked to make sure that none of the local packs would be here. And that Cahaya didn't interact with those packs directly, either. Any pack that Cahaya had interacted with was a threat, what with all his lying. Mori wasn't going to allow Cahaya to hurt Mimi again, not when she'd just started to improve.

When Mori had first met them, back when they were all just three years old, Mimi and Cece lived in their wolf shapes. Mori had learned the yips and barks, howls and whines, of pack speech before he'd learned the words they used when they had human tongues. Wolves' howls came more naturally to Mimi than human speech even now. After Cahaya's stupidity, Mimi had been all but trapped in her human shape, too hurt and betrayed to let anyone see her true self. It was only now that she was starting to recover, though she'd yet to shift around Mori.

At some point, Mori would have to sit their parents down, all three of them. They needed to understand just how much damage Cahaya had done to everyone. And, specifically, how much damage *they* had done to Mimi and Cece by not believing them. By not believing Mori when he told them that Cahaya was a siren, not a were. No one had believed him.

Later, though.

"They have shish kebabs!" Mori exclaimed as he skidded on the grass.

"Oh, they do," Mimi murmured. She faltered as she saw the werewolf pack minding the kebab tent. They were from south of Seattle. Not quite to Tacoma where merfolk lived in the waters as thick as the pixies in the sky back home in Everett. They didn't have the scent of all the merfolk on their fur and skin, but close. One of them smelled quite strongly of medusa. Odd. Mori didn't know that there were medusa in the Puget Sound.

"I'm getting kebabs," Mori declared. "You want some? I'll get three for me. Two for you guys? One? I know, I'll get three of each type and we can eat them as we walk!"

A passing elf with gold and silver chains draped over xyr chest grinned at Mori, only to do a double-take as xe realized that Mori was far older than the cute little dragonling he looked. Then xe saw Mimi. Xe blew out a breath and nodded, very slightly, before walking on—leaving Mori to bounce and clap his hands while Cece laughed and Mimi smiled grimly.

Good to see that other people could spot the damage done to Mimi, too.

"Don't spend all your money in one place, Mori," Mimi said.

Mori snorted, sending twin jets of smoke across the lawn. "I brought more money than *that*. I want to see if I can find more pendants for my hoard."

Cece grabbed Mimi's wrist and dragged her towards the tent where the shish kebabs were sizzling. "I thought you'd changed your mind and wanted to hoard illuminated books."

"I do!" Mori exclaimed. "Those are lovely. Especially the ones with gold and silver ink. But I like pendants, too. Nice sparkly ones with gold and silver wire."

Mimi raised an eyebrow, her magic brightening as her mood lifted back out of the dark depression she'd been coping with. "You just want to hoard *all* things sparkly, like a magpie."

"Not a bad guess," Mori said, allowing his voice to deepen a touch and then forcing it go high and sweet and young again as he laughed and wagged his tail just as they reached the shish kebab tent. "Sparkly things are pretty!"

When they saw Mimi and Cece coming, the weres minding the tent stiffened, their magic going on the alert.

Mori ignored them, standing up on his hind legs to pull his credit card out of his carrying pouch. "We'll have three of every sort of shish kebab other than the one with snake and the one that's nothing but vegetables," Mori declared. "They smell wonderful! What sauces do you have?"

"We..." The were minding the counter was Huan Leon, the pack's Alpha. He was an older male whose magic was starting to soften as his belly spread with age. There was an awkward pause before he took Mori's credit card, and Huan shook his head as if doing something against his better judgement. "We have teriyaki, sweet and sour, a beef gelatin-edible gold flake glaze, and lemon wedges. Which would you prefer?"

"Gold?" Mori asked, peering at the bottles, then snatching up the one labeled "gold" to shake it enthusiastically. "Oh! Mimi, Cece! It has actual gold flakes in it! I want that one!"

"You and your sparkly things." Mimi laughed even though her magic was flinching away from the other pack's attention. "I'll take teriyaki on mine."

"Sweet and sour, please," Cece said.

They ended up with paper baskets full of shish kebabs: pork, beef, chicken, a lovely mixed kebab with all three, and then reindeer and kelpie. The kelpie was appropriately aged and pickled, removing the nasty swamp mud taste, while the reindeer was very fresh indeed. Mori wrapped his tail around his haunches, munching on the shish kebabs and making appropriately juvenile yummy noises.

It took two minutes, sixteen seconds for Huan to calm down and start smiling at the three of them. But who was counting? A minute later—minus three seconds—a cub poked her nose out from under one of the tables' banners. She was followed by two other cubs, boys, who blinked at Mimi and Cece.

Mimi promptly cooed at the girl-cub, whose jaw dropped open and tongue lolled out. Cece took a moment longer to smile, and then they were both sitting on the ground with the cubs in their laps and draped over their backs begging for bites of the kebabs. So predictable.

And so necessary for both of them.

Huan followed Mori, and took the sticks and sauce-stained basket to the garbage bin after he'd finished. Mori let him. Huan clearly wanted to talk away from the others. How else was he to convey what need to be said? Huan couldn't say it openly with his pack and Mimi and Cece right there. No one would listen. And it would hurt his siblings.

Mori wouldn't allow that.

Huan worried a thumbnail in his teeth as he peered at Mimi and Cece playing with and cuddling the cubs. With their identical defensive glares gone, they looked like the teenagers they were.

"Mimi and Cece, they're…kids," he murmured, quietly enough that even werewolf ears wouldn't overhear.

"They're wounded," Mori corrected in his proper, deeper voice. He might be a runt, but his magic was developing properly, so his voice had deepened. It took more and more effort to use the child-like voice that disarmed people. "Cahaya damaged them. He wounded Mimi straight to the soul. I've been working to heal her, but it's hard going when our pack believes Cahaya, not us. And Cece is as damaged as if she'd had her guts ripped open. I almost killed him for it. Only my size stopped me."

"We heard that they'd driven his mate away," Huan said

Mori snorted. The jets of smoke were mingled with more sparks of fire than was appropriate but really, who could blame him? Cahaya's siren magic curled into people's souls, polluting their senses, confusing their minds. He used it like a scalpel, a sword, to chop away what he didn't like so that he could sculpt what remained into his desire.

No matter what it did to the person. Cahaya was *that* person, the one their parents warned them about, who'd break them into pieces for his own purposes. If only everyone else would realize it.

"Jaiden Horn rejected Cahaya on his own," Mori rumbled. "Everything else you've heard is a siren's tale to rip Mimi's and Cece's lives apart. I won't allow it. They're my sisters. He's abusive. Jaiden accused him openly, but does anyone listen? No, of course not. It has to be a seventeen-year-old girl's fault that Jaiden Horn rejected poor, sweet, innocent, twenty-nine-year-old Cahaya Ruzzier, then ran across the continent to escape his violence."

Huan stepped back, eyes wide.

Oops. Mori hadn't intended to let that much of his magic out in his voice. Or be quite that viciously sarcastic. It always made people uncomfortable to hear such adult behavior coming from such a child-like body.

Mori banked his flames, controlled his temper, and then deliberately licked his claws free of any trace of the lovely gold-gelatin glaze from the kebabs.

"Siren," Huan said in a flat voice that was nonetheless a question. "Cahaya is a siren."

"Oh yes," Mori agreed. "Quite powerful, actually. Cahaya is a powerful siren despite, or maybe because, of his were-blood. Rather like I'm a more powerful magic user despite being a runt. Cahaya's were senses help him tailor his voice to get the response he wants. And with werefolk? Your hearing and other senses respond beautifully to his siren magic."

Huan stared, stunned. A moment later he scowled. Mori let his tongue curl around one of his fingers as he hummed thoughtfully.

The slurp when he let go was loud enough to draw grins from Mimi and Cece, plus yips of laughter from the cubs. Good.

The little absurdity did nothing to temper Huan's scowl. Also good. Someone needed to carry word of Cahaya's behavior to the other packs. They would not listen to Mimi and Cece? Fine. Mori would tell everyone about Cahaya's abuse of his siren abilities. He would roar it from the highest skyscrapers in the Magical City, Bellevue, if he had to.

But starting quietly, here in a human enclave? That was a better plan. A more effective plan. Mori knew what his true hoard was. Mori hoarded people.

He hoarded Pack.

Mimi and Cece were his First Items. After them, came Father with his fire magic. Mother with her pure werewolf blood. Also Giang, their third parent, with xyr dryad blood and lovely blooming magic. Their sister Janie and August, her wife, they were part of his hoard, too. The entire pack was his.

All the people he loved were his hoard and he would take care of them, shower them with what they needed to succeed. He would make sure that every single one of them was happy, somehow. He would tear Cahaya to shreds if he had to, if that was what it took to stop him from hurting Mimi and Cece again.

"I wondered," Huan murmured, gnawing on that thumbnail again. "The teens in our pack were upset with how Mimi was treated. But everything seemed so clear-cut."

Mori snorted again. "Only if you listen to Cahaya. He keeps calling our mother, talking with her on the phone. I've been tempted to pull the phone from her hand and smash it to keep him from reinforcing his work on her soul. Might yet do that even if I do get grounded."

"Don't," Huan said. He patted Mori's shoulder, fingers curling instinctively around the warmth and magic that made Mori able to breathe fire and fly. "I'll call her. The three of you should mingle. Talk to people. Let them…see just who they really are."

Mori nodded, wagging his tail like a cub. Cece had glanced his way, frowning so Mori let himself wiggle just a bit to reinforce the young and enthusiastic thing. He let his voice stay deep for Huan. "Why do you think I insisted on coming to this gathering? Other than finding some shiny things for my hoard, of course."

Huan laughed, hooking the gnawed thumb over his shoulder towards the Space Needle, raising his voice a little. Cece was still looking. "The elves have set up crafting and sales tents that way. You'll find lots of lovely shiny things there."

"Oh!" Mori's ears went straight up.

He bobbed his head at Huan, content with the way Huan's magic curled with anger and determination, then dashed over to run around Mimi and Cece. Instantly, the cubs yipped and started chasing his tail, which just made the pack laugh. It took a bit longer for Cece to laugh, and longer still before Mimi chuckled and smiled wryly at him.

"The elves have crafting tents!" Mori exclaimed as he skidded to a stop in front of Mimi and Cece, only to be puppy-piled by the cubs. "We gotta go see! They've got shiny things, guys!"

"Well, I guess we'd best head that way," Mimi said as Huan came to help Mori escape from the cubs climbing all over him and gnawing, harmlessly, on his ears, tail and fingers.

Much better. Mimi's bleakness was gone, replaced by a sort of relaxed joy that Mori hadn't felt from her in ages. Not since Cahaya attacked her. Good. This was going well, though there was still darkness there that needed healing. He'd have to learn a bit more healing magic if he couldn't find something to fix the hole left inside Mimi's heart.

The Space Needle was the weirdest thing Cece had ever seen. Full stop. Just outright weird. It looked like, well, a pair of saucers set on top of funky, curved tripod legs. Why that suggested "space" wasn't at all clear, but hey, apparently to humans it was obvious.

Humans were so weird.

Cece followed Mori as he dashed from stall to stall, checking out all the shiny bits and bobs. Sometimes he acted like he was nearly grown. Other times, like now, he acted more like a little kid. She'd never asked him just how much of the kid thing was an act. Some of it had to be. Dragons didn't mature any more slowly than weres did. He was nearly an adult mentally and emotionally, even if his body was the size of a ten-year-old kid's.

Another thing she'd never dared to ask Mori: how much did he resent the fact that practically no dragon anywhere would ever take him seriously as a lover in the future because he was such a runt?

Mori didn't seem to care. Kinda like Mimi, Mori didn't have the slightest interest in finding a mate. It wasn't even on his mental horizon. Cece could get that. They were all three of them still young. There was time. The thought of a lover or mate or something was a distantly appealing idea but nothing that Cece would work for. Look for. Pine after.

"You're thinking hard," Mimi commented in a low voice as Mori gasped and stared at some sun catchers that a band of elves had for sale, pretty things with amethyst and crystalized feathers and leaves.

"Eh, just pondering the whole mate thing," Cece said with a one-shouldered shrug. "You know, everyone thinks it's such a big deal, and I just don't get it."

"Mm, I know," Mimi agreed. "Never have figured out why Janie's romance novels all go on about not being able to resist their lover. What, it's hard?"

The characters in a romance novel always struck Cece as being sort of like Mori bouncing and crooning and wiggling like an eel as he tried to choose which shiny bauble to add to his hoard. Janie always threw up her hands whenever they just stared blankly at 'hot' scenes from her romance novels. Seriously, though, none of that stuff made sense.

"He is never, ever going to grow up," Mimi said. She leaned on Cece's shoulder, chuckling.

"Nope, not Mori," Cece agreed.

This close, Mimi's scent was still sad, but the bleakness had subsided a good bit. The anger was still there. Just milder, like being here had eased something inside of her.

"Mori's a sneak," Cece commented.

"You just figured that out?" Mimi replied with mock-shocked, wide eyes and raised eyebrows.

"Nah, just figured out that he insisted on coming down to make you feel better," Cece said.

Mimi stared at her, true confusion in her scent until her cheeks went bright-hot from the blush. Cece snickered. One point for Cece. She'd figured it out before Mimi did.

"Oh, shut up," Mimi grumbled but there wasn't any heat in the grumble and her scent was only embarrassed. Plus a bit of appreciation. "Think we could get something for the family?"

Cece grunted. "No, I'm not getting a damn thing for anyone. Mom, Dad and Giang all sided with Cahaya. Janie and August refused to even hear our side. The rest of the pack took off to go to Cahaya's gathering and flat-out left us behind, even when we begged them not to. Not getting them anything at all."

There was a moment of startlement from Mimi, then Mimi practically knocked Cece down with a hug that hid her near-tears from everyone's eyes. Not their noses, though.

"Guys, look, look!" Mori ran back on his hind legs with a lovely bit of crystal and wire and gemstones hanging from his hands. "I can hang it in my window and add a bunch more sparkly things to it! It's designed for additions!"

It was a nice one. Nice thick copper chain that'd been magically hardened to bear as much weight as needed, good wide links every inch or so that would be perfect for hanging more dangling pendants, and the crystalline bits would hold a good, solid ward spell—which Mori was getting pretty good at.

"I like it," Cece said. "Sort of surprised you didn't go for the one with the crystallized leaves on it."

"Mmm, I thought about it," Mori said. His voice slid adult-deep as he looked over his shoulder at that one. "It is quite lovely. But this one is more versatile."

Mimi said, "It's pretty..."

She froze, staring over Mori's shoulder with such dread in her scent that Cece immediately went on the alert. Mori's head whipped around and he started growling at the same time that Cece did. Every single person in the area—human, elf, dragon and were—went still.

Cahaya Ruzzier stood at the far end of the line of tents, one hand over his chest like he was afraid to take another step. The look in his eyes was pure malice, no matter what his body language claimed.

Cece's lip curled.

It was nothing compared to Mori's rage.

"What are you doing here?" Mori roared at Cahaya.

The roar was so loud that all the tents in the area billowed. Every wind chime and bell clattered as if about to break. The darkness of the evening went red as Mori started to glow from within by the power of his magic.

His fire.

"No, don't!" Cece shouted as she grabbed Mori, yanked the chain out of his hands before he could melt it, then hauled back against one arm at the same time Mimi grabbed his other arm and tried to pull.

Neither of them did the least bit of good. Small Mori might be, apparently immature, but his magic flowed like water through a garden hose nozzle, magnified by his size.

"Mori," Mimi said. "You can't kill him. You'll get arrested."

"I don't care," Mori snarled. "He won't hurt you again, Mimi. I won't allow it!"

The air around them heated in ways that hurt, even though Mori always, always, always worked to keep his fire from harming either of them.

Cece hissed in pain as Mimi cursed and let go.

No, not that! Don't let go!

Cece stepped in front of Mori, putting her face right in front of his so that the flames wreathing his face scorched her skin and curled her hair with a stench that made Cece's stomach turn.

Mori gasped and backed off a step, abruptly banking his flame.

"The only one hurting us right now is you, Mori," Cece said.

Cahaya's voice came from behind her. *Too* close behind her. "This is exactly why—"

"Oh, shut the fuck up, Cahaya," Cece snapped over her shoulder at him. "Do you always have to be a dramatic bitch or what?"

For the first time ever, Cece saw, and smelled, true shock in Cahaya's scent. Unlike everyone else in the area, Cahaya had gotten closer during Mori's rage. He was only ten feet away, well within Mori's blasting range. A normal dragon's flame wouldn't go that far, sure, but Mori could hit thirty feet with pinpoint accuracy, and had been able to do so since he was just eleven years old.

Cahaya's lip curled up to reveal a canine that wasn't nearly long enough for a true were. When he spoke, his voice resonated far too much, almost like he was trying to growl and talk at the same time. "This is exactly why your sister was forbidden from attending any pack events. The damage she could cause—"

Cece rolled her eyes. "Will you give it up?" She stepped over to grab Mimi's wrist before Mimi could stomp off in a rage. Or a sulk. Or worse, start crying. "For fuck's sake, it's Mori who's going to fry you, not Mimi. And knock that stupid growly thing off. It's annoying."

"Really is," Mimi said, the words directed at Cece, not at Cahaya, whose eyes Mimi wouldn't even meet.

"That's...not possible," Cahaya said. This time his voice came out higher, more hissing like waves over fine gravel than a growl. "You aren't... It's not possible!"

"Siren!" Mori roared, and Cece realized she was no longer between him and Cahaya.

The flames were back, much bigger and brighter than before. Behind Mori several dragons were rushing over, one in the sky and one on the ground. Both of them were older, full-grown, but they looked terrified.

The werefolk stood way, way, way back, all of them in their animal shapes. Lots of wolves, two African lions who were one hell of a long way from home, a horse, and six foxes who whined and hid underneath a trio of centaurs who were very carefully not stamping their hooves.

Siren.

Cahaya wasn't full were. He'd never once shifted that Cece had seen. To be unable to shift with were blood meant you were way down into one great-grandparent only having been a were. Which meant that Cahaya wasn't actually a were at all, despite his claims.

He was a siren.

Who'd had his lover escape after Mimi scolded Cahaya for treating him badly. Jaiden had not only left the pack, he'd left the state. He'd traveled across the country to escape from Cahaya, once Mimi gave him a chance to break free.

In return, Cahaya had punished the only person he could get his hands on. He'd destroyed Mimi's place in the pack, in all the packs, trying to drive her away just as Jaiden had run away.

Cece growled, "He's controlling people with his voice. That's why he sounds so weird."

"How is he not controlling us…?" Mimi paused, then visibly decided not to think about it now. "That's… yeah, no. Mori's gonna go to jail if he doesn't stop."

"I got Mori," Cece said.

Mimi took a quick breath and looked at Cahaya, gritted her teeth, then squared her shoulders. "And I got *him*. Go."

Cece didn't hesitate. She whirled toward Mori and leaped straight at him, just like they used to when they were toddlers. It was like jumping straight into a bonfire.

The flame winked out as Mori's eyes went wide.

Cece crashed into his chest, knocking them both to the ground. The earth under Mori's feet was more like poorly fired pottery than grass and dirt. Mori's magic wrapped around her, keeping her from being really hurt. Cece promptly sat on top of him, holding him down, then shoving his shiny new pendant thing into his mouth to keep him from objecting to whatever Mimi was going to do.

Hopefully it would work. Whatever it was that let the two of them resist Cahaya's powers, it had to last until Cahaya was taken care of.

Otherwise, all three of them were not only going to jail, they were gonna be thrown out the pack for real.

Mimi studied Cahaya. He was making this low humming noise, a rumbling thing rather like what Mori did when he decided not to speak with his mouth, using only his magic. How had she not noticed that before?

Of course she hadn't noticed, not if Cahaya was more siren than were. He'd sculpted everyone's awareness to make sure that they didn't catch on to what he was doing.

The two other dragons rushed in, only to skid and flip head over tail, as Mimi held up a hand at them, as if they were so scared of Mori's fire that they'd take any excuse not to charge in. Couldn't blame them, really. An Oriental dragon had far too thin of scales to resist Mori's flame and a Kiren wasn't armored at all.

"He's *my* problem." Mimi turned back to Cahaya. "A siren, huh?" Half of her wanted to run for the hills and the other half wanted to rip Cahaya's throat out. "Explains a lot."

"I have no idea what you're talking about," Cahaya said in that weirdly vibrational voice that didn't actually involve his jaw moving. Lips? Yeah, they moved. But his jaws and throat stayed perfectly still.

"That's so strange," Mimi said as she peered at him. "You don't talk with your throat. Your voice box never moves. It's all magic, isn't it? Never noticed that before."

Cahaya's head went back, his eyes flaring wide and scent going alarmed. "Don't be ridiculous!"

Mimi turned toward the two older dragons. "You *are* seeing this, right? He's not actually talking. It's just magic-speech, like you guys do."

The dragons were both from south of Seattle; she'd seen them around but never spoken directly to them. Neither of them had been very nice to Mori, because of the "runt" thing.

"I see it," one of the dragons agreed. "He is a siren."

"No, I'm not!" Cahaya insisted, his fear-scent rising until it was a sea-salt stink in the air. "I'm a werewolf! I'm part of a pack, not spawn of a school!"

Mimi studied him. Closely. Watched the way his ribs heaved as he glared at her, watched his hands flutter but the fingers stayed firmly together. Webbing? Probably.

Question was, did Cahaya have poison spines to go with that webbing? Probably not. His fingernails didn't look like a siren's claws, but just like those of Mimi's human form. Sirens with venom had claws, not nails.

A siren with no weapons but his voice. A siren who'd fled from the vicious, blood-thirsty life under the water to the land. And a siren who, apparently, hadn't learned that life on land, and especially life in a pack, meant that you worked together with people instead of attempting to control them.

"You're lying to hurt me," Cahaya said, glaring at Mimi, "just like you always do. You want to hurt me. You want me to be destroyed!"

The rumble coming from Cahaya's throat stepped up a notch.

Mimi turned and looked at the people watching. All of them were now frowning disapprovingly at her. Just like the last time when she'd scolded him for treating Jaiden so poorly.

Well, all of them but Mori and Cece. And the two dragons.

Mimi jerked her chin at the two dragons, "You're still seeing this, right? He says something about me trying to threaten him and I don't respond to it, but everyone else does. And then he gets all freaked out that I'm not responding as he wants."

"That's...very accurate," the Oriental dragon agreed.

"What I don't understand is why you're not responding," the Kiren said. He stamped one hoof, tossing his horns while his ears went back to hide in his mane. "Even I can feel it. What he's doing is strong enough that its edge is touching me."

The first dragon nodded in agreement. "Very odd that the three of you aren't affected."

"We're all asexual," Mimi said with a shrug, carefully watching Cahaya's response from the corner of her eye. "Also aromantic. Got no interest in mates at all. So his magic has nothing to grab onto."

Cahaya skittered back about ten paces. His expression was so terrified that, yeah, she had to be right. Not only was he more siren than were, he was the sort of abuser who needed control. Control made him safe. Lack of it made him lash out.

And anything he couldn't control, like—say—Mimi, had to be destroyed.

"Kill them!" Cahaya shouted.

No, not shouted. *Sang.* It was a song, a rising wave of sound and vibration that carried the message "kill them." It was barely even words.

The crowd starting staggering towards the three of them. Even the Oriental dragon and Kiren had dull eyes and a sort of stupor over their movements as they turned towards them.

Okay, so yeah. Cahaya was the siren version of Mori.

Finally, Mimi realized that none of this would end until Cahaya was taken down.

Mimi stepped back towards Mori and Cece, but they were both on their feet already. Mori calmly shoved his sparkly new purchase into Cece's pocket. Then flame billowed around him. Cece shifted forms, snarling at everyone around them.

Mimi grabbed a heavy, fist-sized chunk of crystal from the nearest table and whirled and flung it straight at Cahaya's head. She grabbed for a second one, then a third.

The first one hit his upflung arm and there was a nasty crack. Cahaya's song didn't stop. Faltered for a moment, but that was all.

Mimi flung the second crystal and cursed as Cahaya ducked under it. The others were coming too fast—they were already too close. She took a step back toward Cece and Mori.

"Here!" Mori exclaimed.

Flame wreathed the three of them, a blazing fence that kept anyone from getting close. Even the Oriental dragon and Kiren backed off, eyes fluttering as they shook their heads.

Mimi held the third and final crystal toward him.

His magic enveloped both the crystal and Mimi's fist. The bright flames didn't burn her, but that didn't mean they were harmless.

"Cahaya, catch!" Mimi flung the flaming crystal at him with every bit of strength she had.

It lanced through the fire wall, picking up even more flame. Cahaya's song turned into a scream of terror as the crystal hit him right in the chest and Mori's flame enveloped him.

Mimi jumped through the ring of protective fire and ran straight at Cahaya, trying to ignore his screams, trying not to smell the stink of fish burning on an open grill.

Mimi impacted Cahaya's chest the same way Cece had hit Mori, knocking them both to the ground.

The moment she hit, Mori's flame winked out.

Cahaya wheezed, fell and tried to get up.

Mimi hit him with all her might, pile-driving her fist right into the side of his head.

Silence.

Mimi panted, staring down at Cahaya's still form. No movement. No song. Nothing.

She stood. The flame wall was gone. Cece was still in her wolf form. Mori huffed smoke from his nostrils.

And the rest of the gathering attendees who had stopped advancing. All of them looked frightened. Worried.

None of the fear was directed at Mimi.

About damned time. Too late by far. Mimi almost laughed as she licked her lips and raised a chin at the crowd.

"Hey, anyone got a working cell phone?" Mimi asked the crowd at large. "Someone ought to call the cops, get a limiter down here so that Cahaya can't control anyone when he wakes up."

Something like thirty phones appeared in people's hands.

Mimi laughed as Cece and Mori crashed into with her, knocking her to the ground. Thankfully, Mori cushioned her fall so that she wasn't bruised. Didn't even have the air knocked out of her lungs.

"You did it!" Mori cheered, with a voice so deep it was a rumble. He bounced and squirmed just like normal, though, ears up and forwards and tail wagging his whole body. "You did it! You stopped him!"

"Finally," Cece agreed. She grinned at Mimi. "Seriously, that asshole needed to be whumped ages ago."

"Oh, agreed," Mimi said. "Just didn't know how badly or why."

She stayed on the ground, letting Cece and Mori high-five over her head. They were way too excited. If she tried to get up, she'd only end up flat on her back again as the two of them tackled her.

The Oriental dragon and Kiren very quickly got the crowds under control, casting spells to contain Cahaya in the event he woke up, and huffing streams of fire as they ordered everyone back to their business.

Which didn't work terribly well, but people did pull back.

Three minutes later, the cops showed up, running through the gate with wands, guns, and swords at the ready. The older dragons explained everything. Giving her deposition was the work of about two minutes. Getting Mori to stop adding in details was a lot harder, but hey, that was fine.

By the time it was done, the three of them had already passed their curfew.

Mimi stared up at the stars overhead, what few shone through the light pollution of Seattle and the clouds drifting by. She smiled before turning to Mori, who perked up even though he didn't stop playing with his new shiny.

"I'm hungry," Mimi announced.

"I could eat," Mori said slowly, his tail starting to wag.

"You know I'm always up for food," Cece agreed when they turned to her. "What're you thinking? There are still some vendors with food here."

"Nah, I want burgers," Mimi declared. Mori promptly started vibrating with excitement. She smirked. "Greasy burgers with all the fixings."

"And cheese?" Mori asked in such a high-pitched voice that he sounded like a hatchling. "Maybe double cheese?" As if he should eat even a single slice of cheese with his lactose intolerance.

Cece hooted with laughter. "Your stomach is going to hate you! We're not that far from the diner you like so much, Mimi. Head down there? They've got great milkshakes, too. I'd love a milkshake."

Mori crooned with joy. He tucked his shiny away, then launched up into the air, blowing smoke rings and flying through them. He flitted towards the parking garage, swooping and barrel-rolling so obnoxiously that even people on the ground glared up at him.

"Let's go!" Cece exclaimed. She shifted to wolf and ran off, only to stop a few paces later when Mimi didn't immediately shift to follow her. The moon had come out from behind a cloud, its sliver bright enough that Mimi could see the curve of its dark belly against the dark night sky.

Suddenly, Mimi shifted and dashed straight at Cece, who leaped out of the way with a startled yip. Mimi ran right past her, tongue lolling out as she laughed. Cece's gruff bark made Mimi laugh harder, especially once Mori stopped fooling around and winged straight towards the parking garage as the three of them raced each other.

They were going to be grounded already for being late getting home, but Mimi didn't care. Because she was free. Cahaya wouldn't ever hurt her again. Mimi laughed as she ran with her siblings, free and happy and, yeah, time for some greasy diner food and maybe a nice long drive that lasted until sunrise. The moon was still up and they could do whatever they wanted now. Who needed anything else when you had your siblings at your side and a good ride?

That was all Mimi wanted, now that Cahaya'd finally harvested the chaos he'd sowed.

About the Author

Meyari McFarland has been telling stories since she was a small child. Her stories range from SF and Fantasy adventures to Romances, but they always feature strong characters who do what they think is right no matter what gets in their way.

Her series range from Space Opera Romance in the Drath series, to Epic Fantasy in the Mages of Tindiere world. Other series include Matriarchies of Muirin, the Clockwork Rift Steampunk mysteries, and the Tales of Unification urban fantasy stories, plus many more.

Find out more about Meyari at:
mdr-publishing.com

Exit Ramp

Jeff Wood

Everything smelled weird.

They'd all been riding inside the family Oldsmobile for three long days, Jimmy and his parents and Jimmy's dog, Cecil, so that accounted for some of the smell, but not all of it. Jimmy sometimes melted plastic army men out in the woods behind the back yard, and that's kind of what the place smelled like: the black smoke that spooled off of the bubbling dots of plastic. But some other scent hid behind the melting army man scent, too, Jimmy noticed. Like rotting fish. Burnt hair. The sack of old lawn fertilizer out in the shed.

When the car's tire blew out, Dad had yelled, "Damn it, just my luck, why do I have to get a flat right now!" mumbling variations on that theme as they rolled down the exit ramp.

Dad used to say people who believed in luck weren't accepting responsibility for their own actions.

Not anymore.

If Jimmy's dad hadn't lost his job six months ago, they never would have had to make this trip at all. If he hadn't lost his job, he wouldn't be so stressed out all the time, wouldn't be fighting with Mom so much, wouldn't be dragging his entire family across the country for a job that he didn't want, in Mesa, Arizona, a town none of them had heard of or wanted to live in.

It was like he was a different person since he lost his job.

Their car limped off the exit ramp. They descended under the jumble of roadways and into the parking lot of the Skelly station. Jimmy rolled his window down, and that's when the weird smell hit him. And not just the smell: everything sounded weird too. The air filled with a high-pitched whirring the instant he rolled the window down. The sound ebbed and flowed with the wind, though never entirely disappeared. It sounded like something breathing.

The car rolled to a stop.

Mom and Dad got out and stood outside the car by the hood, talking quietly. Probably about money. Jimmy stayed in the car with Cecil.

Lately the beagle felt like Jimmy's best friend.

Sometimes his only friend.

Whenever his parents were talking in hushed, secretive voices at the kitchen table, or arguing in the bedroom in louder ones, Jimmy would slip out to the garage and play with Cecil, rolling on the cold concrete together, snuggling on the ancient dusty sofa.

Sometimes he'd melt army men out there too.

Jimmy watched Dad and Mom hug. Dad walked off in the direction of the garage. Mom headed back to the car, opened the door and got in.

"What's going on, Mom?"

She turned in the passenger seat to face him.

"Nothing, honey. We have a flat tire."

Duh, thought Jimmy. "Now what?"

"We're going to have to get a new tire. But they have to get it from another gas station."

He knew what was coming next. "We have to spend the night here, don't we?"

She smiled. "Yes, we do, honey. Just one night. It'll be fun. It'll be an adventure."

"It smells here, Mom."

"I know it does," she said.

"It's not an adventure. It's not gonna be fun."

She said nothing for several moments. "No. Probably not. Dad really wants this job. We all do. So we need to support him."

"I know," he said. "I will." Then, "I promise."

"We'll eat fast food. Or order pizza! We'll watch TV in the motel. As late as you want."

"Even *The Time Tunnel?*"

Mom winced. "Even *The Time Tunnel*."

She turned to the front of the car. They watched as Dad talked with the tire guy in the Skelly station office and handed him several bills from his wallet.

Inside the garage, several cars sat suspended on lifts. Their car would be up on one of those lifts soon, to get the tires changed. Three mechanics stood in the front of the garage, backlit by the bright fluorescent lights. They seemed to be staring directly at Jimmy and his mom sitting in the car.

Jimmy stared back.

Their eyes looked weird. They were blue, but a weird blue. They reminded Jimmy of looking into a lake, or the depths of the ocean. He half imagined he could see schools of fish swimming beneath the surface.

Dad and the tire guy walked across the lot toward the car.

To Mom, Dad said, "There's a motel a couple of blocks away. They'll take the car overnight. We'll spend the night in the motel and leave in the morning."

Mom nodded.

Jimmy did not react.

"Come on, Jimmy," Dad said. "Let's carry Mom's bags for her."

Jimmy stifled his urge to protest. It would do no good. Besides, he'd noticed something else.

The tire guy's eyes were that weird underwater blue, too

Jimmy picked up Cecil, cradling the dog protectively in his arms, and got out of the car.

The winding walk to the motel seemed to last forever. The three of them walked at the edge of the street, luggage in hand, Cecil trotting dutifully at Jimmy's side.

The looping entrance and exit ramps of the newly-built I-40 towered over them, groaning and rumbling with the passage of cars overhead. Occasionally Jimmy could hear the screech of brakes, the sounding of horns. The overpasses blotted out the sun, leaving Jimmy and his family in nearly perpetual shadow as they walked.

It was a different world. Even though the ground had been nearly entirely paved with concrete, no sidewalks had been built. The place wasn't designed for humans, but for cars and semis.

Motels and gas stations and diners were sandwiched between the thick slabs and columns of concrete of the roadways above. Small, oddly shaped factories stood at regular intervals. Bright light leaked out of the windows and cracks in the doorways. Fumes that smelled like rotten eggs belched from brick smokestacks at the sides of the buildings. Pipes ran over the cracked and shadowed roads, connecting the buildings to short, squat storage tanks that bristled with levers and gauges and valves leading into the ground.

Dad said, "Those buildings look a little like the refineries back in Texas where I grew up. Pump oil out of the ground, store it in tanks. I guess we're in oil country now."

Eventually they saw the dim neon sign for their motel. The Little Moon Inn. They trudged across the paved lot toward the office. Jimmy saw faces peeking through the shades of several motel room windows, watching.

The woman at the front desk had normal eyes, unlike the mechanics at the garage. She told them the motel had only a few vacancies, because a lot of people stayed in the rooms long-term, paying a monthly rate. No extra charge for pets. She checked them in, took Dad's cash, told them where the ice-maker and the vending machines were. Check-out time was at 10 a.m. She handed Dad keys on a plastic diamond keychain with the room number stamped on it.

Jimmy and his dad hauled the luggage in. Mom checked the bathroom for whatever it was that Mom always checked motel bathrooms for, then started to put away their belongings. Cecil stayed outside until Jimmy brought his doggy bed into the room, then trotted inside to lay down. The whir and grind from the outside followed them into the room too, as did the smell from the smokestacks. The sound made them speak in louder, more distinct voices. The smell made them mildly nauseous.

They ordered a pizza.

Dad turned on the old TV. Loud white noise filled the screen. He played with the positioning of the bunny-eared twin antennas until he finally got a reasonable picture. Static occasionally threatened to take over the screen, and the picture would collapse into a wall of gray. Once or twice Jimmy thought he saw figures within the dancing static. Open, toothless mouths. A face with no eyes. Tentacles.

They watched *Voyage to the Bottom of the Sea*. They watched *The Time Tunnel*. They watched the evening news and Johnny Carson's monologue, and then it was time for bed.

Jimmy couldn't sleep.

He listened to his parents snoring. He listened to the wheeze and drone of traffic rumbling on the interstate. He listened to the endless thrum outside their door.

He breathed through his mouth to avoid the smell.

He thought about what it would be like in Mesa, Arizona, if Dad got the job. He'd be going to a new school. He'd have to make new friends. He wondered if anyone would like science fiction, or the Cubs, or Roger Miller. What would their new house be like? Would they have a big backyard? Would he be able to play wiffle ball back there? Would he have any friends to play wiffle ball with?

When the clock hit two a.m., he decided he needed to get out. Just for a little while. Go to the U-Tote-Em on the far side of the intersection and get a candy bar, maybe a Slushie. He contemplated how to do it. His first instinct—sneaking out the door with a five-dollar bill from Mom's purse—he discarded almost immediately. His family had gone through a lot lately. He didn't want to have one of his parents wake up and see he was gone.

And he couldn't steal from Mom.

He woke her up as quietly as possible, gently shaking her shoulder. "Mom." Then louder: "Mom."

She rolled over and blinked several times, waking, then focused on him.

"Mom," he whispered. "Can I go across the street to the store? I'll just be a second. I'm hungry and I can't sleep."

"Absolutely not." She turned to go back to sleep.

"Please, Mom."

"No."

"You can watch from the window."

She sighed and paused, which meant she was at least thinking about it.

He pressed on. "Sit and watch from the window. I'll walk across the street. I'll buy a candy bar and a drink. I can get you something!"

She didn't respond right away. Her eyes widened slightly and she looked off to the side and he knew he had a shot.

"I'll get you whatever you want. You can watch me the entire time. There's nobody out there. It'll be fine. I'll take Cecil with me. He'll bark if anything goes wrong."

Mom whispered, "Okay. Get me cigarettes. If they'll let you. Don't push it. But if they let you. Virginia Slims 100s."

"You don't smoke."

Mom smiled for the first time in what seemed like days. "You and your dad are not the only ones stressed out on this trip."

She rolled silently out of bed, handed Jimmy a five-dollar bill from her purse, and walked to the motel window. She pulled the shades open. The lights of the U-Tote-Em shone across the street. Empty streets yawned between the window and the store.

"Okay," she said. "Take Cecil. I'll watch from here. Make it snappy, mister." She kissed him on the forehead. "And don't tell your father."

Cecil already stood by the door. When Jimmy walked toward the door, he jumped up and down, tail wagging, ears flopping.

Jimmy opened the door and stepped outside.

The air loomed thick, almost like fog but too warm, too dry. It felt like dust, sticking to his skin.

Jimmy looked left. He looked right. He made sure Mom could see him turn his head. No one around. No cars, no pedestrians. He walked across the street and into the brightly lit asphalt parking lot of the U-Tote-Em. A little girl, maybe a couple of years younger than him, sat on a yellow concrete curbstone in front of the parking spaces, so small and so quiet he almost didn't notice her.

Jimmy patted his leg to bring Cecil closer, then looked back at his mom's face in the window. He waved. She waved back.

Hers was not the only face watching him from the windows of the motel.

Jimmy gave the little girl a wide berth, opened the door and followed Cecil inside. The clerk's eyes were more bloodshot than blue. At least he didn't seem to mind having a dog in the store. Jimmy grabbed a Caravelle bar and a cherry Slushie and headed to the register.

He asked for the cigarettes, heart beating a little faster. "They're for my mom, not me." He gestured at the motel. "See? She's right there."

The clerk didn't even look. He handed the package to Jimmy with no questions.

Jimmy handed the clerk the five, collected his change, and grabbed the brown paper bag. Cecil and he walked out the door.

Across the street, Mom still watched from the hotel window. Others from the motel still watched as well. The little girl still sat on the concrete outside in the parking lot. She watched him with the same wariness he watched her with.

Then her eyes widened. She pointed behind Jimmy. "There goes your dog, mister."

He turned to see Cecil running around the corner of the building, disappearing into the night.

Jimmy walked along the middle of the street, slowly, grocery bag still in hand, calling Cecil's name every few steps. He peered into the shadows thrown by the streetlights.

Mom had probably seen Cecil bolt from the parking lot and Jimmy run after him. She'd be worried. He considered going back to the motel room to reassure her.

No. He'd lose valuable time. He kept looking.

He passed gas stations, tire shops, cheap motels, convenience stores, pizza parlors, more tire shops, a few run-down apartment complexes, and a couple more tire shops.

Between two tire shops stood one of buildings his dad had called a refinery. A big smokestack pumped out stinky fumes. Surrounding the property was a chest-high, sagging chain-link fence with *KEEP OUT* signs. Rusted locks shuttered each of the gates. Bright lights lit the interior.

Walking with weary steps, a small group of workers exited the doors. A streetlight shone on their faces, revealing to Jimmy the same weird underwater eyes.

A large pipe connected the building to a tank across the street. Heat radiated from the building so intensely he could feel it all the way from the fence.

The paved lot beyond the fence looked quiet and dark. Just the kind of place Cecil liked.

Jimmy climbed the fence. He crouched down as he searched through the weeds and tall grass, quietly calling for Cecil.

Jimmy heard a commotion inside the building. He crept closer to the window. The melted army man odor grew stronger as he got closer. He peered inside.

The window was scratched and grimy. Blinding light shone from the center of the room. It appeared to be from a fire; Jimmy could occasionally make out large flames leaping from the center of the blaze.

Figures danced in a circle around the light in a slow but building rhythm. The intense glare made it hard for Jimmy to see the figures very clearly. Mostly he saw the shadows of bodies as they passed between the fire and the window.

All at once the fire roared, the light thrown from the flames turned bright red, painting the walls with color so that they looked like they'd been splashed with blood.

The figures leapt and cheered.

Something screamed. A man, an animal: it was impossible for Jimmy to know.

He ran from the building, not even slowing as he placed his hands on the top of the fence and vaulted himself over.

He kept running, not even wondering where he was headed, determined to put distance between himself and what he had just seen. Only after stopping to catch his breath did he realize he was lost.

He wandered the concrete landscape, looking for anything recognizable: a street sign, a billboard, a fence. Nothing seemed familiar. He was scared, and so far away from home.

Then Jimmy found a road he remembered, and saw it led to the maze of overpasses where the motel and the gas station were. Where his parents were. He stuck to the road, calling for Cecil from the center of the street, peering into the shadows rather than exploring them.

He only strayed from the path back to the motel once.

As he passed another refinery, Jimmy heard moaning coming from a storage tank. A kind of toneless singing, not too different than the humming made by the refineries. He walked closer, careful not to pass beyond the boundary of the fence this time.

A man was caressing one of the pipes that led from the tank and the ground. He had wrapped his arms and legs around the curve of the metal, tightly but tenderly, as if embracing a loved one. His face was pressed hard against the surface of the pipe. His eyes were closed, his mouth open wide. He was humming.

As Jimmy watched, two more men came out of the refinery door. Jimmy dropped to the ground. The men didn't see him. They focused only on the man draped over the pipe. They walked toward him, eyes and mouths open, the same tuneless hum coming from their lips. Both of the men had those weird underwater eyes.

Jimmy crawled away.

Summoning his courage, Jimmy stood up. He could no longer see the men, but he could still hear the humming, louder than ever. The sound seemed to come not only from the men and the pipes but from deep in the ground, like a living, breathing thing. The stink was so strong here Jimmy found it hard to breathe.

Jimmy hustled back to the street, making his way home. He called to Cecil from the asphalt, peered into shadows, looked into trees and under cars. He noticed with a start that he'd seen no other animals. No birds. No squirrels. No stray cats.

No dogs.

Jimmy felt a familiar sinking feeling in his stomach, the same feeling as when Dad lost his job. When he listened to Mom and Dad fight. When he learned they were moving across the country and he'd have to leave his school and his friends and his hometown behind.

He knew he'd never see Cecil again.

Jimmy turned a corner and saw the motel sign stood alight and shining only a few blocks away. Mom and Dad would be there. Maybe he could make his dad feel better by saying he knew they had to hit the road tomorrow. That if Cecil hadn't come back by morning then Jimmy was willing to move on without him. Maybe he could sneak Mom her cigarettes.

The first streaks of light signaled the approach of dawn.

Jimmy turned the corner and walked across the asphalt parking lot to The Little Moon Inn. The curtains of their room had been left open. Jimmy decided to look into the window first, to gauge his parents' reaction.

He peered inside. The lights were on, the beds unmade, blankets and sheets tossed aside, a stray pillow left on the floor.

His parents were gone.

They were out looking for him. Looking for Cecil too, probably.

Jimmy looked around either side of the motel. An empty weed-filled lot on one side. A nest of electric lines on the other.

He looked across the street.

The U-Tote-Em.

Streetlights stood on sturdy metal poles at all four corners of the well-lit parking lot. He could sit on the curb and be within eyesight of the clerk inside the store. The little girl still sat on the yellow curbstone.

Jimmy walked across the street. He asked the girl, "Can I sit next to you? I'm waiting for my parents. And my dog."

She said, "You're scared."

"A little."

"You bought cigarettes when you were here before. You still got 'em? There in your bag?"

He'd forgotten he was even carrying it. "Yes."

"Gimme a cigarette. Then sure, you can sit."

Jimmy shot a hand into the brown paper bag and searched for the box of Virginia Slims. He pulled the pack out and tried to open the top. He'd never handled a pack of cigarettes before. Eventually he just handed her the whole box. She expertly tore off the plastic wrapping, opened the triangular top of the pack, loosened the foil, and tapped out a cigarette.

She pulled a tarnished Zippo out of her pocket, lit the cigarette, handed the pack back, then patted the space on the curbstone next to her.

Jimmy sat down. He opened the bag and pulled out the candy bar. As he unwrapped it he said, "So do you live here?"

"You mean in the parking lot?"

"No. I mean, you know. Here. In this place." He gestured around.

"You mean, like, this neighborhood."

"Yes. Here under the interstate."

She turned. "Yeah. I live here. I have for a while now."

"How long?"

"Feels like forever." She took a drag off her cigarette and let the smoke drift out. "Maybe it has been forever."

"Did you move here? From somewhere else?"

"Sorta."

Silence overtook them. He ate his candy bar, she smoked her cigarette.

"I saw you come down here," she said at last.

"Down where?"

"Down the exit ramp. Your car had a flat tire. You pulled into the Skelly at the bottom of the ramp. You got a room at the Little Moon."

"Yeah," he said. "How did you know?"

"I watched. Not from here, from a few doors over, in front of the apartments." She took another drag. "That's what I do. I watch. I watch the cars from the exit ramp. Sometimes I follow people. See where they eat. See where they spend the night."

"Don't you go to school?"

"There's no school here," she said.

Silence again. Candy bar. Cigarette.

Jimmy finished his Caravelle, stuffed the wrapper back in the bag. He considered the cherry Slushie. "How did you end up here?"

"My dad got a flat tire." She exhaled a puff of smoke.

"That's what happened to us," said Jimmy, hesitantly.

"I know."

He wanted to ask a question, but didn't know how.

"Leave," she said. "Just leave."

"Why?"

"We got a flat tire. The next day they said we had engine problems too. So we were here for a few days, waiting. Next thing I knew, my dad got a job at the factory. And we had an apartment, fully furnished, down the street. We didn't even need a car anymore."

"What does your dad do? At the factory."

"I dunno."

"Does he have…those eyes?"

She stared down at the ground.

"What do they do in those factories?" he asked. "What do they make?"

"I dunno."

"Tell me."

"I really don't know." She looked up from the asphalt to meet his gaze. "Yes. My dad has those eyes."

Jimmy wanted to reach out a hand to comfort her. He didn't.

She continued, "It's the acid in the air. That's what someone told me. Some grown-up. There's gunk in the air that messes with your eyes."

"Does it come from those smokestacks?"

"I think so."

Jimmy said, "It doesn't make sense. These refineries, they're pumping something out of the ground. Oil, right? And storing it in those tanks. I get that. But there are no pipes carrying anything away. And no oil trucks coming in to haul it out. Where does it all go? Nothing comes out of the refineries. The gates are all locked. The locks are rusted shut."

The girl's eyes narrowed. "It's not oil. And they aren't pumping it out of the ground."

"Then what...?"

"They're pumping it *into* the ground."

Jimmy stared at her, not understanding.

The girl said, "The refineries make something. Some kind of... stuff. They store it in the tanks. And then they pump it into the ground."

"But why? That's just wasting it, right?"

"I don't know."

Jimmy refused to accept the answer this time. "What do you think?"

"I think they're feeding something." She shrugged.

Silence. Jimmy listened to the whirring grind of the refineries, the hum of the pumps. The stench in the air filled his lungs.

"Nothing here makes any sense." Jimmy said, "Everything's weird here."

She smiled for the first time. "Yeah. Weird. That fits. I like that."

After a moment, she said, "I'll get out of here someday."

"Am I...is my family ever going to be able to leave?"

She said, "Sure. Probably. Most people leave." She crushed her cigarette out on the painted concrete. "Some come back, though."

"What do you mean?"

"They come back. Same car, same people. Different eyes."

She held out her hand for another cigarette. Jimmy offered the pack. She slipped a cigarette out and put it behind her ear.

Jimmy asked, "How does the eye thing work? The blue eye thing. You said some people don't get it."

"I don't know. It never happened to me."

"Because you never got…recruited?"

"The eyes never turn blue right away. It takes a few days. If it happens at all. Sometimes it doesn't."

Jimmy screwed up his courage to ask the next question. "Does it only happen to people? What about animals?"

The girl looked to him.

"Where did all the animals go?"

He never heard her answer.

Cecil came bounding around the corner of the parking lot and leaped into Jimmy's arms. As the dog licked his face, Jimmy laughed loudly, the first joyful noise he had made since they had driven into this shadowland. He hugged Cecil close to his chest, feeling the warmth against his skin. His best friend.

Jimmy's parents appeared a few minutes later from the opposite side of the U-Tote-Em lot. He had expected them to rush toward him when they found him. Run to him and scoop him into their arms and hug him. They walked toward him calmly, unhurriedly. Jimmy stood. When they got close enough, his mother opened her arms to him.

"Welcome home, son," she said.

His dad smiled. "Thank God you're safe."

As they turned to walk back to the motel, Jimmy looked over his shoulder.

The little girl had vanished.

Mom never did ask for her cigarettes.

Convincing Dad to leave first thing in the morning turned out to be easy. He agreed at once. "I've got a job waiting for me in Mesa, and we're behind schedule."

They spent a little over an hour at the gas station, watching the trio of mechanics install the new tire.

Maybe Jimmy imagined their interest earlier.

Maybe he imagined the eyes.

Maybe he imagined the lukewarm reaction of his parents upon finding him last night.

Welcome home, son.

When the tire had been repaired they loaded their luggage into the trunk, piled into the car, and took a twisting route through the maze of cracked streets toward the interstate exit. Night had passed, and daylight lay a hundred yards above them, shining on the cars roaring past on the roadways overhead.

Jimmy's dad finally found a bright blue sign pointing to the interstate ramp and made a sharp left. Seconds later they were driving up and out of the dark. Jimmy felt like he was on an airplane, flying under a black blanket of thunderclouds, about to break through the storm and rise into a boundless, sunny sky.

They emerged into daylight. Dad hit the turn signal and they merged into one of the middle lanes, then settled into traveling speed.

A sign a short distance later told them they were 327 miles away from their new home.

Jimmy should have felt more optimistic than he did.

Parents were weird. Parents were parents. They could turn

into aliens, or monsters, or whatever it was that was happening to the people they'd just left behind. Parents turned into different people all the time. It had already happened to his dad when he lost his job. Dad had already turned into a different person. And Mom with her secret cigarettes, that was different too.

Sometimes parents just changed.

Sometimes they turned into monsters.

Jimmy woke his dog, picked him up, and sat him in his lap. He held the dog's head in his hands and looked into his eyes.

Cecil looked back. The weird smell was fading, and the humming sound had long since disappeared. Dad turned on the radio and the car filled with sunny pop music. Mom reached out and took Dad's hand in hers. They smiled at each other.

A few days, the girl from the parking lot had said. It took a few days. If it happened at all.

Jimmy and Cecil settled down into the back seat for the rest of the drive. 327 miles. Jimmy did the math in his head. They'd be in Mesa in five or six hours. Nothing to do now but sit back and wait. And hope.

Always hope.

The highway stretched before them like an unanswered question.

About the Author

Jeff Wood lives in Colorado Springs, where he spends way too much time staring at the night sky, and a little too much time watching baseball. His stories have appeared in over 30 publications such as Boston Phoenix, New York Press, Wild Musette, Fiction at Work, Bright Desire, The Greyrock Review, Bellowing Ark, and Java Journal. He has a children's play included in the anthology *Childsplay*, in the company of such authors as Sam Shepard and Maya Angelou.

Find out more about Jeff at:
jeffmwood.wordpress.com

Wiggle-Wiggle, Shake-Shake

Rebecca Hodgkins

Honey, let me explain the sad condition of your bouquet. And... about the hula girl.

Thirty-eight years married, you've forgiven your old Horse a lot, mostly because I think you like hearing my stories from the road. This last time out was a doozy.

I oughta explain this brand-new tape player, too. You're gonna like it. It's better than that old eight-track. You can put any songs you want on the cassettes. I made one for you. First up, that song you always used to tease me about, "Horse with No Name."

That's where my story starts, too: listening to America and The Eagles and good old Jimmy Buffett, thinking of you while I'm hauling produce through the Nevada desert. The refrigerated—reefer—trailer was suffering from deferred maintenance, oh joy, causing it to run above the regulated thirty-two degrees for pork and fresh corn. The corn was the bigger problem because that stuff would build up heat as it rotted on the way to market, and the farther I went down the road, the warmer it'd get. But, the warmer temps let me keep your usual bouquet of flowers in the back. Instead of freezing, they'd stay cool and fresh.

I'd gotten a late start and the sun was shining straight into my eyes on its way down. Grocery warehouses are the worst for making you wait. So what's new? Still, it's cooler riding at night, which means I can get away with keeping the thermostat up a bit, get one more trip outta it before a tune-up.

I'd planned on rushing right by that weird refinery they got going north off US-50 just west of Austin, Nevada. Place always gives me the creeps with its weird smells, and I'll be damned if I can tell whether they're pumping something into or out of the ground.

So I was driving a little faster than I should have, and I was feeling mellow from a different kind of reefer and singing along to "Horse with No Name."

I was singing that last verse, the one about the heart lying under the cities, when a weird sound rose over the song, a sort of roaring. I got concerned, thinking it was the rig, but the sound was coming from farther away outside. It sounded like a chopper, but higher-pitched one minute, and lower the next. The sun had dropped behind the mountains and the sky was clear and orange, and I got paranoid that maybe it was a bear in the air clocking me and that I'd been nailed.

Then *boom*. Something hit the truck hard enough to rock it.

I pulled over as fast as I could without tipping my gal over. I didn't know if I'd hit an animal, a retread—or sweet Baby Jesus forbid—a person. Not likely out here in the middle of nowhere, but I was right up by that refinery, so who knew?

I got out to look at the front. No blood and nothing mashed into the grille, thank God.

All was quiet, but here's the funny part, I swear I heard the faintest ukulele music coming from the cab. It couldn't have been the eight-track or the CB, because I'd shut them off.

I was gonna get back in the cab and maybe just roll on outta there, when a slight breeze carried the smell of something chemical and burnt toward me, with an underlying fleshy rot. I couldn't hear the helicopter no more, either. I got concerned that the sound had come from the truck after all. Maybe the stink, too.

I came around the north side of the reefer, expecting God-knows-what, hoping I wasn't smelling rotting pork and coolant.

All I could see in the fading light was a big dent in the trailer's side. Whether it was caused by a plant, a bird, a rock, or a thing, I had no idea. "By sand or hills or rings," I sang, thinking about the lyrics to "Horse with No Name" and cracked myself up. Guess I was still feeling the joint I'd smoked an hour ago.

I laughed until I heard a squeaky-creaky voice laughing right behind me.

I spun around.

It was a skinny teenaged boy standing beside the road. He wore a long brown leather duster that sparkled in places like it was covered with mica, and a dirty old white ball cap pulled far down and about half covered with reddish mud that had dried like paste. Under the brim's shadow I could see his wide open smile, making him look a little simple. It took me a second to put two and two together.

I scowled at the kid. "You just throw a rock at my rig, boy?"

His smile spread even wider and he nodded vigorously. "Rock at my rig, boy. No, sir. I need a ride, sir."

Maybe he'd thrown something, maybe he hadn't. Maybe I couldn't blame him for wanting to be away from this stinking stretch of no-where road. Might be an hour or more before another rig came along. Might be all night out here in the desert, with nothing but the flames from that refinery to keep him company. Hell, I'd throw a rock, too.

"Trying to get back home," he added.

I thought of your good cooking, babe, the way you danced with the kitchen radio on, how much I missed you, and that decided matters. "You and me both just trying to get home, kid. All right." I banged on the passenger door. "Get up in there."

Looking at that dent again, I decided the kid would about have to throw a boulder to make one that big. Too heavy for that skinny kid to manage. I convinced myself probably something happened at the warehouse while I was off getting lunch. I decided to find a payphone and call the warehouse, leave a nasty message for the day shift. Still, I wondered what just happened. Maybe a gust of wind hit the rig same time I found a pothole.

I expected the kid to unearth a bag from under the sagebrush along the road, but he just hopped up onto the bench seat and slammed the door after himself. The stink of the refinery followed him in, clinging to his duster.

"Home must not be far, huh, kid? You got no bag?"

"Got no bag. Sir. Home must not be far." He pointed west.

I started up the rig. I had the CB turned down—not much point along this stretch of US-50—and the eight-track turned up. America came back on, the la la la part near the end.

"You live in Fallon?" That was a good hour-and-a-half away. About the only thing in between here and there was the diner I always stopped at along this route.

"Fallon. Fallon. Fall…on." Kid gave a high-pitched laugh that convinced me he was indeed simple. Or maybe on something. Acid, most likely, maybe speed. Not PCP, I hoped.

"What's your name, kid?"

He waved me off with another laugh that sounded like the yawp of a young blue jay. "No name."

That actually made *me* chuckle. The coincidence was too good. "Okay, No-Name. I'm Joe Palomino, but my good buddies on the CB call me Horse. You and me, I guess we're Horse with No Name, huh?"

He didn't seem to get my joke.

"You a music fan? America?"

"America." He shook his head no.

I pulled the cassette out of the eight track and shoved in Jimmy Buffett. Margaritaville's latest oil-slicked tourist began singing, claiming there was probably a woman at the bottom of his troubles and it wasn't his fault.

I pointed at the player. "That fool just doesn't know how easy it is to keep a lady happy. Never go to bed mad or you'll end up sleeping alone and cold. Take the blame when you're wrong, keep her warm and fed on love and attention, and she'll keep *you* warm and fed to the end of your days."

No-Name says, "Fed fed fed to the end," and he let out this little giggle, very un-teenagerlike, and I heard this *scritch, scritch* sound. He was scratching at the seat and I figured he'd got some long-ass nails to be doing that, but I couldn't see his hands on account of the duster's long sleeves.

I started wondering just who I'd picked up. Something was off for sure. Miles down the road, the refinery smell still clung to him. A stink almost like roadkill.

Then, like he was reading my mind, he went and sniffed the air in the cab, making my skin crawl the tiniest bit. He was looking at me again, scritching-scratching at the seat, like maybe he was tweaking.

I cracked my window to bring in some fresh desert-night air. The little hula girl pasted to the dashboard danced in the wind. She was holding a little ukulele like she was gonna start jamming with Jimmy any minute, her big hula skirt made of real dry grass moving to "Margaritaville." Wiggle-wiggle, sway-sway. Really more like wiggle-wiggle, *shake-shake*. She didn't sway much for a hula girl.

As you know, babe, my little partner in crime on the dashboard had a secret.

No-Name reached for her and I slapped his hand. He pulled it back quick with a sharp *hiss*. It happened so fast, I only got a quick look at his hands—filthy like he'd been digging in the dirt, and long-nailed like I'd thought.

I told him, "I know you have two questions about her and I'll answer them both. Yes, I've looked. And no, she's not anatomically correct."

No-Name kept his gaze locked on her and sniffed the air again. He glanced at me, then back at her, like a hungry puppy at a bone. That's when I realized what he was really after.

"Look, buddy. I know the cab smells like I'm holding, but I smoked my last one over an hour ago," I lied. How he honed in on my hula girl and the Maui-Wowie stashed in the spring under her skirt along with my mini-Zippo, I'll never know, but I wasn't about to share my last joint. It was a long way from Austin, Nevada, to Fairfield, California.

No-Name went quiet except for them nails going scritch-scratch on the bench, and I got to studying him out of the corner of my eye. The highway was straight and empty enough I could've turned my head to get a good long gander at him without fear of going off the road. I didn't want to be obvious. I had an idea about my hitcher. Maybe I'd got him all wrong. Something about that high-pitched voice, the long nails. The small, thin fame. Birdlike.

Maybe this wasn't a teenaged boy at all, but a girl. A girl or woman traveling on her own, she's not gonna wanna advertise something like that. She's gonna want to let you think she's a boy instead and hope you're not into that.

I coughed to get her attention, then scratched my right ear with my left hand, to show off my gold band. I thought it might reassure her.

She did look, real quick, then went straight back to staring at Miss Maui-Wowie.

"You really like my hula girl, huh? My sweet wife bought her for me as a kind of joke."

No-Name tilted her head, reminding me of a bird again. She kept mum, either still smarting from the smack I gave her hand—something I regretted, because you know I don't hit women—or disappointed she wasn't going to score any weed.

I pulled Jimmy Buffett mid-song without a never-you-mind, and plugged in The Eagles' Greatest Hits for a peaceful, easy feeling while I talked.

"It was about twelve years ago. I was hauling dry goods on I-15 east of Vegas, and all I wanted was to get home, but Mother Nature had other plans. My good buddies up ahead sent the word out over the CB. There was a huge dust storm coming, followed by torrential rain. Highway patrol were shutting the roads down. No choice but to stop in Vegas for the night.

"So me and some boys, other truckers I'd known a while, well, we met up to do a little gambling, a little drinking and a lot of bullshitting. We were having a good time when this guy Shorty gets the idea to hit a tittie bar, some tiki place way off the Strip where we could spend our winnings in a friendly way. I didn't wanna go. Like Paul Newman says, why would I go for a burger when I've got a steak at home?"

No-Name cackled. "Steak at home. Home at steak. Steak. Steak."

Her crazy talk made me wish she'd go back to being quiet. I hit the gas, hoping the diner up ahead was still open and I could let her out.

"Yeah, 'home at stake' is right. Getting in trouble's fun. *Being* in it, well, not so much."

"Trouble." No-Name cooed the word.

"Speaking of trouble, we had a Holy Roller among us in Vegas, liked to bullshit well enough, but didn't drink, didn't gamble, sure didn't go in for strippers. Me and him went back to the motel instead, me with a hundred bucks in my pocket that I managed to steal from one of them one-armed bandits. Don't know what he did back his room, probably prayed, but I went straight to bed and hauled ass outta Vegas next morning, soon as I could.

"Smart move, because it turns out Holy Roller didn't just pray that night. He called home and confessed to his wife, who spread the word about the tiki bar to any trucker's wife or girlfriend who'd listen. And boy did they, especially Shorty's wife. But because I'd been a choir boy, I was off the hook."

"Off. Off the hook? No. Sir." No-Name adjusted her leather duster and some of the glitter scattered onto the bench seat.

"This old Horse was indeed off the hook. When I got home a couple days later, my wife meets me at the door, standing there in a grass skirt and a coconut bra, doing her own wiggle-wiggle, sway-sway. Let's just say, as a reward for being a choir boy, I got Hawaiian lei'd that night. That's when she gave me my little hula girl, too. A surrogate to keep me company on the road." I tapped Maui-Wowie on the head to make her wobble and she did her dance—as well as she could.

Up ahead was an old cottonwood with some pretty funny-looking clumps hanging from it. It was a sight for sore eyes. I knew that tree. The diner was only a few minutes away.

Baby, you remember that tree, don't you?

I relaxed but didn't ease up on the gas. I tried to think of a nice way to leave No-Name at the diner. I'd buy her a burger, explain how I...what? Couldn't take her another fifty miles up the road to Fallon because I couldn't take her stink? I didn't know. I picked up my storytelling, hoping to think of something. Glenn Fry sang about having a world of trouble on his mind.

"See that cottonwood?" I asked No-Name. "That's the world famous Shoe Tree. Some newlyweds got into an argument under it years ago. The missus threatened to walk home and he threw her shoes up into the tree so she couldn't. They made up after that. People still come and throw their shoes for a happy marriage. See them all hanging up there, nearly toppling that tree? My wife sometimes used to come over the road with me and we stopped once, threw our own shoes. Guess it works."

"Guess it works," No-Name echoed with that blue-jay laugh-cackle.

Then, baby, she did something that turned my stomach.

All she did was stick her feet out from under that long leather duster. She didn't have any shoes on. In the dashboard glow and the moonlight I could see her bony feet and her long, thick nails. Like scaly talons. By the dashboard light, they looked to be dripping with blood, glistening with pus. God, that smell. It wasn't from the refinery after all. Even when I rolled the window all the way down, it stank up the cab. Pretty sure if I hadn't smoked that doobie, I'd of puked out the window all over the side of the rig.

I damn near missed the turnoff for the diner. Don't know what would have happened if I had. I don't think I'd be here telling you my story. You wouldn't have any flowers, mangled or not.

But I didn't miss the turnoff. That neon Open sign in the diner window was the second prettiest sight I've ever seen, next to you in a grass skirt.

I parked beside a pump and encouraged No-Name to go into the diner. I was tempted to drive off without her. She must of kept reading my mind because she waited in the cab while I filled the rig's tank. She sat staring and staring at Maui-Wowie, only she wasn't smiling. She looked fierce, like she was staring down a rival.

I got back in and pulled the truck forward.

"Come on out to the diner," I told her. "I can't let you be alone in the truck. It's against regulations."

I got out, but she still wasn't budging. She just pulled that old cap down lower over her forehead. Probably embarrassed about her feet, or afraid I'd pegged her as a girl and had bad intentions. The passenger door wasn't locked so I opened it wide.

"Look, I'll buy you supper, okay?"

"Supper," her voice scratched out.

"Anything you want. You've gotta be hungry."

"Anything," she said. "Hungry."

"I know we're almost to Fallon, but I might as well feed you. It's late, and I don't know if they're expecting you home tonight."

"Home tonight." No-Name smiled her simple smile. She slid off the bench, leaving behind more glitter or mica or whatever it was that sparkled under the arc lights. I winced for her feet when she hit the ground. I hoped the diner didn't have a "no shirt, no shoes, no service" policy. I should have gone back to the tree and pulled a pair of shoes off. At least her duster was long enough to hide her feet.

I intended to keep the reefer unit running to keep the corn and pork cool. But I could hear it making noises, letting me know I'd let it go for too long without some TLC. I needed to make sure all was cool in the back. A little peek, not enough to let all the cold out. Just enough to reassure myself that all was hunky-dory.

Especially your flowers.

"Go on in," I told No-Name. "I gotta check something."

Soon as I turned my back, I heard her scamper back into the cab.

Maybe it was best we went in together anyhow. I walked past the dent and cursed the warehouse guys. There were long scratches that I'd missed. I ran my finger over them. They went through the paint all the way down to the metal. I thought, what the hell did those bastards at the warehouse do to my gal anyhow?

I went on around to the back and cracked the door open, grabbed the flashlight I kept right inside, and checked on your flowers. There they were, roses and lilies and baby's breath, the stems wrapped in wet paper towels and plastic wrap. They looked good. I could smell the lilies over the warm ripeness of the corn and the faint tang of fresh meat. You love them lilies and that's why I get them for you, babe, but to tell the truth the smell always brings up bad memories for me.

My stomach turned and I was anything but hungry.

Then I heard it again, a ukulele playing real faint. Usually, ukulele music gives me a chuckle, it just sounds so funny. But this was different, quick rhythmic strums like the pounding heart of a little animal, cornered and scared for its life. Made my ears perk up and my attention snap back to where I was, alone in the shadows behind my rig.

Until I felt a presence, and my heart went to pounding like that music.

Something was out there with me, shuffling in the gravel and snuffling and pulling in big lungfuls of air.

I've heard coyotes and I've heard bears, and this wasn't neither. This sounded bigger and hungrier—for the meat, the corn, for me, maybe all of it—I didn't know and it didn't matter. I wanted my sawed-off that I'd left under the bench in the cab. I had half a mind to jump into the reefer, take shelter. But wouldn't it have beat all to get trapped and freeze to death in my own trailer?

That's when I saw the eyes peering out of the black not five feet from me. They were a sickly pale blue-gray, catching on the edge of an overhead light just past the shadows, reflecting like an animal's in the headlights.

Those eyes told me to just lay down in the dirt and let what was gonna happen, happen.

Honey, there was a moment. A moment where I wanted to do what those eyes told me to do.

But damned if that thing didn't snuffle again. Smelling your flowers.

That pissed me off, and I swung my flashlight beam straight into that monster's face.

Then I had to laugh at my own imagination getting away from me, because it was just little No-Name cowering there, shading her eyes with her duster and that dirty old ball cap.

"You gave me a fright, No-Name."

"A fright." She still cowered with her head down, probably blinded from the flashlight.

For good measure, I swept my flashlight across the dirt and gravel parking lot, making sure there wasn't anything else out there. Nothing. I didn't hear no more snuffling, but I did catch a helicopter's roar off in the distance. I'd have to watch my speed up the road. Looked like the only bears I had to worry about were the ones wearing badges.

No-Name raised her head, took a long sniff of the air, looked into the darkness of the reefer. It gave me a polluted feeling, having her near those flowers.

I slammed the door.

"Let's go feed you, No-Name. I think you're hungry."

"Hungry," she nodded. "Sir."

I deliberated once more on leaving her at the diner. She felt to me like a stray dog who cowered and wagged its tail all right, but that you just couldn't trust not to turn on you if you accidentally cornered it.

You remember that diner, baby? That old Pony Express station, all dark wood beams, exposed ceilings, and wagon wheels, a well-stocked bar and tables with red-and-white-checkered tablecloths. Me and No-Name were the only customers.

Our waitress was a nice old gal about twenty years younger than me. As we walked in she glanced at the clock over the bar—twenty minutes till closing time—but never so much as frowned, just seated us with menus and water and told us about the new Monster Burger Challenge. Eat five pounds of food, including a tower of burger patties and a pile of fries, and win a tee-shirt saying you done it, you "Ate The Monster."

The picture of the Monster Burger caught No-Name's eye. She scritch-scratched at the menu like a dog at a door wanting out to chase a rabbit. Then she looked up at me, and I got my first good look at her face.

Those eyes. Pale blue, cloudy, bloodshot. Not a teenager's eyes. Not a sane-person's eyes. Baby, what I thought that very moment I put right outta my head as too fanciful. But I shouldn't have.

I thought: Those ain't even a real person's eyes.

"Hungry. Sir."

"Yeah. I promised you anything you wanted, didn't I?"

"Anything."

"You got it, No-Name." I signaled our waitress, who was over talking to the cook. He had the door to the kitchen open and I could hear the radio playing, smell the grease from the griddle. They both looked our way and she came over, looking nervous now that she and the cook had had time to suss us out a bit, saw the little things I'd missed in the trickster light of sunset, then the darkness of the cab.

No-Name coulda also been called No-Hair. Bald as a cue ball under that dirty white ball cap, coated with what looked less and less like red mud. And that brown leather duster, well, it made me think of how wild things camouflage themselves. How some insects looked like leaves even when you got right up close to them.

"What'll it be?" our waitress, name tag of Nancy, asked with the prettiest little Southern lilt to her voice. Her eyes didn't leave my face, never strayed to No-Name's.

"Just a big cup of coffee for me, and a Monster Burger for that one."

"That's a lot of food," Nancy said. "Takes a while to eat."

No-Name looked up. "Hungry."

Nancy took a step back and touched a tiny gold cross around her neck.

No-Name rolled her shoulders and the duster creaked and popped.

Nancy gave me a look. I got real concerned that she wasn't gonna fill the order. Then what was I gonna do? She must have seen something in my face because she frowned and gave her head a little shake, then trotted back to the cook.

He must have made that burger in record time. Nancy come back with our orders after about ten minutes. By then, my eyes had wandered everywhere but in No-Name's direction. I didn't want to look into them eyes again. My attention was caught by a wall of patches pinned up near the bar. Some police and state patrol patches, but mostly from military units. And there, in the dead center like a round black hole in the wall, was one that gave me chills. Outta that round black patch stared two eyes like the ones I'd seen outside in the shadows. Angry blue bloodshot eyes. I couldn't quite make out the name of the unit.

Nancy came back with a tray. "Here's your food, lemme know if I can get you anything else." She set down my coffee and a big stoneware platter with the Monster Burger and a greasy pile of fries. She walked away before I had a chance to say anything but thank you.

No-Name tore into the burger. Didn't pick it up, just left it on the plate and took big, gouging bites from the top of the bun on down.

Nancy and the cook stood in the doorway watching. I watched too. Don't rightly remember if I even touched my coffee, because I was too caught up in witnessing No-Name devour that thing. Like nothing I ever seen. Well, I take that back. I have seen it, the way No-Name came at the burger.

I seen plenty of that, driving through the desert. Buzzards, pecking and tearing at roadkill.

All the time them hands gripped the edge of the table and the thick yellow nails dug into the tablecloth like talons and I knew the wood would be scratched up underneath.

No-Name finished off the burger, then pecked at the fries until nothing was left on the platter but a smear of ketchup and mustard. Even the long, frilly-ended toothpicks holding the burger together disappeared down that gullet.

And then, I swear to the Sweet Baby Jesus, No-Name started in on the stoneware platter. Took a bite right out the edge and crushed it up before swallowing.

All I could think was, there go the pebbles for the gizzard.

"Stop, stop," Nancy come running over waving her arms. "You don't have to eat the plate to win the tee-shirt."

No-Name looked up, face all smeared with secret sauce and dusted with ceramic. Nancy took one look at them eyes and stopped. No-Name went back to demolishing the plate while Nancy just said, "I'll get the shirt," and turned tail back to the kitchen.

Not five minutes had passed since Nancy had brought the food.

I pushed my chair back, stood and said, "Welp, I'd better pay up." I backed away toward the kitchen. No-Name paid me no never-you-mind, just kept smacking and crunching. My back touched that swinging door and I just kept on going till I was inside.

The cook brandished a cleaver in one hand and a meat mallet in the other. Nancy preferred a butcher's knife and a little old can of mace.

Nancy said, "Lemme see your eyes, mister."

I couldn't open my eyes any wider than they already were. She looked into them, nodded to the cook and said something quickly, sounded like, "No, he ain't blue."

Before I could ask her what that meant, she went on: "Now, you mind telling José and me about that."

She pointed back out toward the dining room, where we could still hear No-Name gobbling down that plate over the music from the radio.

"I'm Horse, that's No-Name, and—"

"Like the song?" José asked.

Well, gosh darn. Somebody besides me was an America fan.

I told them about picking up No-Name by that refinery but left out the story about Maui-Wowie, and about you, Babe—no offense. We were in kind of a hurry.

"That old refinery always give me the creeps too, man," José said. "Trucker went missing around there last night, matter of fact."

"Boys, listen," Nancy held up her hand for silence.

And that's all we heard from the dining room. Silence.

We all three peeked out the round window in the door, just to make sure. Empty table—no plate, no salt and pepper shakers, no napkin dispenser, not even a Sweet'n'Low wrapper.

No No-Name.

"What do we do?" José asked.

That's when we heard the snuffling start, somewhere right up close.

Like No-Name wanted dessert.

I motioned for Nancy to give me her butcher's knife, then for her and José to step back while I pushed the swinging door open just a crack.

Nothing.

That snuffling was still so close I could practically feel No-Name's breath on me. Where the hell was it?

I went into the dining room while Nancy and José watched me out the window.

"No-Name? You still out here?"

I thought I'd give it a shot.

The snuffling got quieter the farther I got from the kitchen door. I passed by the wall of patches. Close up now, I could read the name of the unit on the monster-eyed patch.

HS-5 "Nightdippers."

Fear must have sharpened my brain, babe, because a crazy thought came to me all at once.

HS meant Helicopter Squad.

And what do helicopters do? They hover above you.

The beams in the dark wood ceiling ran the length of the building from dining room to kitchen. There was about a foot-and-a-half gap between each one, and it was plenty dark in the gaps between the beams.

I made eye contact with Nancy and José, still looking through the kitchen window.

"We got some pie for you, No-Name, you want to *come out* for it. My treat."

I beckoned to Nancy and José, still in the kitchen.

Nancy's mouth opened as wide as her eyes. Then they both crouched and scurried through the door, José still with his cleaver and Nancy with a new butcher's knife in one hand, mace still in the other.

Just as No-Name hissed in the rafters above them.

It had itself wedged up there good, that duster pulled tight around its body, no trucker's cap anymore to give it away. It stared down at Nancy and José.

That was a mistake.

Nancy sprayed her mace right into that monster's eyes.

No-Name screamed like Mick Jagger at the beginning of "Sympathy for the Devil" announcing himself as Lucifer.

And then it scurried down that channel between the rafters straight at the front door like some big old cockroach crossed with a bat. No-Name swung its body down legs-first and kicked the door wide open. And that duster, well, it spread like a pair of wings as No-Name made its escape into the night.

All that worrying about how I was gonna leave No-Name, and No-Name done left me.

Then I thought about the truck, the scratched-up dent, all that snuffling around the reefer. The corn and pork. Your flowers that I promised you. And my little hula girl from my big hula girl.

I would have run out that door fast as I could, but Nancy and José held me back.

From the window I could see the rig, runner lights glowing orange, reefer unit humming away with the occasional sputter, keeping things chilly-willy. Nancy made a point of locking up and turning off the neon Open sign for good measure. We walked back into the brightly-lit kitchen. The radio was still on, playing like nothing had happened. A song I didn't know started up, but there was something familiar about it.

"What do you s'pose we should do?" José asked me.

You hear stories about things happening on the road. You know, the young girl looking for a ride who turns out to be a ghost. Chupacabra sightings. I felt like I'd just been through both at the same time. I listened to that song playing, and I recognized that base line was exactly what the ukulele had been playing earlier. It felt like a message from you, babe.

The song ended and the DJ announced, "New one by Jefferson Starship, going out to all you folks on the road tonight. That was 'Find Your Way Back.'"

José said, "You should stay here with us. We got a place out back, plenty of room."

I told José, "I just wanna get back on the road, get on home."

"You ain't serious, man. What if that thing's just out there waiting?"

With the refrigeration unit going on the fritz, I'd have a reefer full of rotten food if I waited and didn't haul ass right now, and that wasn't something I could afford.

"I was the one who brought trouble down on you good people's heads. Maybe if I leave in my rig, No-Name will follow."

José had no answer to that.

Nancy stepped past José. "Don't let nothing stop you on the road again, especially nobody with those haint blue eyes."

"Excuse me, ma'am, did you say haint blue?"

Nancy shrugged. "It's a Southern thing. Maybe it's superstition, but…" Her hand went to that little gold cross again. "That thing's not the only one I've seen with haint blue eyes, but it sure is the worst."

José made me keep one of the knives, even though I told him I had a pistol-grip shotgun under the bench in the cab. Luckily, I still had my flashlight with me, tucked in my pocket. Nancy handed me a wadded-up t-shirt and said, "It got won, so you might as well take it."

She tried to give me the mace too, but I made her keep it, just in case.

I unfolded the shirt. Printed on the front in ketchup-red letters across a cartoon burger was, "I Ate the Monster."

I put it on, for luck.

Nancy unlocked the door for me, then hesitated like she wanted to lock it right up behind me. But she and José stepped out on the porch and I was grateful for that.

I stepped off the porch and looked up. Nothing blocked a single one of those billion desert stars. No bears in the air and no No-Name.

I jogged over to the rig. Nothing. I looked under it.

Nothing still.

I walked all the way around my rig with my flashlight. The reefer unit sputtered regularly, telling me it was on its way out. But the back was locked up nice and tight. I opened her up quick to check. The reefer felt warmer than it should, of course. I grabbed your bouquet and took it up front with me. It didn't feel right leaving it back there out of my sight no more.

Nancy and José stood on the diner's porch watching me,

brandishing their assorted cutlery, for all the world looking like they was getting ready to carve up a Thanksgiving turkey.

I jumped into the cab—I have to say I had a bit more spring in me than usual—and waved to Nancy and José to let them know I was safe. I never knew before then that a wave could lie.

I didn't feel a bit safe. No-Name had been back in the cab.

She—funny how I thought of "it" as "she" once I was back in my rig—had torn poor little Maui-Wowie right off the dashboard. She'd left deep gashes behind, reflected in the windshield.

At first, my heart dropped into my gut, but I found Maui lying on the passenger-side floor. I braced my hand on the bench to lean down and get her.

The seat felt gritty where No-Name had sat.

All that glitter was fine quartz sand. I sifted a bit of it through my fingers, trying not to think about where it coulda come from because *that* could be bad news.

I shifted into first, waved one last goodbye to Nancy and José, rolled down my window to clear the bad smell outta the cab, and rolled my rig back toward westbound US-50. The town of Fallon was fifty miles up the road.

I figured I'd be A-OK if I could get there.

But twenty-five miles before Fallon was Sand Mountain, two miles long and six hundred feet high.

This time of night with the moon shining on it, that quartz sand dune would be all shades of shimmering, haint blue.

"You think that's where No-Name calls home?" I asked Maui-Wowie, who sat on the bench next to me, alongside the butcher's knife and the flowers. I'd checked under her grass skirt and had been shocked to find the joint and my lighter still there. "If so, why do you think she was so far up the road?"

If Maui-Wowie knew, she was keeping the answers to herself.

The miles rolled smooth and fast under my eighteen wheels as we plowed through the night. The land on either side of us started to rise into jagged hills and the road went from straight to curvy. I dropped her speed a bit since I didn't know what might be waiting around a bend. A sign said thirty miles to Fallon. Only half an hour and some change.

I thought we still might make it, honey.

At a bend in the road, I passed a conical hill to the north and there was Sand Mountain, just as cold and blue as I'd imagined it. Like a shoulder of the moon had slipped off and hit the ground, it was so pale against the rest of the desert. People said when the wind hit it just right, the sands shifted and the dune sang. I tried not to look at it, but couldn't help myself and took my eyes off the road just for a second.

But that was just enough time for me to miss seeing the goddamned bull in the middle of the road. I had enough time to think it looked wrong, too skinny, and that it was falling over dead before I even hit it.

I overcorrected. As my brakes locked, I almost rolled. I heard a couple tires go and tasted the stale air that came out of them.

The truck stopped with the windshield facing Sand Mountain.

I looked back out through the passenger window and saw the bull—or what was left of it. Bare ribs poked up from the chewed-up carcass. White sand had piled up like snow drifts on the road. Rocks big enough to shred a tractor tire poked out of each one. That, and bones. Too many to be from a single animal. A gust tore at one of the drifts, revealing more of what was buried underneath. I shone my flashlight out the window on it.

A chewed-up human corpse's yellow-toothed grin smiled back at me, maybe the missing trucker José had mentioned. And on its head was the dirty white ball cap, left there like a little note to let me know No-Name made it home just fine. Turns out her family waited up after all.

I bit my knuckles. The wind blew harder.

The dunes of Sand Mountain sang.

The sound was low and deep, like something trying to make its way out of the ground. Or like the hum of a giant hive busy making honey from blood.

In the distance, dark specks crawled over the sand and took to the air. I watched that mountain through the windshield and I couldn't move.

Even when I saw the black specks getting bigger as they flew closer. Half a dozen at least, and who knew how many more waiting under the sand. I wondered which one was No-Name, and if the others would give her first dibs.

And then for the last time, I heard that ukulele music.

It cut right through that hum and tickled my brain awake. I saw you smiling and doing your wiggle-wiggle, sway-sway, and knew what I needed to do.

I reached under the bench and grabbed my shotgun. I had eight rounds and there were six of them haint-eyed Nightdippers, as I'd come to call them. Good odds.

I turned on my flashlight and gripped it under the gun barrel with my left hand. I leaned out the window and waited.

Them buggers was fast. I raised the shotgun with the flashlight and blinded the first one as I fired.

Two more slammed into the reefer. Their claws were worse than nails on a chalkboard as they gouged their way in.

I took down the fourth.

The fifth and sixth joined the party in the back and tore at the trailer.

I was thinking about the merits of getting out and trying to shoot 'em, versus staying put and hoping what was in the reefer would be enough for 'em to eat, when I heard a helicopter's roar over the hum.

Baby, I'd never been so happy to hear a police chopper in my life.

I stuck my head out and looked up.

The shape blotting out the stars was nothing like a helicopter. It was shaped exactly like a Mama Nightdipper carrying a boulder.

Which she dropped right on the reefer. The fact that it wasn't on my head was the only thing I had to be grateful for.

When I realized what was coming next, I stuck your bouquet and Maui-Wowie under one arm and held onto the gun and the flashlight. I opened the door and jumped just as Mama dipped down outta the night, picked up the rig, and tossed it off the road.

I hit the ground and rolled behind the half-eaten steer. I felt every bump of that road the whole way.

My head came to blows with a rock and all the stars went out.

When I came to, I couldn't quite remember where I was or why. There was a war going on. It seemed familiar. Helicopters, roaring machinery, the screams of dying men as their tanks ripped open. Strange thing, though. Maui-Wowie and your bouquet were on the ground next to me. I grabbed them.

Then I remembered.

I lifted my head an inch, then back down it went. It weighed more than the rig and it hurt. I didn't have no chance anyway. What was I gonna do, twenty-five miles from nowhere, nothing but scrub for miles in any direction? I couldn't run from these things. Especially from that big mama. Hell, she'd use my shotgun to clean her teeth after she ate me.

Honey, I just kept thinking how disappointed you'd be if I didn't come back with the flowers.

That's what got me up and moving again. How cold and lonely you'd get at night wondering where I was at and if I was ever coming home. I couldn't have that.

I peered between the steer's ribs and watched Mama and her babies gorge on spilled corn and pork. The truck was a twisted thing, a broken piñata. I smelled diesel and coolant and any number of other juices that had kept her and me on the road, now leaking out all over it.

That gave me an idea.

But it meant I'd have to give up something you gave me out of love and that I'd never, ever get back.

I took out the doob and the lighter and set Maui-Wowie on the ground. I gave her head one last tap to see her sway in the manner she was meant to. I lit my doob and got a nice hot cherry going.

Then I set Maui's dry grass skirt ablaze while I sucked on what I figured was my last joint, and threw her in a Hail Mary pass, right at the rig.

Enough time had passed that all them good explosive chemicals had time to build up plenty of vapor.

Which exploded.

Diesel won't burn so fast as gasoline, but it sure will keep the fire going once it starts. So will corn, when it's warm enough.

For the second time that night, all the stars ran away.

—

They said the patrolman who found me tried to take your bouquet but I fought him off. I don't remember none of that. First thing I remember was waking up in a hospital bed looking at them flowers sitting in a cheap vase and wondering who hated me enough to give me such a sorry-looking arrangement. To add insult to injury, the lilies still smelled nice and strong.

Two insurance claim adjusters and their lawyer paid me a visit on my last day at the hospital in Fallon to sign some paperwork. They said it looked to them like none of it was my fault, that it was a combination of the windy weather and a mechanical failure, not to mention a steer or two that some rancher shoulda taken better care of.

You know what, baby? All three of them had fancy suits, letterhead with the same logo as the refinery up the road, and haint blue eyes.

I signed on the dotted line.

They gave me a bus ticket home and here I am. Settlement money spends the same as any, and silence keeps me from ending up under my own pile of singing sand. You're the only one I'm ever gonna tell, and I know you'll keep mum.

And that's why the flowers ain't in the best shape and little Maui-Wowie is gone. But something tells me that you'll forgive me for that. In fact, something tells me that you already knew this story before I even opened my mouth. That somehow you were there with me the whole damn time.

And baby, I'd go through all this again if only it'd happened seven years ago when you first got the cancer and the money would have done us some good.

I'm just gonna sit here by your marker and enjoy the rest of this beautiful Sunday with you, if that's all right. I'm gonna play your mix tape and imagine you doing a little wiggle-wiggle, sway-sway in my arms.

I hope you forgive me. But I guess it'll be a while before I get to know. We'll both be sleeping cold till then, honey, but not on account of going to bed angry. Just lonely.

Figure I'll buy a new little hula girl to keep me company on the dashboard, assuming I ever go back on the road. Thing is, hauling freight's all I know. That, and that the loneliness of the road is better than the loneliness of an empty house.

Yeah, I'll get me a new little hula girl. She won't be the same as the one you gave me, but maybe you'll take a shine to her, and you'll both accompany me down the long miles left to me.

Like always, I'm hoping to get back to you.

About the Author

Rebecca Hodgkins is a freelance editor for hire and the author of five novels. Her short stories range from science fiction to just plain weird and have been published in *Edward Bryant's Sphere of Influence*, *A Fistful of Dinosaurs*, *Vagabond*, Daily Science Fiction, and in numerous other online zines. She spends her time between Colorado and an island off the coast of Texas. Her plan for world domination consists of being ruthlessly nice to everyone.

Find out more about Rebecca at:
rebeccahodgkins.com

Stowe Away

Mark Leslie

July 31, 2015 – 5:54 A.M.

You'd think, after all this time, that I'd be used to it.

But no matter how many times I wake up naked, with my body mostly hidden away in some sort of greenery and no memory of the previous night or how I got there, it is still a startling way to begin my day.

Since I have no conscious memory of the change between man and wolf, I have to rely on how Gail, my closest friend, has described it. She says it looks like a cross between an episode of violent childbirth and the Wicked Witch of the West melting as, over the space of about sixty seconds, I change from a six-foot-two, two-hundred-pound human into a one-hundred-pound, six-foot-long grey wolf.

The memory loss is likely a sanity-preserving side effect of the terrifying physical transmogrification.

I imagine these mornings are similar to what career drunks or drug addicts might experience waking up in strange places every morning, those first few confusing seconds at least. For me it's a little different. Sadly, there's no manual, no *Werewolves for Dummies* book to help explain my specific situation or predicament. But I have, at least, established a bit of a routine, or a process, of dealing with the cycles of the wolf I experience every month. I tend to plan out most of my transformations in the large green space of southern Central Park in Manhattan, and have the presence of mind to hide a change of clothes for the next day.

Where else, after all, can a werewolf safely make his change in such a large metropolis?

As I sit up and pay attention to my surroundings, I take in the sights, sounds, and smells and recognize the part of the park where I am, an area known as the Ramble, across the Lake from Strawberry Fields, the well-visited memorial to John Lennon.

One of my usual clothes-stash areas is just a few meters north of Bow Bridge. I have a half-dozen stash areas. Sometimes a crafty homeless person comes across one of them, or a small animal tears the bag apart to use some of the clothes for nesting material.

I listen for anyone nearby.

And, despite being male, listening is something I do extremely well. Or at least, in an enhanced way. When in human form, I retain heightened senses, extraordinary strength, and a super-charged immune system. Those side-effects come in extremely handy.

The closest human-generated sound is a pair of joggers on the other side of the Loeb Boathouse about a quarter of a mile across the lake. Dozens of birds are singing a multitude of beautiful choruses and zipping about in the treetops. There's a rabbit about twenty feet or so north of me that pauses in its shuffling and tenses into high alert the moment I started to stand up. And a few feet to my left, a squirrel is scurrying up a tree.

But, other than that, I'm alone. It takes me less than a minute to make my way to the fortunately unmolested stash of clothes, tucked in a small crevasse between the thick roots of a tree trunk.

One can't simply walk down 5th Avenue butt naked, after all.

I pull the day's ensemble—a cheap pair of track pants, a t-shirt and sneakers—out of their plastic bag, a bit damp from the rain and heavy fog yesterday afternoon.

At least I have clothes.

As I pull the pants on, I cringe slightly at the dampness. Once I have them on, I see a fully soaked spot about two inches wide, located dead center at my crotch. Great. The wet spot, which, on the grey material is as subtle as a slap in the face with a trout, makes me look like I've wet myself.

When I finish dressing, I head over to the trail, cross Bow Bridge, then head south through the park. There's something calming and peaceful about being in the park this early, before it starts to fill with local joggers and dog walkers, and later on with tourists. I quite relish this part of my walk. It's a great chance to recharge and refresh the mind, preparing me for a decent hour or two of writing.

My writing time will be limited this morning because of my plans to meet Gail, the only woman I've ever loved or trusted with the truth of my condition, at eight a.m. for breakfast. We're meeting at a café in the East Village not far from Gail's metaphysical supply store, Enchanting Magic. Gail has owned the shop for more than a decade. She has three staff members who work for her, but she regularly likes to be the one to open the shop, which she does at eleven a.m. most weekdays. It is typically quiet there until mid-afternoon.

The fifteen-minute walk to The Algonquin Hotel, which is my full-time residence, is a chance for me to contemplate the next scene in the Maxwell Bronte novel that I'm working on. Although, to be honest, picturing Gail's smile across the diner table from me keeps interrupting my thoughts.

Gail and I had something truly special once. A love like nothing I had ever experienced before. And I screwed that up. But at least we are friends, dear friends. Despite the fact I wish there could be more, despite the fact I can sense she does too, though she isn't able to be more than friends right now. She is still coming to terms with recently finding out her ex-fiancé was an underworld criminal. And I have no intension of pushing her. So I'll be there for her as a friend, and I'll wait patiently until she is ready, the way she patiently attends to me when I am forced to spend the night as a wolf when I'm trapped inside.

But in the meantime, I really need to get a new hobby. Something to stop me from obsessing over her.

"We're good friends," I mutter as I leave the park on my way to cross West 59th Street. "We're good friends." It's a mantra I have to keep repeating to myself.

"Buddy, we just met," says a gruff male voice off to my left. "How about you buy me a coffee and at least ask me my name before we get that intimate?"

I look over to my left to see a homeless guy leaning against the low brick wall at the edge of Central Park. He looks like he is in his mid-sixties, with weathered, sun-baked and leathery skin, smelling of sweat from wearing the same clothes for weeks. He has a hearty and healthy heartbeat, and, obviously, a good sense of humor and a solid mind.

I smile at him as I pause on the sidewalk, turn towards him, and pat at the tops of my legs where pockets would be if I had any. "Wish I could, my friend. Afraid I'm fresh out at the moment. I'm Michael."

"S'all good," he says. "You can call me Saul."

"Good to meet you, Saul. We'll have to take a rain check on that coffee, okay?"

"Sounds good," Saul says. Then he notices the wet spot on the front of my pants. "Tell you what, Michael. If you come into any dough, maybe you should invest in a pair of Depends. Sound like a plan?"

I laugh, looking down at the still obvious blotch of dark wetness.

"It's a marvelous plan," I tell him, and then turn to continue my walk.

"You have yourself a good day, Michael," he says. "May the wind be ever at your back."

"You too, Saul." I call over my shoulder.

Over the years my extrasensory abilities have allowed me the chance to really understand the unique comraderies of the people of this city, all of them—from the ones living in the richest towers to the ones who struggle to find a spot to sleep at night. On the surface, the Big Apple can appear cold and harsh. But underneath, it's no different than any other city or town. Sure, there are jerks. But there's also some decent heart.

I manage to make it back to the hotel without anyone else making commentary about the wet spot across my crotch. That's not to say people don't notice. I can sense and scent their reactions. I often wonder if the unspoken judgements we hold against strangers could sometimes be harsher than words spoken in truth.

I make it up to my room and am greeted by a blinking light on my phone. There is a voicemail waiting for me.

The first message is from Gail at 9:20 p.m. last night.

"Hi Michael. It's me," the message says. "Just letting you know that I won't be able to meet you for breakfast in the morning. I'm on my way to the airport to catch a flight to Vermont. It's my Uncle Albert. He had a stroke. I'm grabbing the first flight. I'll let you know when I get in."

The devastation in her voice is intense. Uncle Albert wasn't just a favorite uncle to Gail. He was, and still is, a father figure to her. He practically raised her.

The next message is also from Gail. It came in at 3:41 a.m.

"Hi Michael. I'm at the University of Vermont Medical Center in Burlington. I'm with Uncle Albert. He's not doing well. He's still unconscious and his vital signs are weak."

I can almost smell the fear and helplessness in her voice.

The third message from Gail came at 5:01 a.m.

"There's been no change. I don't know," her voice breaks and she lets out a stifled sob, "I don't know what I would do without him, Michael." There is a long pause while she struggles to gain some composure. "Also, my phone is down to one percent battery. I didn't pack a charging cable, so I likely won't be able to call again for a while. I will when I can."

Uncle Albert is well beyond a favourite uncle and mentor; he's the one person in the family she could count on for support and guidance when things went south for her and she stumbled in her teen years. He is the inspiration and the support she counts on in order to pick herself back up, to keep going any time she feels herself slipping. His presence, his love, and his compassion were among the main reasons she didn't take her own life when she was in her darkest, weakest moment. Uncle Albert is the one person she can count on to be there for her when she needs it the most.

The immediacy of the moment hit me hard. I understand how alone, how vulnerable, how terrified Gail must feel.

I needed to get to Vermont.

11:52 A.M.

As the train left the Bronx northward on the bridge over Pelham Bay, I peered out the window on my right. I got a glimpse of the most rural landscape I had seen in several years. If I'd been looking in the opposite direction, I would have still seen the signs of the city, urban landscape and tall buildings jutting upwards.

New York has plenty of green spaces and beautiful landscapes. But there was a greater sense of an open landscape here that I reveled in as we began the journey out of the city and the rural landscape of New York State began to reveal itself. Prior to moving to Manhattan more than ten years ago, I'd lived in a small town in Ontario, Canada. My back yard had been wilderness. And, as the greener, more rural landscape rolled past, I felt an odd sense of comfort, despite the anxiety that compelled me to be on this trip.

I had to get to Gail. She needed a friend now more than ever.

A flight to Burlington, Vermont, would have been about an hour. But I couldn't do that. I became a permanent resident of the US more than six years ago and am a fully-fledged dual US and Canadian citizen. But I had let my passports expire, and, living in a city with a world-class public transit system and more taxis than you can shake a stick at, I had never bothered to get a driver's licence for the State of New York. I couldn't even imagine trying to learn how to drive in a big city like that. I hadn't been much of a driver before, either, apart from the occasional tractor, quad or snow machine in the rural north.

With a quick call to Mack, my literary agent, I'm sure there would have been a way to fly, even with an expired ID. But I was still behind on my latest deadline, and wasn't about to reach out to him and provoke his wrath.

So I purchased the train ticket.

The Vermonter train left Pennsylvania Station at 11:30 a.m. and performed nineteen stops on its way to Essex, Vermont, in just under nine hours. From there, I'd take a transfer to an Amtrak bound for Burlington, where Gail's uncle was in the hospital.

The only clincher in this plan was the fact that the train arrived in Essex Junction at 8:18 p.m. And, according to a quick Google search, sunset in that county in Vermont would take place at 8:17 p.m. during a full moon. Which meant my transformation into wolf form would be happening as we pulled into our last stop. And I had no plan for how to handle that.

So, I did what I often do. I acted first, determined that I would figure something out along the way.

It's how I ended up in New York, after all. Hitchhiking into the city with a dream of fulfilling my dream of being a writer.

Yep, I often acted the way that I wrote. A man with a basic plan or idea; a rough outline, and the belief that I'd figure it out somewhere along the way.

It seemed to work out okay for my novels.

And, so far, it served me well on the life journey.

So I wasn't as nervous as I likely should have been.

After all, I had eight hours to figure it all out.

As I returned to gazing out the window at the landscape, I kept experiencing fleeting memories of the night before as experienced by the wolf-part of my mind.

Running through the underbrush of the forest-laden hills of Central Park, and the accompanying sense of pure unadulterated joy.

The satisfaction of quenching a deep thirst by lapping at the cool water at the edge of a lake.

Pausing to sniff the air, aware of the nearby sound of a human shuffling slowly down a trail just a few yards away, and, at the same time, the wail of a siren echoing from somewhere behind the safety of the park.

Clips and short memories of various moments are pretty typical of most of my nights as a wolf. I have often wondered if my wolf form has visions of the things I have done during the previous day, or any idea that it has another form as a human.

The retrospective clips of the night before were interspersed with flashes of the memory of Gail's cool-green eyes staring back into mine on the night of our first date, of the intensity of her passion in those same eyes when we were in the clenches of making love.

Similar to the fleeting glimpses of my experiences as a wolf, those special memories of moments with Gail were distant, and further muted over time.

Both were similar in their almost dream-like existence.

Before leaving, I had tried to call Gail several times. It kept going straight to her voice mail, which suggested that her phone was still dead. I left a couple of messages. One to let her know I got her message and was planning on coming to be with her. A second one to let her know I had booked a train ticket and was on my way up there.

I hadn't bothered leaving any other messages before rushing to the train station. I instinctively reached down to pat my pocket for my mobile phone, thinking I should try to reach out and call Gail, then remembered I had decided to leave it at home. I don't like having things on me that I could easily lose track of when in wolf form. All I had with me was a backpack filled with a few changes of clothes, minimal toiletries, and a thin wallet with some cash and the single credit card I had used to purchase the train ticket online with.

As the countryside became more rural outside the train window, I was reminded of the encroaching deadline to figure out a proper plan on what I was going to do when the clock struck "moon-rise" and I began to turn into the proverbial pumpkin.

I needed to figure out a plan.

1:41 P.M.

I woke up as the train was pulling out of New Haven, Connecticut. There was something about the gentle and rhythmic pulse of the train that had coaxed me into sleep. Yes, even with the concern over Gail as well as my worry over needing to figure out a solution before the train arrived in Essex.

While my supernaturally enhanced strength and senses were heightened during my monthly wolf cycles, I was also occasionally overcome with fatigue when in human form, perhaps because my human mind didn't get the sleep needed for a properly functioning, average adult.

Based on where we were, I figured I had gotten a good solid hour and a half of sleep. I also figured I should stop procrastinating and get my butt into gear figuring out a plan. I got up from my seat and started to walk towards the front of the train. I wanted to figure out the layout of the train, and what sorts of cars it contained. Perhaps there would be a useful hiding spot I could use. Trying to find a hiding spot inside an enclosed space for a wild animal might seem like a preposterous idea, like taking one's bull into a china shop, but it had worked. At least a few times.

Gail, who'd been with me for most of those times, explained that it appeared my wolfish form recognized the danger that came with being discovered. Perhaps it was instinct; perhaps an indication of some of my human consciousness leaking through. I did have fleeting memories of being in wolf form in an enclosed space while Gail was with me. Those snippets came with an overwhelming feeling of what I can only describe, in human terms, as trust, love, and respect.

It's easy for me to understand how any mammal, human or otherwise, could have those feelings for Gail; she has a presence and energy that immediately commands respect and trust; the love, I imagine, is likely a side-effect of the human blood pulsing through my wolf form.

I made my way from the coach train car I had been sitting in and moved forward into the next one, which was a lounge. A few people were relaxing there, enjoying a coffee and seats that faced the windows. The car after that was the dining car, where the overwhelming smells of food almost changed the course of my mission. Sure, I had eaten a hearty breakfast, but I could certainly use more food. The calories I burned transforming from human to wolf form and then back again were substantial. I picked up my pace to get the dining car behind me.

As I moved onto the next car, a sleeper, I took note of the indicators of the bunks. So far, all of them were occupied except one. I had intended to attempt to try to open the unoccupied one, but a man entered from the car in front, so I just kept walking.

The man, who had the large, muscular frame of a body builder and a pencil-thin black moustache, looked to be in his mid-twenties. He smelled of garlic and the woody oak scent of whisky, with a skunky base of pot. I sensed heightened anger, both in his scent and in the strong and heightened beat of his heart, as he moved quickly and purposely through the car and toward me. The anger wasn't directed at me but on something else. Something he seemed to be desperately searching for—and extremely angry about.

My instincts suggested it was most likely a partner he had had a falling out with. His eyes kept moving from me to the doors of the sleeper car rooms, the way a hungry canine might eye dog treats on the floor. As we passed one another, both squeezing to get by in the confined space, he smiled at me, one of those smiles that causes the lips to form the proper shape but fails to make it to the eyes. His glance at me also came with an air of annoyance, like I was a mosquito buzzing around his ear. I wondered who had pissed in his cornflakes.

I didn't, of course, have to wonder long.

I made my way through the sleeper car. Cornflake Guy exited into the dining car behind me. At the far end of the car, I picked up a distinct scent from the room marked as unoccupied.

I recognized the scent immediately: a woman filled with absolute fear.

I had first picked up on it going down the escalator to the train at Penn Station. The odor had been pervasive as I descended to the track level. It had been from someone who had moved through the same space only a minute or so before me, and the anxiety and fear was so palpable to me that it stuck in my mind, although I hadn't been able to follow it at the time.

A colleague of mine, Barney, who manages a bookshop on the upper East Side, once explained it to me. Having been a bookseller for more than thirty years, Barney couldn't not notice a reader. It could be someone reading a book on a park bench, carrying a paperback or a Kindle eReader. Wherever Barney looked, readers jumped out at him.

He couldn't not see them; couldn't not notice them.

It was the same for me.

Me, I couldn't not sense those who needed help.

I had lived most of my life with an underlying, Stan Lee-infused philosophy of power and responsibility. Growing up on a steady diet of Spider-Man comic books, I had a sense of wanting to use my powers to help others in any way I could.

As a wolf, picking up on scents of those who might need help had become second nature to me.

I couldn't detect the woman when I was boarding the train, but her scent had stood out. And now it was far more intense than it had been at the train station.

The woman was inside the bunk to my right. I could hear the rapid beating of her heart and the short, quick breaths she was taking in an attempt to be as quiet as possible. She was fearful for her life.

I looked back to ensure that Cornflake hadn't returned, then opened the door.

The woman's anxiety ratcheted up all the way to eleven as her "fight or flight" mode shifted to attack mode.

The room was small, with two large armchair seats across from one another at the window, and a mirror and a sink to the left. The upper bunk was still pushed all the way to the ceiling. Her scent was coming from above and almost behind me. There must be some sort of luggage storage compartment above the door where she was tucked away.

"It's okay," I said in a voice that was almost a whisper as I slowly inched my way into the room. "I'm not here to hurt you. I know you're scared."

A voice came over the train's PA system as the train began to noticeably slow down. "Meriden is the next stop. We are arriving in Meriden."

Her fight or flight response kicked up even higher. Either this was her stop, or she was calculating her chances of being able to get away from me and escape off the train once it came to a stop.

"Is this your stop? Do you need to get off here?"

There was no answer. But her breathing changed subtly, as if she had opened her mouth and considered speaking.

"Listen, I know you are hiding from someone and I won't let them find you. I promise."

The train was beginning to slow down as it pulled into the station at Meriden.

"My name is Michael Andrews. I'm on my way to Burlington, Vermont, to visit a friend whose uncle is ill. I'm a writer. I promise I mean you no harm, and only want to help you stay away from whoever it is you are hiding from."

Her heartbeat jumped a split second after I said my name. Then her anxiety changed to a scent that included a sense of wonderment.

I could hear her drawing in a deep breath.

Muffled, almost as if from behind a wall, she said, "*No way!*" Her voice sounded young.

I chuckled. "What? Are you heading to Burlington to see a sick friend too?"

"Are you really Michael Andrews? The author of *Print of the Predator*? *Tomes of Terror*? The guy who created Maxwell Bronte? You've got to be freakin' kidding me!" She giggled.

As a writer, I was used to most people not recognizing me, despite the fact that a Hollywood movie starring Ryan Reynolds had been made from one of my novels. I had been a multi-time *New York Times* bestselling author, had been on *Late Night with David Letterman*, had been featured in hundreds of newspapers and magazines around the world, and my book signings commanded long lines. But the average person has no idea who I am.

So it was still rare for anybody to recognize my name.

"Uh, yeah. That's me."

"*The* Michael Andrews?" she said, her voice and scent filled with a slight bit of incredulousness.

"In the flesh."

"No way!"

"*Waaaaay*," I said.

She giggled again.

The train came to a complete stop. The male voice over the PA system said, "Meriden Station. This stop is Meriden Station."

"Listen." I said. "I'm stepping all the way inside so I can close the door. I don't want whoever you're hiding from to know you're here. Is that okay?"

Her anxiety raced up again. "Y-yeah," she said. "Okay."

"You don't need to get off at this stop, do you?"

"No," she said. "This isn't my stop."

"Okay. I'm closing the door." I closed it, then turned down the latch to lock it. "It's locked. They won't find you." I paused, thinking about Cornflake, about the purposeful way he had been storming through the car, his eyes darting to the doors on each side. He had been angry and searching. I now knew who he was searching for. "*He* won't find you."

"How did you know I was hiding from a man?"

"I think I saw him. Tall. Muscles on top of muscles. Thin moustache. Is that him?"

Her fear shot up again. I didn't have to hear her confirmation to know I was right.

"Yes," she said in a hoarse whisper. "That's him. Where is he?"

"I just passed him in the hall outside. He was—"

The PA told us that the train was now on its way again as the train began its crawl out of the station.

I continued, "He was heading toward the back of the train. But I could tell he was looking for something, or someone. He was moving with purpose and—"

The sound of the door between the railcars creaking open came with the return of his fresh scent. I stopped. "Don't move. He's coming back."

The door in the dining car opened. Cornflake's scent began moving back in our direction. As I stood facing the door, I could hear Cornflake's footsteps as he moved onto the car, the sound of the door to the car closing behind him, smell his anger and determination.

This time, he was pausing to check the doors as he moved through the car.

The curtain over the window in our door was closed. The one over the small window beside it was mostly closed, but the Velcro tab wasn't attached, leaving a half-inch crack.

As Cornflake neared our room, he spotted me looking out from the crack in the curtains. We made eye contact for the briefest moment. His scent and heartbeat gave away his surprise at being caught. He stopped midway through the motion of reaching for our door latch, but stopped and immediately shuffled past.

A few doors down he tried the latches again, then made his way to the end of the car and exited through the door there.

"Okay," I said. "He's gone."

Her heartbeat slowed from the race it had been on and her fear abated a little.

"Who is he?" I asked.

Her head popped over the edge of the small open luggage compartment above me as she looked down. She was young, very pretty. Wavy, light-blonde hair. Piercing blue eyes. She looked maybe sixteen or seventeen, but the tone and intonation of her voice gave her away as someone a lot younger.

"No way," she said, staring at me with wide eyes. "You really are Michael Andrews."

"Who is he?" I asked again. "That guy stalking around out there."

"Can I climb down?" she asked. "It's really cramped up here."

"Yeah," I said, stepping back to stand in front of the two seats facing one another near the window. "Do you need help?"

"I'm good." She wiggled out of the luggage compartment and used the steps designed into the sink and toilet to make her way down. She was slim but quite tall; watching her lanky body come out of that tight luggage storage space over the door was akin to watching clown after clown pile out of one of those tiny cars at the circus.

She stepped down. She was almost as tall as I was. I stepped back as much as I could, not that there was much space for two people standing in that tight area. She let out a sigh of relief and reached down to rub the backs of her legs. "My legs were getting so cramped up there."

Suddenly her blue eyes couldn't leave mine. "Oh my God, I can't believe I'm meeting *the* Michael Andrews. I've read all of your novels. I love them. I've read all of your books. Even the short story collection. I know that the reviewers didn't like it, but I thought it was fascinating to get to read stories that weren't about Maxwell Bronte. I thought—"

"Thank you. I am truly honored," I said, putting out my hand. "But you've got one up on me. You know I'm Michael Andrews. But I don't know your name."

She took my hand and gave it a firm shake. The confidence and strength in that handshake again made me think she might be an older teenager. But I doubted she was. Something about her speech, her mannerisms, even her pulse rate, suggested someone younger. Much younger.

"I'm Bridget." She said. "Bridget Wells."

"Pleased to meet you, Bridget."

"My friends call me Bridge," she said. "I've read all your books. Read so many articles about you and interviews. I feel like I know you. Call me Bridge."

"Pleased to meet you, Bridge. There's not a lot of room in here," I said. "Why don't we take a seat?" I inched my way to the one chair on my right.

She smiled and plopped into the chair across from me.

"Who is that guy?" I asked.

Her heart began to race again, there was a sour scent of fear. "I've read all of your books. I wanted to ask if you'll be putting out any more story collections like that last one."

I smiled. "Thank you. I'm honored."

She smiled, and I could tell she thought she had again successfully steered the conversation away from having to answer.

"Who *is* he, Bridge?" I repeated.

"Bruce," she said, letting out a long breath. "His name is Bruce. He's a friend of my dad. He was younger than most of them. And I thought he was cute, too. We used to talk about stuff together. I thought he was cool. But last night, that changed. He's not cool. He...he's a pig."

I just listened. I knew there was more coming as she took in another long breath.

"My Dad was having a party. He has lots of parties. Lots of people. Everyone was drinking, smoking up. And dancing. I was standing in the hallway watching them. Bruce saw me and asked me to dance. I love dancing, and Bruce and I always got along. We enjoyed playing the same video games, talking about the same movies. So I joined in. Everyone was laughing, having a good time. Then, a few minutes later when I was in the kitchen getting a soda from the fridge, Bruce came up behind me, put his hand around my waist, turned me around. He was drunk. I could smell the booze and the pot on his breath. Then he leaned in and kissed me."

Bridge paused and looked out the window and took a deep breath before continuing.

"I was shocked. It happened so fast I didn't know what was happening. I tried to back away, but the open fridge door was behind me, so I bumped into it. Bruce kissed me again. And he put his tongue in my mouth and moved his hand lower, over my butt. I could taste the alcohol, the weed from his tongue. Disgusting.

"Cheryl steps into the kitchen then. She's another friend of my dad. She's a lot older. 'What are you doing?' she says.

"Bruce steps back and just smiles at Cheryl. 'Nothing.'

"'Bruce,' Cheryl says. 'She's only a kid.'

"'We were just goofing around,' Bruce says. 'She said she wanted to learn how to kiss. I was helping her out.'

"Cheryl walks over to me and asks if that's true. Bruce is staring daggers at me. 'Yeah,' I say. I take a can of orange soda out of the fridge, open it and drink some, no big deal.

"'Cheryl leans toward me and I can tell she's high. She whispers, 'Might as well learn from the best. He is one hell of a kisser.' She steps over to Bruce, slaps his butt, then puts her arms around him and says, 'It's been a while since I've had a kissing lesson, honeybun.'

"Bruce and Cheryl start making out. I go to the washroom, and I throw up. The orange soda I just had comes out. That makes me even more sick."

She began to gasp for breath, as if re-experiencing the nausea, then quietly shook her head. For a moment she was unable to speak

"I stay in the washroom for a long time. I can't believe what just happened. Or how stupid I was. But thinking about what Bruce did is what makes me sick again. Only nothing comes out. I was so stupid."

I said, "You did nothing wrong, Bridge."

She remained quiet. Her heartbeat was beating a mile a minute.

"How old are you, Bridge?"

"Thirteen." Her eyes filled with tears. "I'd only ever kissed a boy once, at summer camp. Last summer. We were playing spin-the-bottle. I had a huge crush on him. It was a quick peck on the lips. But with Bruce it was hard and my lips hurt. His breath was horrible. The tongue! It was disgusting."

I am feeling disgusted myself. Anger and resentment at the as-shole I'd seen in the hallway. Frustration that this innocent child had something like this forced on her. I was ready to kill the man. I had to take a deep breath.

"That's because it wasn't a kiss, Bridge. He was assaulting you. He had no right to do that to you."

"But instead of telling Cheryl when I had the chance, I helped him cover it up."

"You did nothing wrong."

"Oh yeah?" Tears started streaming down her face. "Then why didn't my dad believe me? When I was sitting in the washroom, I was scared Bruce was going to do something like that again. So I washed my face, used mouthwash to rinse my mouth, and went out to the living room to tell my dad. He was dancing with a bunch of other friends. I pulled him into the kitchen.

"When I told him he just stood there looking at me like he didn't know what I was saying. He was high and drunk.

"But before he could say anything, Bruce and Cheryl walked in, arm in arm.

"'Bruce,' my dad says. 'Is this true? Did you just kiss Bridget in the kitchen?'

"Cheryl says, 'I was there when it happened. She wanted to know how to kiss. Bruce said no but she kept bugging him.'

"My dad turns to me, and do you know what he says? He says: 'Why would you make something like that up about my friend?'

"Then the three of them laughed about the wild imagination of teenagers, lit up another joint to share, and moved off to the living room together.

"My Dad didn't believe me. But then Cheryl says I was asking for it. I know she wasn't even there when it started, but I can't help second-guessing myself. Maybe I remembered it wrong. Maybe I was acting in a way with Bruce that brought him on. Maybe I *was* flirting with him. I did like hanging out with him.

"I know what I thought happened. But I don't know what to believe."

Bridge dropped her face into her hands.

I sat silently across from her, forcing myself not to touch her. The last thing she needed was to worry about a stranger getting too close for comfort.

Finally, she lifted her head up and looked up at me. "I'm sorry. I couldn't help crying. I know I sound like a baby. But I couldn't help it."

"It's okay. You have nothing to apologize for. Bridge, you did nothing wrong. This was something uninvited, unwelcome, unwanted, that happened to you. But you have to tell me, because I don't understand. How did you get here?"

"Afterwards, I wandered around the party. Bruce and Cheryl went into my dad's bedroom. I decided to go to sleep. But I couldn't sleep. The music and the voices, the shouting, the singing, all of it was too loud. And I could hear Bruce and Cheryl doing it. They were really loud. I went to the washroom and tried to throw up but there was nothing more to come out. I went back to my bedroom, put on my headphones and played some music to drown out all the noise.

"I woke up later. It was quiet. The partying was over. Then I look over and see Bruce standing on the side of my bed.

"He's naked. And…um. *Up.*

"'Bridget,' he whispers. 'We aren't finished, you and me. I've seen the way you look at me. I know you want me. I'm here to teach you more. I'm here to help you become the woman I know you want to be.'

"He pulls the blankets off of me, then he puts one knee onto the bed and grabs on to my shoulder.

"'No,' I say.

"He says, 'Don't be like that. You know you want it. I could see it in your eyes. You want a taste of old Brucey.'

"I don't know what to do. He pushes me onto my back. He's so strong and I can't move at all. Then he lifts one leg over to climb on top of me.

"I jab up with my knee as hard as I can. I knee him right between the legs. He gasps and lets go of my shoulder. I knee him between the legs again. Even harder. He doesn't move. I shove him off the bed. He must have passed out from the pain, because he doesn't get up.

"I get out of bed and grab the jeans and t-shirt I was wearing before bed. I grab some cash and a Metro card I left on top of my dresser and shove them into my pocket. But my phone is on the nightstand on the far side of the bed, right beside Bruce.

"I start to walk over to grab it, but he's moaning and getting to his knees. I give up on the phone and open the door to leave and I hear him hiss behind me.

"'You little bitch,' he says. 'I was going to be gentle with you. But not now. Now I'm going to fuck you so hard. Because I can tell you like it rough.' I slam the door behind me. I run down the stairs to the street and keep running. I don't know what I'm doing. Finally I just stand there.

"I hear him. He's calling my name. Then he spots me. He's about a block away. He yells that he needs to talk to me. But I know that's not what he wants.

"I run to the nearest Metro station and take the next train, hoping he doesn't get there before it leaves. I go to Manhattan. The only thing I can think of is to get to Pennsylvania Station so I can take the train to Vermont. My mom and I moved there when I was nine. I'm only in New York to spend the summer with Dad.

"As I'm looking out at the tracks, I see Bruce. He's all the way on the other side of the train platform coming down the escalator. He's looking right at me.

"I get up from my seat and start looking for somewhere to hide. This was the only place I could think of. He's going to catch me. I'm so stupid."

She dropped her face back down into her palms.

"I'm so sorry, Bridge," I said.

Like a little kid, she put her arms out for a hug. I put both arms around her and just held her quietly for a moment while she cried, almost soundlessly.

I whispered to her, "I won't let him get close to you. I will not let him hurt you. And I'll make sure you make it to your mom safely."

She stopped crying and looked up into my eyes.

"Thank you."

In her eyes as well as in the emotions I could smell, was her complete and unadulterated trust. It was that complete innocence, trust and belief in those thirteen-year-old pale blue eyes staring up at me that melted my heart.

How could someone do what they did to this kid, this bright young child?

This girl had already been through enough.

And from people she had put her trust in.

I would not let her down.

"I promise, Bridge. I won't leave your side until you're safely back with your mother."

She snuggled herself tighter against me. Her anxiety was replaced by waves of safety, security, trust, and comfort. "Thank you, Michael." She said it in a voice so low, so weak, so exhausted, that a normal human ear would not have been able to detect it.

But I heard it. And I felt the confusion, fear, and angst that filled this poor child's being.

Is this how a parent felt when they watched a child hurting? It was almost unbearable. How did parents handle it?

The train began to slow again.

The male voice over the PA system announced. "Hartford will be our next stop. We are arriving in Hartford."

I wondered how I might try to accomplish getting her safely back to her mother...when I would be turning into a wolf well before we made it to our destination in Stowe.

4:32 P.M.

I woke with a start.

Bridget was still sleeping in the chair across from me.

Outside, the sound of someone trying the door. That was what had woken me. It was Bruce. Again. I knew him by his odors and his still-angry emotion, by that familiar heartbeat. He wasn't giving up. He knew she was on this train and hiding, and he was determined to find her. But I had sealed the curtain with the Velcro strip, and he couldn't see in at all.

I could hear him trying other doors along the way. A few doors down, one of them opened. I heard him shuffle inside and look around. More anger flared when he didn't find who he was looking for. Then he moved on.

He had repeated that same relentless searching both times. The exact same pattern. Try every door; search through the ones that were open, and move on.

Conflict raced through me. Just like it had the previous time he'd been outside the door.

I wanted to stand up, throw open the door and wring his neck. I wanted to hurt him for hurting Bridget.

But my priority was keeping Bridget safe and hidden from him. And getting her to her mother.

Bruce finished his search through the last empty compartment, then exited the car.

Earlier, I hadn't even realized I had nodded off until I woke up. Again, I wondered at the gentle and rhythmic underlying pulse of the train and the effect it could have on a person. Across from me, Bridget was still sleeping in the seat. Bruce hadn't disturbed her at all.

The poor dear had slept for almost two hours. Not long after she had relayed her story to me, the sense of relief had finally allowed her to succumb to exhaustion. Her facial features had softened. She looked a lot younger than she did when she was awake.

I wondered where these overwhelming paternal instincts were coming from. I'd never really wanted kids. But I knew that male wolves were paternal. After I'd figured out what had happened to me, I read everything I could to understand wolves. Wolf blood ran through my veins, providing my human self with incredibly powerful wolf-life senses and strength. Was that same blood now infusing me with the same attentive and fiercely protective instincts?

"Hey," Bridget said, startling me out of my thoughts.

"Hey," I said. "Did you sleep okay?"

She sat up, yawned and stretched. "Like a baby. Wow, I was right out of it." She looked out the window. "Where are we?"

"We just left Massachusetts. We're in New Hampshire."

She gave off the essence of relief. She was that much closer to the safety and comfort of her mom. But then her emotions twisted, as she remembered the man she was hiding from.

"Any sign of Bruce?" she asked.

I wanted to tell her *no*, but I couldn't lie to her.

"He keeps searching; but he hasn't found us. He won't find us."

"But if he does…"

"He'll have to go through me first. I know I don't look like much, but I'm a lot tougher than I appear."

She smiled. "You're big. You're a thousand feet tall in my eyes. You're my favorite author. Besides Kelly Armstrong, that is."

I grinned and decided to use Bridget's love of fiction to distract her from the present moment. It was a subject I could talk about all day. "Oh yeah? I've met Kelly. She's a Canadian, like me. We met at a Comicon a few years ago. She is really sweet. A great writer; she writes some really dark stuff, but she's a genuinely really nice person. You'd really like her."

"I've been a fan of hers for a long time too. I loved her *Women of the Otherworld* series. Have you read them?"

"I've only read a few of her books. Just the first few in that series. I enjoyed the ones about Elena and the werewolf pack."

"Me, too. I love the whole series, but the first books about Elena are still my faves. Elena's one of my favorite characters. Have you seen the TV series based on Elena?"

"*Bitten?*" That was the name of the first book in that series. "No, I haven't seen it, but I hear it's pretty good."

"It's great! I really love it. It's in season two now. I like the books more, but the TV series allows me to get more of Elena."

She paused for a moment and looked back out the window.

"Funny, I actually just dreamt that Elena and I were racing through the woods together. We were searching for something, I'm not sure what, but we were running, side by side. She was in wolf form. I was me, but I was able to run fast, keep up with her. It was amazing."

I marvelled at the fact she had dreamed she was running alongside a wolf while, in reality, she had been racing across the countryside with a man who was also wolf. Was that some sort of preternatural instinct in her? Or just a strange coincidence?

It also made me worry again. I had to figure something out soon.

Or else, shortly after this train stopped in Waterbury, Bridget might just be *literally* running in a field beside a wolf.

We were pulling out of White River Junction in Vermont when Bridget woke up the second time. This time as she had slept, I hadn't nodded off at all. I just sat there and watched her sleep, again marvelling at the beautiful innocence that overcame her features once she drifted off.

While she was asleep, my stomach began to growl and rumble. I needed to eat. Unsurprisingly, I was a voracious eater during this time of the month. Sure, I'd had a hearty "trucker's special" style breakfast before heading to Penn Station. But I was ready to eat again. I was pretty certain Bridget must also be starving.

I wanted to get up and go get us something to eat from the dining car. But these doors didn't lock from the outside, only the inside. Bruce had come back two more times. The desperation in him kept growing the longer he stalked back and forth through the car, continually searching, finding nothing.

"Hey," Bridget said, shortly after opening her eyes. "Where are we now?"

"We're in Vermont. It's almost six thirty. We just left White River Junction. Three stops and we'll be in Waterbury."

Waterbury. The final stop before she needed to head north to Stowe. Her train was scheduled to arrive at ten to eight. Less than half an hour before the sun went down.

She smiled at me. It was a genuine smile, one of wonder and friendship and trust.

"I still can't believe I'm hanging out with Michael freakin' Andrews," she whispered. "The brilliantly talented author, and now my hero."

"And I can't believe I'm hanging out with Bridget freakin' Wells." I replied. "Seriously. You're the most well-read person I've ever met. When did you become such a voracious reader?"

"My whole life. Mom tells me when I was really young, I started to read words aloud along with her as she read to me. She'd thought I just memorized words from the page, because it was a book she'd read to me countless times. But then she tried a new book, and when I started reading it along with her, she said she knew.

"I read everything I could get my hands on. I couldn't get enough. I started reading young-adult novels by the time I was six, and since about age eight I have been reading regular novels. A lot of the classics. Dickens, Brontë, Tolkien. My favorite is *Howard's End* by E.M. Forster. But I like new books, too. Once I discover a writer I like, I try to read all their books, if I can get my hands on them at the library. I picked up one of your books when I was ten and have read all of them."

"You've likely read more books by age thirteen than the average adult will read in a lifetime."

She nodded, with a big grin on her face.

"That is so awesome!" I said. "Us writers need to know there are more voracious readers like you out there." I lifted a closed fist into the air between us.

She mimicked my gesture. We did a fist bump and she giggled.

Her giggle brought out her actual age, not the maturity level she displayed in her speech and interactions, not the maturity of her reading level, not the much older teenager she appeared to be on the surface. But a thirteen-year-old.

"You must be hungry, Bridge." I said.

She laughed. "I'm starving."

"I was waiting for you to wake up. These doors only lock from the inside. I'm going to get us something to eat. I need you to lock the door behind me."

Her nervousness was palpable in the air suddenly. "All right," she said.

"It'll be okay," I said in a reassuring voice. "He's not out there right now. Lock the door behind me and make sure the curtains are tightly sealed. I won't be long. When I come back I'll use a code word to let you know it's me."

She smiled at the playfulness of that.

"I could use something like *Forester*. The author of your favorite novel."

"No," she said. "Let's use *Bronte*. Because I also love the books by both the Brontë sisters and that's also the name of the main character in your books."

I grinned. "*Bronte* it is."

As I slipped out of the car, Bridget pushed the door closed behind me. I could hear Bridget slide the lock latch closed, as well as the rapid beat of her heart and increased rate of breathing.

I made my way out of the sleeper car and back through the coach car I had been sitting in originally. My backpack was sitting on the seat where I'd left it, completely unmolested. I grabbed the backpack and found my way through the other cars and to the dining car. I could detect Bruce's smell throughout each car, but I didn't actually see him anywhere along my route. Which meant he must be in one of the other sleeper cars, toward the front of the train.

I settled into the queue of people lined up at the service bar in the dining car. The overhead PA announced that we would be arriving in Randolph Station.

When the train pulled to a stop at the station, I was still in line, bemused at the reactions of the people ahead of me: the mixed emotions and feelings of hunger, anger over the wait and, in the case of an impeccably dressed older lady who looked like she should be having high tea with the Queen of England rather than on a dining car on an Amtrak train, a continually ongoing case of serial flatulence. Her farts were silent to normal ears, but the ungodly smell was detectable to everyone. Most of the others in line threw annoyed glances at a nearby biker dude. I was amused at how they assumed he was the perpetrator of the gaseous infestation, and not the sweet old lady.

I finally got my food as the PA announced that the train was about to leave the station, and I started walking back through the diner and lounge cars as the train began to slowly move forward.

As I entered the first coach car, I smelled the distinct scent of Bridget's fear.

It wasn't a lingering scent from before, but a fresh, more powerful one.

And, oddly, it wasn't coming from the cars ahead of me.

I was picking it up off the air vent, tinged with a burst of fresh air.

Bridget was outside!

I looked out the window to my right and spotted her rushing down a street beside the train station.

With Bruce right behind her.

The train was picking up speed. They disappeared behind a warehouse-sized building.

I rushed back to where the coach car connected with the lounge car. The exit door was unlocked. Dirt and gravel sped past as we continued to accelerate out of the station.

I leapt out, clearing the gravel. My feet hit the hard-packed dirt, and the forward momentum pitched me forward. I tucked and rolled, losing my backpack and the sandwiches in the process.

The train rushed past.

I came out of my tumble and raised myself to my feet.

I ran along the trail of Bridget's scent, picking up where Bruce's odor intersected with hers. He was closer, gaining on her.

I followed their scents to the open doorway of a rickety, three-story wooden structure that looked like some sort of mill.

Just as I was stepping into the shadowy interior of the warehouse building, wood cracked as it connected with flesh and bone. The sound echoed through the mostly empty space, along with a yelp of surprise and pain from Bruce.

About twenty feet ahead of me, at the door of an inner room, Bridget had ambushed him with an old two-by-four.

He was still standing. A long slash on the left side of his head was just starting to bleed.

The board was old and weathered. It had done some damage, but not enough.

I ran toward them.

Bruce grabbed her wrist with one hand and easily twisted her off balance. She squealed in pain as she flopped to the floor on her side.

"You stupid bitch. That's twice you've hit me," he yelled, dabbing at the blood streaming down the side of his face. "I wanted to talk to you about what happened. Explain. But now I'm going to fuck you so hard you won't be able to walk! Then I'm going to shut you up for good."

"No!" Bridget said, striking at him with her free hand. "Let me go!"

A split second before I reached Bruce, he turned his head to look.

I slammed into the side of his chest with my right elbow. He was a solid guy. Even through that quick hit, I could feel the tight and thick muscles on his chest. But the blow was hard enough to knock him off his feet and sending him flying against the old wooden wall. Weathered, like the board Bridget had found, the wall cracked and buckled.

"You're not touching her again!" I growled.

He shook his head and started to pick himself up.

I bent down and put out my hand to Bridget. "You okay?" I helped her to her feet.

Bruce was upright now. "This is none of your fucking business. I'm gonna fuck you up."

The man's muscles and fighting stance made me pause.

As I've said, I'm not a fighter. Never have been. Prior to me coming into my supernatural powers, I'm pretty sure I'd have been a quick knockout.

Bruce rushed at me and sent a right hook for my chin. His anger made him sloppy. I dodged away from it, my right arm pounding into his ribs. Beneath the layer of tight muscle on his ribs, I felt and heard them crack. I realized I hadn't tried to pull my punch, as I always did since I'd been turned. My own anger had gotten the better of me.

"Fuck!" Bruce shuffled a few steps away.

"Language!" I said to him. "There's a young person in the room."

I had always wondered why Spider-Man was such a wise-cracker. Since my change, I'd learned that, at least for me, it was a way to relieve the tension of conflict. In a tense fight situation, it just spouted out of me.

Plus the cheeky ribbing I'd just given him—get it, ribbing?—angered him more.

I could tell Bruce was tensing for a surprise attack just before he ducked down and lunged at me. But I didn't have enough time to get out of the way of the full body tackle.

He hit me hard enough to throw me off balance and we both stumbled to the floor. As we landed, he rained quick, fast blows with his right hand to my own ribs.

With no give between his fists and the concrete floor, I felt one of my own ribs crack.

"Copy-cat!" I blurted as the wind was knocked out of me. "Try one of your own moves."

He raised his left arm up and elbowed me hard in the mouth. I could immediately taste the blood. Then his closed right fist hit the right side of my face.

"That's better," I quipped, hoping my voice could be heard through the sudden ringing in my head. "Good for you. You get to advance to the next level."

The truth was, I was hurting. But I didn't want him to know that.

Bruce slammed his elbow into my nose and sent another punch to the side of my head.

Then I heard another crack.

Bridget stood over him with a broken two-by-four in her hand, the other end bouncing away across the floor. It hadn't hurt him but provided a much-needed distraction. I'm not a fan of being pummelled.

I bucked, bringing my knees up and lifting him into the air to launch him over my head. He hit the floor with his right shoulder as he rolled onto his back.

"Thanks, Bridge," I said as I shifted around to my feet.

Bruce was in the process of getting up, still in a crouched position as I rushed him. This time my right elbow connected with the soft spot between his left shoulder and neck. He crumpled down to his knees.

With my right hand, I grabbed him near the back of his neck and lifted him off his feet. Then I shoved my left hand into his face and stepped forward, pushing him back against the wooden wall with the back of his head leading the way.

The wood splintered and cracked.

I let him drop. He managed to stay on his feet.

I punched him in the ribs again, this time with my left hand. I didn't pull the punch. There was a much more audible cracking this time. He buckled forward and let out a yelp. I slapped his face hard with an open right hand, snapping his head to the left, then followed that with a backhand that caught him dead center and broke his nose.

I paused, smelling that the fight was out of him. He was in full defensive mode, trying to back away. He backed into the wall and put one hand out to keep his balance, barely able to stay on his feet.

As I was trying to figure out what to do next, Bridget stepped up from my left, got right in front of him and thrust her right foot up, her shin catching him squarely between the legs.

He crumpled to the floor, unconscious.

"Nice legwork, kiddo," I smiled at her.

She smiled back at me. "Nice work yourself." Her scent became infused with worry. "Oh no, your nose is bleeding. So is your lip."

"I'm okay." I said. "I'll be okay." I cradled my left side. "My ribs feel a lot worse than my face looks." Blood from my nose and lip had leaked onto the front of the gray t-shirt I was wearing. I grabbed the material and used it to dab at my lip and nose.

"We've got to take care of him," I said.

"Let's call the police!" she said.

"No," I said, thinking about the time. It was going to be sundown soon. "Not yet. Not right now. This might sound strange, but I can't be involved with that."

"Oh," she said. "You're a celebrity. You don't want the tabloids to know. That makes sense."

Best to let her believe that. "Thanks for understanding." I said. "But we also need to make sure he can't follow you. Not that I think he'll have it in him to do much more than go crawl somewhere and lick his wounds."

I explained that if we took his clothes, tossed his wallet into a ditch somewhere a few blocks away, it would limit his ability to follow any longer. What I didn't tell her was that, since Bruce was a bit larger than me, his clothes would at least come in handy for me to wear in the morning—as soon as I figured out the logistics of how that was going to work, now that I had a travelling companion.

We left Bruce completely naked. I suppose we could have left him in his underwear, because I certainly hadn't planned on wearing them. But I wanted to leave him completely naked and vulnerable. I had certainly woken up enough times in that state. I was an old pro at it. But the experience would likely be a new one for him. Catching Bridget would be the furthest thing from his mind.

I wrapped his t-shirt around his jeans in a tightly wadded ball. I also wrapped his boxers around his wallet. One bundle to keep for later; the other to dispose of. "Okay," I said. "We need to get out of here."

"There's blood on your shirt," Bridget said. "People will notice."

The front of my t-shirt was most certainly a mess. The right side of my chest was a dark-red Rorschach blob.

"We'll have to try to take a way where nobody sees us," I said.

"Why don't you just wear his shirt?"

"I have another idea for how to use his shirt," I said. "I'll explain later. Let's get going."

"Why don't you just wear his t-shirt over top of yours for now?"

Smart kid. I grinned at her. "Good idea." I unwrapped Bruce's t-shirt from the bundle and pulled it over my head.

"Okay," I said. "Let's move. We have to get as much space as we can between us and Bruce, as quickly as possible."

We made our way out of the old wooden warehouse. Nobody was on the narrow side-street on the other side of the train tracks; nobody would see us leaving the warehouse and thus connect us to the naked, unconscious man inside.

"This way," I said.

We walked down the back street to where it hooked around to the left, then connected with a larger street, still running parallel to the tracks. The stop sign at that intersection told us it was Weston Street. We turned right onto Weston.

"How did you know I'd gotten off the train?" Bridget asked. "How did you find me?"

"I saw you running. I guessed that you might try to hide in that empty warehouse."

She looked at me funny; her scent told me she knew I wasn't being entirely truthful.

"How did Bruce find you?" I asked. "Did he get in the cabin? How did you get away from him? Did you hit him?"

"Oh," she said, and her scent took on an air of embarrassment.

"I was stupid." She shuffled forward a few steps, absently kicking at a stone on the path in front of us.

"It's okay," I said. "You don't need to tell me. It doesn't matter what happened. All that matters is you're all right. And you're not stupid, Bridge."

"No," she said after a pause and more pebble kicking. "I *was* stupid. I had to pee. The toilet in the cabin we were in didn't work. I *really* had to pee. The train had stopped to let people off. I peeked out the curtains and didn't see anyone in the hall. I figured I'd try one of the other cabins and use the toilet there. But the minute I stepped into the hall, Bruce called to me.

"He was at the corner at the end of the car. So I ran in the opposite direction. I didn't know how far down the diner car was. When I got to the car with all the regular seats, the door was open. I felt trapped. I went out the door and the second I stepped off the train I ran."

"See," I said. "You weren't stupid. You knew the best option to get away. You were right. Being on the train was a dead end."

"Maybe," she said. "But at least being on the train meant I was going to get to my Mom's. Now I don't even have that."

"We'll find a way."

We were both quiet on the rest of our walk up that long street. I could tell Bridget was worried, wondering about how we were going to get to her mom's. Me, I was trying to figure out a plan to keep her safe. I didn't want to get tickets for the next train out of Randolph. We needed to be as far away from Bruce as possible, just to be safe.

I couldn't be around Bridget overnight anyway. I had to get her somewhere safe so she could continue her journey to her mother without me. I didn't want to leave her alone, but it wasn't like I had much choice. In less than an hour, I would be turning into a wolf.

I didn't know how to tell her I'd be leaving her after promising I wouldn't.

It took about ten minutes for us to make it to the end of Weston Street, where Weston and the tracks again met.

The sound of running water was not far ahead.

"Let's follow the tracks from here," I said. "Put a little more distance between us and Bruce."

"Sure," she said. "But give me a minute. I can't take the sound of running water. Remember the reason I left the train car in the first place."

She rushed off the side of the trail into a set of the bushes. I was confused.

"Look the other way," she called out, even though she was barely hidden behind the foliage.

"Where are you…?"

"Michael," she said. "Turn around. I have to pee."

"Whoops, sorry." I laughed, turning around.

I tried to block out the sounds as I stood there, completely embarrassed for both of us, while waiting for her to finish. For a man with extra heightened senses and abilities, I sometimes really didn't pick up on the subtle things.

In a hundred yards, the tracks crossed a brook. I stopped on the bridge and opened Bruce's wallet, removing the cash and handing it to Bridget. "You might as well hang on to this." I wrapped Bruce's underwear around the wallet again and tossed it high into the air over the water.

The underwear unfurled and landed on a branch hanging over the water. The wallet itself came down another twenty feet or so past that, and landed with a satisfying splash in the brook.

"There," I said. "I don't think he'll find that any time soon."

"Anytime, ever," Bridget giggled.

We kept walking in that same direction along the tracks, trees on both sides. We continued in our silence. The quiet, the trees on both sides of us, were conducive to me coming up with a plan.

After another fifteen minutes or so, we got to a longer bridge, this one crossing a larger body of water. I figured it must be close to eight o'clock. I had maybe fifteen minutes before I turned into my canine form.

From the sounds and smells, to our left was a large expanse of forest. Up ahead there were more people, some roads, traffic, the scent of wood-burning stoves and campfires. Likely another small subdivision of homes, maybe even a campground.

I figured that stashing Bruce's t-shirt and jeans (as well as my own jeans) under the tracks might work. This could be a good spot for me to change. I just had to send Bridget on up ahead.

"Did you ever see the movie *Stand By Me*?" I said, as we stood in front of the bridge.

"No," she said. "But I read the novella by Stephen King that it was based on."

"Of course you did," I laughed.

"You're thinking of the bridge scene," she said.

"Yeah. Every time I see a set of train tracks over a river, I think of that."

"Are you worried about a train coming?" she asked.

"No," I said. "I can tell there isn't one coming."

"How?"

"I don't hear anything," I said. And I reached down to feel the tracks. "And you can actually feel the vibrations if there's one not that far away."

"Okay, I don't get it, Michael." Her scent was filled with confusion. "What does this have to do with that Stephen King book?"

"Listen, Bridget," I said, reaching into my pocket for my small wad of cash.

"Bridge," she said. "My friends call me Bridge."

"Bridge. You're the same age as the kids in that movie. And you're much smarter than they were. I need you to keep going along these tracks until you find a house where you can call the police. I can't go any further with you. I really wish I could. But it's something I can't really explain."

"What?" she said, her tone and scent completely incredulous. "Why aren't you coming?"

"I...I don't know how to explain. Just trust me. Look, it's going to be dark soon. You should get going. There are some houses up ahead. You can get help." I pulled out my cash and handed it to her. "Here. You might need this. Just in case."

"No!" she said.

"Bridget, I can't go on. I want to help you get to your mother. But I can't go any further. I can't be seen after dark. I need to be alone."

"What?" she said. "Do you turn into a pumpkin at midnight or something?"

"Please," I said. "I need to know you'll be safe. Go on ahead. Find the first house. It's not that far ahead. Tell them what happened. You'll be okay."

"How do you *know* that?" she asked.

"Just go, Please."

"No! We're in this together. I need to get to my mom. You said you needed to visit a sick friend. And besides, you promised me. So I'm not going anywhere without you."

"Please," I said. "Bridge, there isn't much time."

"Time for what? Michael, we are friends. You helped me. I can help you. Just let me know and we can get through this."

She was thirteen going on thirty in terms of her emotional intelligence and maturity. A bright and brave kid. And an open-minded one. And I knew, because I could smell it on her, that was not going anywhere, no matter what I said, no matter what I did to try to convince her.

For a moment I considered running, sprinting really fast, losing her in the woods. But if she followed me, and she would, she might get lost. At least here, she was on the tracks. There was a clear direction. She knew there were some houses up ahead.

I needed to convince her it was better for her to go on without me.

But after what we'd already been through, what could I say, in fifteen minutes or less, to make her leave without me? Maybe, instead, in the time I had, I could explain it to her.

She had already been lied to, been betrayed; the thought of being anything but honest with her started to skitter away.

I at least owed it to her to try.

I sighed.

"Okay," I said to her. "I'll explain. But it's not going to be easy to tell you."

"Do you think," she said, "that it was easy for me to tell you about what Bruce did to me, and what he tried to do to me?"

"No, you're right. You trusted me. So it's time I returned the favor and trusted you. I'm about to share a secret I haven't ever told anyone else before. In fact, only one other person knows, and I never even told her. She figured it out on her own."

A deep and rich empathy flowed from Bridge as she reached out and took my hand. "Please tell me."

I shouldn't have been surprised. This was in keeping with the rest of her incredible maturity; but it was also startling that this girl whose childhood had been snatched from her less than twenty-four hours ago was suddenly comforting an adult.

Perhaps it's easier to comfort another person than to wallow in one's own predicament.

But nonetheless I was impressed.

"You remember that dream you had about running in the field with Elena the werewolf from Kelly Armstrong's novels?"

"Yeah."

"Well, what I'm going to tell you, it's like…that."

"No way," she said, and I could tell from her scent that she had already pieced enough of it together, slowly, in her head, to believe me. "*Noooooo waaaaaaaay!*"

August 1, 2015 – 6:12 A.M.

I woke up curled up in a ball, or maybe more like a fetal position. Normally, when I woke up, it was more of an awakening of my consciousness. Like I had just recently resumed human form from the wolf persona. But this was a waking from sleep; as if I had actually morphed into human form while asleep as a wolf. It wasn't sunrise, but shortly after. I just know these things. Like when you just know that you can't trust a particular fart.

I was naked, lying on a wooden floor inside some sort of structure. I could feel something draped over me. It was a t-shirt, laid overtop of me like a blanket. Someone was pressed up against my back, and I could feel and hear the rhythmic sleep-breathing of the person nestled tight up against me, as if we had been snuggling while we slept.

The person was female. But it wasn't Gail.

I knew her, though. The scent seemed oddly familiar.

The cloth on top of me offered a familiar scent, and I immediately recognized the scent on it as Bruce, the guy I had nicknamed Cornflake when I'd first spotted him on the train.

Then it came to me all at once. Bruce. *Bridget.*

I wiggled my naked body away from her, feeling like some sort of perverted old man. I tried to remind myself that she had been snuggling with a wolf, not all that different than curling up to sleep with a dog. Thank goodness she was still asleep.

As I looked at her peaceful, sleeping form, I wanted nothing more than to protect her from the darkness of the world, help bring her the same sense of peace she experienced in sleep, when she woke.

I was reminded of my promise to get her to her mother.

Looking around, I deduced we were in some sort of small shed. The earthy scent of shovels and other yard tools clued me in to that as much as the visual overview. There was a single, small window beside the door to the shed. Scuttling further away from Bridget, I kept myself covered with Bruce's t-shirt. No sense freaking her out if she woke up. I spotted a pile of clothes to my right. My jeans, Bruce's jeans. My t-shirt. Bruce's t-shirt. Socks. My running shoes. No underwear. I figured I must have had those on when I'd changed the night before.

Damn, I hate piecing together missing time.

I often had very little memory of the last five to ten minutes before turning into wolf form. I didn't know exactly what Bridget and I had spoken about or what had happened. I knew what I had planned on telling her. But all I could remember was that I had started to tell her and that she seemed to believe me even before I could get to the details.

Then my memory went blank.

Probing the fleeting memories of the past ten hours, I was able to come up with a few images of walking alongside a young human female beside a set of train tracks. Of course, my wolf mind didn't know they were train tracks, just that they seemed to be some sort of unnatural, human-built structure. But, looking back at that wolf memory, I knew what they were.

Another memory. It was of a vehicle passing by on a nearby road. The human female was hunkered down beside me, whispering that it was okay. I remember being frightened of the bright light and the roaring sound of the engine as the vehicle passed us.

There were two other memories, mostly auditory. The first one was the human female saying, "It feels weird calling you Michael when you're in this form. How about Mikey? That seems like a much more fitting name for you. Mikey." The second one was the same voice saying, "Okay, Mikey, you need to settle down. It's time to get some sleep." That memory came with the feeling of being snuggled into a tight hug.

I pulled my jeans on, then Bruce's t-shirt. I made a note at how forward-thinking Bridget had been. She must have carried my clothes with her last night while I was in wolf form.

Like I said, a bright kid.

I got to my feet and looked out the window.

There was a dirt laneway and a large, barn-shaped structure on the left, and, past that, on the right, a white house with red shutters. I could smell at least five distinct human scents coming from the general direction of the house.

To the right, down the laneway, a hand-painted sign with some sort of flower in the middle and a cursive script read *Johnnycake Flats Bed & Breakfast.*

I had to assume we were still in Vermont. Perhaps a bit north from Randolph. I had planned on telling Bridget to just keep following the train tracks north; it was the best way to get us where we needed to be. Eventually. But how far north had we made it? How close were we to Waterbury, which was the Vermonter's last stop?

Bridget was still sleeping peacefully. I marvelled at how she had rolled with the punches, accepted what I was, and continued on the quest to see her mother. She had obviously put faith in me as her canine companion. We must have walked for miles in the dead of night.

Was I ever this bright, this brave, this flexible, when I was thirteen? I sincerely doubted it.

Her heartbeat and breathing started to change as she moved out of a deep sleep and into a lighter mode. She was beginning to wake. I stood and watched her for a minute until her eyelids fluttered open.

A huge smile beamed across her face as she lifted her head. "You're back!"

"I am. Thanks for taking care of me when I was in wolf form, Bridge."

"Are you kidding? Thanks for taking care of me. I was terrified out there. It was pitch black in some spots. Sure, there were some houses along the way, some streetlights and traffic on a nearby road here and there. The main highway and the train tracks kept splitting off from one another. But most of the time, the only light we had was the full moon."

"That full moon can be both a blessing and a curse."

She laughed. "I imagined we were Mowgli and the wolf-pack leader Akela on a midnight romp through the jungle." Of course she was familiar with *The Jungle Book*.

"Did you sleep okay?" I asked.

"Yeah, I think so."

"Was it scary? Watching me turn into a wolf?"

She said, "I watched this childbirth video last year in health class. It was both scary and disgusting. But that video had *nothing* on watching what happened to you. I thought you were dying. I didn't know what to do. And then you were standing there on all fours, looking at me, your tongue hanging out. You seemed to recognize me. It was freaky, but not scary. Um…I called you Mikey. You reacted to that."

"Do you know how far we went?"

"I don't know. All I know is that I was tired. I tried this shed door. It wasn't locked." She got up and came over the window and looked out. "Nice place," she said. "Where are we?"

"It's a bed and breakfast."

She rubbed her stomach and I could actually hear its low rumble. "Oh yeah, I could use some breakfast."

8:28 A.M.

"Sincerely, it's truly my pleasure," Jim said. "I only wish I could take you the whole way there."

Jim was driving. Bridget and I cozied up beside him on the bench seat of his pickup truck, me on the far right and Bridget nestled between us. Tight fit, but not uncomfortable. Jim drove with both hands on the steering wheel, as conscientious a driver as he was a host of the bed and breakfast he and his wife Debra owned and ran, Johnnycake Flats. Their passion for hospitality, conversation, and just plain neighborly love was unfounded.

Bridget and I had walked from the shed and up the main building at Johnnycake Flats. We gave them the story that I was

Bridget's uncle and we were on our way to visit my sister-in-law, her mother, in Stowe, when our car broke down several miles down the highway in the middle of the night. We explained that there was nothing we could do to fix the car, so we'd spent the night walking and hitch-hiking, hoping to get somewhere we could call Bridget's mother. We made up an excuse that we didn't own cellular devices, preferring old-fashioned conversation and human connections, and asked if we could use their phone to call Bridget's mother.

Jim and Debra immediately welcomed us in. Their scent didn't reveal a drop of mistrust or disbelief in either of them, although they thought it was strange about the cell phones. They were both very trusting souls. And generous, too. No sooner had they showed Bridget where the phone was, that they were offering us coffee and suggesting that we sit down to eat because we must be exhausted from the walking.

Bridget called her mother, but it went straight to her mobile phone's voice mail. She ended up leaving a message, telling her that she was on her way and would be there later that day. She didn't leave any specifics.

We had the most amazing farm-to-table breakfast I think I have ever had in my life. Debra kept piling more onto our plates in a seemingly never-ending buffet. When the meal was finished, Bridget tried calling her mother again and, for a second time, got her answering machine. Jim insisted on driving us into town. He actually said that if he hadn't already promised to do a favor for a friend at nine a.m., he would have been delighted to drive us all the way to Stowe. Even their dog, a border collie named Toby, was friendly and personable. He stayed right at my feet the entire time we were sitting at the dinner table, and I could smell off him the special kinship he'd felt toward me. Most animals could sense the canine elements running through me, and sometimes made strange with me. But not Toby. We were immediate pals. It was as if he were cut from the very same "friendliness" cloth as Jim and Debra.

I hated lying to such a sweet and trusting couple. But what was I supposed to tell them? *So here's the deal, Jim. I'm a werewolf, originally from Canada, but now living in Manhattan. I'm trying to help this thirteen-year-old, who I just met and who escaped nearly being raped, to get to her mother's place.* I didn't think that would fly. Better for this delightful couple to think I was Bridget's uncle and that she was much older than she appeared to be. Better for them to not have any questions.

As Jim pulled into the bus station in Montpelier, he apologized—again—for not being able to take us the whole way there. I assured him that he was a huge life-saver and that we appreciated everything he and his wife had done for us. We shook hands and thanked him again, and he wished us good luck before his pickup truck pulled back onto the street.

As Jim's truck pulled away, Toby stared back at us with his mouth partially open in what appeared to be a huge grin.

Naturally.

8:58 A.M.

The bus we were on between Montpelier and Waterbury wasn't much larger than an extended-length van. There were six rows of seats. Bridget and I were in the fourth seat from the front. Half a dozen other passengers were on this route, which left Montpelier at 8:42 a.m. and was to arrive in Waterbury about half an hour later. We had opted not to take the Greyhound, which wouldn't have left for several hours. A youngster a couple of seats ahead sang a song from a popular children's television program.

The situation reminded me of a scene from one of my favorite movies. Bridget and I were like John Candy and Steve Martin in *Planes, Trains, and Automobiles*, trying desperately to make our way from New York to Chicago in time for Thanksgiving, failing, and having to resort to multiple transportation options.

I watched her as she started out the window.

"Oh," she blurted, turning from the window. "I never told you what I said to my mom when I left her that message. I mentioned that I didn't have my phone on me and that I was on my way. That I was with a friend, I was safe. And I would explain everything once I got there."

"Uh, yeah," I said. "I know. I could hear you."

She giggled. Then she whispered. "I keep forgetting you have enhanced senses. That must be so strange."

"It was at first," I said, also in a low voice. "But I've gotten used to it. I do have to sometimes consciously block things out, but I can easily fine-tune and hone in on a specific sound. Like, right now I can focus in on just the beating of your heart and I'm blocking out the other sounds—the other folks talking, the music coming from the earbuds of someone at the front of the bus. The sound of the engine. The gum-smacking of the driver."

"So with all the smells you can smell," Bridget said. "You must be able to read people. Like you're a human lie detector."

"It is handy," I agreed.

"So you're really good at reading and understanding people, right?"

"Pretty much."

"Then how did you lose the woman you love so much? How did Gail break up with you?"

I paused, stunned. "How did you know about Gail?"

"You told me about her last night before your change. You were explaining that only one other person knew, and that was the friend you were going to see who had a sick uncle. I asked a few things about who she was, and you shared that the two of you had once dated, but that she broke it off years ago and you were now good friends."

I chuckled. "You don't need my special senses to read me like a book."

"So are you going to tell her? Are you going to tell Gail how much you still love her?"

"No," I said. "I'm going there to be the friend that she needs. Just a friend."

Bridget was silent for about a minute before she spoke up again. "Why didn't you call Gail when we were back at the bus station?"

"Yeah," I could feel my face turning red. "Here's the thing. Because I don't actually remember her phone number. It's programmed into my phone."

Bridget laughed. "Too bad you weren't bitten by a radioactive elephant."

"What?"

"You have all these extra wolf powers and abilities, right?"

"Uh-huh."

"But an elephant. That would bring you super memory."

"Funny," I kept a straight face. "That, and the fact I'd always have a trunk to pack a change of clothes in."

She rolled her eyes. "That's bad. That's stupid dad-joke material."

Then she fell silent. I think saying that made her think about her father. I could smell the anxiety and anger and confusion boiling within her emotions.

I reached over and took hold of her hand, squeezing it gently.

She squeezed back, letting me know she was okay.

We held hands for the rest of the bus ride without saying anything else to one another. In some ways, Bridget reminded me of Gail. Gail was also quite adept at reading people, at understanding and accepting them. And, like Bridget, Gail's younger years hadn't been all that easy. But she had managed to make her way through it and become a remarkable woman that I respected and admired so much.

While Bridget was going through a tough time now—her parents' separation, Bruce's attempt to molest her, the startling realization of some of the darkness of the world—she would likely make it through this and become even stronger. Just like Gail.

As the bus was pulling into our stop, right beside the train station, I could detect the scent of a woman filled with an extreme amount of anxiety. Her scent carried a familiarity to it. Bridget's mother.

I squeezed Bridget's hand. "Good news," I said. "Your mother's here."

Bridget's heart rate sped up. "Really?"

"Yup."

She turned and smiled at me. "Thank you, Michael."

"I couldn't have made it here without your help. Thank you, Bridge. But, as we discussed, it's best to leave me out of this. I was just a stranger whose name you never learned. Much easier for me not to have to explain. Go, be with your mother."

"But my Mom can drive you to Burlington. To Gail."

"I'll be fine," I said. "You take care of *you*. I'm almost there. I'll be there soon enough. If I have to stop to answer questions, it'll keep me from getting to Gail in Burlington. I'd prefer to just remain anonymous in this story. A friendly stranger. It'll be easier."

She let go of my hand, turned in the seat and gave me a giant hug. "Thank you. For everything. You've been like a big brother to me." In my ear, she whispered, "You know I won't tell anyone about your secret. It's one hundred percent safe with me."

"I never doubted that for a second, Bridge," I whispered back.

As the bus finished parking and stopped, Bridget moved back from the hug. "Can I call you? Can I stay in touch?"

"Of course," I said. "I'll need to know you're okay."

"What's your number? How do I contact you?"

"I don't even know my own cell number. I never call it. But I live at The Algonquin Hotel in Manhattan."

She slugged me in the arm. "I'll figure it out."

"Go," I said. "Your mom smells like a giant ball of nerves. She'll be over the moon to see that you're safe."

She smiled as she got out of the seat.

"I hope Gail's uncle is going to be okay," she said. "You should talk to Gail about how you feel about her."

I just offered a tight-lipped grin.

"Off you go, kiddo," I said.

She moved off the bus and I heard her mother squeal in delight upon seeing her. The scent of love, of concern, of overwhelming relief was almost overpowering as I could hear her mother embracing Bridget in a beautiful, motherly hug.

I focused on trying to block out their conversation, not wanting to eavesdrop. I waited until everyone else on the bus got off before I got up. I wanted to give Bridge and her mother time to move on and away. The bus driver told me the best way to get to Burlington was to take the 86 route, which was the fastest, or the Greyhound or the Red Line, if I preferred. "You've got plenty of options," he said, smiling at me. "But they'll all get you where you need to be."

Where I needed to be.

I needed to be with Gail. And, thanks to the support, friendship, and wisdom of my new friend Bridget, I would arrive there a much wiser person. Maybe this time I wouldn't screw it up. Maybe I would follow Bridge's sage advice. She had, after all, pulled my skin out of the fire more than once in the past day and a half.

I climbed off the bus. Bridget and her mother were walking arm in arm several yards away.

Just as I looked, Bridget turned her head and offered me a wink and a smile.

"Thank you, Bronte." She whispered in a voice so quiet not even her mother could hear it.

But she knew I could.

Thank you, I mouthed back. But she had already turned away.

About the Author

Mark Leslie would be the first person to admit he's still afraid of the monster under his bed, and he continues to channel that fear into most of his fiction. Mark's dark fiction is often compared to "Twilight Zone" or "Black Mirror" in terms of style, but he usually just adopts the term "horror" when describing the types of tales that he writes. He also writes non-fiction true ghost story tales.

Find out more about Mark at:
markleslie.ca

Trail of Fears

Ron Collins

No one was prepared when the beast first rose from the Florida surf in those early hours of July Fourth.

Even then, before it had grown to what it eventually became, the beast was a monstrous presence, twice as tall as the resort it set upon, made of matted refuse—of plastic and tin cans, of rancid food and other trash from beer coolers men had tossed over the sides of everything from PT boats to streamlined yachts. The beast was clogged with poisons from factories and refuse from ageless landfills, held together by clotted petroleum that had seeped in from all the seven seas. It had teeth made of shark hide, tentacled arms lined with purple and pink suckers. It roiled with slime-slicked sounds as it thundered with thick, plodding steps out of the churning sea.

There was blood in the beast, too. Bodies of the long dead. Tendrils of looped twine and ripped nets. Old cannons from sunken ships. Kodachrome photos of lost loves. Boxes of hooks and nails. Twinkies. Peeps.

The pain that rode with the beast was the cold touch of death in the towering shadows of its body, and the glistening of the morning sun off its dark frame as it emerged from the ocean, waves sliding from its hunched back. The roar it gave as it breathed its first oxygen was loud enough and low enough that it rattled windows for miles up the north coast. Odors of algae and human waste hit like blasts of humid foulness as, unimpeded, the beast shambled across the pristine beach, its sludgy motion half dinosaur and half octopus. Its height and girth made the ground rumble as it left primordial pools of rotting waste in footprints sunk deep into the wet sand.

The swimming pool, built on the oceanside to provide the illusion of nature, was the first man-made thing to feel its wrath, crumbling with a single stomp of the beast's massive foot, its concrete tub exploding with chalky retorts that gave testimony to the beast's incredible strength.

Proceeding without pause, the beast tore into the resort's finely manicured lawn, ripped copses of perfectly trimmed palm trees from their roots, and mashed the fibrous debris between enormous jaws that churned together like grinding wheels.

The first human sound of the morning came in the form of a scream: deep, raw, and twisted with equal parts anger and panic.

The beast's maw reeked of methane as it saw a lone man on the shrub-lined pavilion outside the resort, the clean glassed doors to the manor still open behind him. Vomitous revulsion built like a wave. The beast roared with hunger and crashed a bulbous tentacle against the tallest roof of the building, feeling glorious release as the dry crack of destruction filled the morning calm.

People came awake then.

Men and women with alcohol-blurred hangovers and agendas for the rest of the day.

People retired and spending the interest on accounts they'd tucked away in places out beyond where the darker currents of the ocean had spawned the beast itself.

Others who were enjoying vacations on the links nearby while their wives and husbands spent the days drinking margaritas by the pool or sipping champagne in the spa with a view.

They emerged, these people who'd paid hundreds of thousands of United States dollars simply for the right to spend even more.

They woke to the sound of destruction, and emerged from their suites like moths from cocoons, stepping out of their dreamlives to realize something horrible was happening—or at least to discover that their early morning tee-times were no longer valid.

They ran then. Screaming like the man before had screamed.

They fled the small island, some running toward the bay, others down the salt-lined asphalt of Ocean Boulevard which, only the night before, had seemed so lovely and fragile cloaked in its perfect lace of silver-toned moonlight. Some hid and had to be found. Others froze in panic, leaving themselves easy prey, their quaking forms simply disappearing into the beast's foul morass as if they'd never been there to begin with.

Others ran toward the parking lots, where their finely engineered automobiles sat waiting to burn the petroleum products the people had filled them with in the days before.

The beast inhaled them all—the people and the cars, the buildings and the roads, shuddering with its own joyous ecstasy as oils and gasolines soaked into the mass of its body.

It feasted on those too slow or too weak.

Gnawed on those unaware of the danger they'd let free to run in the world.

It added each of their bloating bodies to its own body, chewing tires and bending metal, salivating at the taste of fear, and groaning with delight as the sting of hubris burned its way down a grease-lined gullet.

The beast tore the roof from the resort, bending like a boy turning rocks to watch crayfish dart for safety.

Passages exposed, the beast's sludgy tendrils found men still comatose from inebriations, and others, dazed from sleepless nights spent trysting with their best friends' husbands or wives, or brokering darkened deals that would sway the world in ways no one else would ever see. The beast found hospitality workers, too, women and men who had left their children before the sun had crested the horizon, giving them kisses on the heads and making promises they now would never be able to keep.

The beast destroyed without deference.

Absorbing the very matter that made up their bodies, the carbon and the water, the enamel of their teeth, the keratin of their nails, flailing as it had been born to flail, crushing constructs and eating as it had been birthed to eat. The beast tossed antique sofas that had been gilded with gold into the clear morning sky, shattered chandeliers that had hung forever in great dance halls, pulverized plaster of Paris that had been laid a hundred years before. It slaked itself on the presence of ostentation that coated the place like grease, wallowed in the cold grace of money that seeped from the building's pores like the sweat that once rolled off the backs of dark-skinned slaves in the swampy fields to the west.

The beast raged until nothing remained but a flatland of mud and rubble.

Only then, when the fall of Mar-a-Lago was complete, did the beast turn northward to take the path it had been called to travel.

If it had understood its purpose, perhaps the beast would have felt something profound at this point, or, at least, something hopeful in the destruction it had caused. The idea of rebirth could have come to it, a sense of revival. But the beast was not born to feel profundity, pathos, or any other form of empathy. All it understood was that this was the path it had been born to walk, so that is what it did, turning to the north to wade through the ocean shallows, growling with unsated hunger as it did, gurgling, belching, and moaning with a long, discordant chord of sound that might have been composed by conductors dead and rotted since before the ages of true music, leaving behind a pile of its own digestive refuse as it vacated the land.

As the beast traveled up the coast, early-morning beachcombers scattered before it like pools of minnows. It did not, however, deviate from its path. Instead, the beast swung its putrid legs farther northward, farther along the coast. Step by thundering step, beach town by slumbering beach town, it traveled northward, leaving in its wake a slimy trail of grossness that covered the surf with its prismatic reflections before riding the sluice across the waterline to ooze into houses and hotels, restaurants and laundromats, the blocks of convenience stores and the hundreds of quaint, touristy boutiques where humans bought happiness for five dollars a shirt.

As it travelled, the beast digested what remained of the resort, its body expanding with its sup. With each step the beast grew stronger. With each stride its resolve more firm.

It passed Jupiter, then Vero Beach and Palm Bay.

As Cape Kennedy lay ahead, two military jets arrived at Mach speed, armed with machine guns and missiles, their screaming afterburners glowing white, their highly trained volunteers simply doing their duty.

Slugs from the guns splattered decaying bits of the beast's foulness across the surf, but the beast trudged on.

The planes turned for another pass, pilots screaming hard against g-force that ripped at their eardrums and broke vessels in their eyes. Rockets burned brilliant streaks across the sky, ripping holes as big as highway trucks into the beast's body.

Black clouds of squalid smoke blotted the sky.

The beast's roar shook the ground.

With astounding speed, it snapped a tentacled arm around the closest jet.

Though the force of speed ripped the tentacle away, the plane buckled and fell from the sky, burning, its shrieking engines clogged with smoldering odor as both plane and appendage made brine-filled splashdowns into the cold, dark water. The beast crashed the second plane, too, and when the skies were clear, a pall fell over the coastline—a deep, deafening silence that rode under the whipping wind and above the water's timeless churn, a silence, too, that lay beyond the fading calls of gulls that glided so endlessly over that churn—a resounding lack of sound that carried power stronger than the sound itself.

Injured, the beast lurched into the sea.

Its wounds burned as salty waves closed over its head.

Broken now, its body waved with the current, its bipedal form spreading to a flattened mire that skimmed the silty bottom to slide toward the wreckage of the first jet. The flayed edges of its touch caressed the columns of ocean current that ran below it and above it. Its skin quivered like that of a stingray.

As it moved, the beast found itself becoming calm.

Life comes from water, it would have thought if it could.

The oceans are home.

The planes, when the beast digested them, tasted of aggression, the pilots of coppery determination.

Do your job, the idea flared as the beast brought its lost parts together and turned northward again, skating along the ocean floor unfettered by the newly arrived airplanes it sensed above.

Perform your duty.

—

When the beast next crawled from the surfy waves, it had grown both thicker of body and even more putrid. The sun, burning hot from above, baked the beast's stench into a stomach-churning wall of clotted floridness. In the distance, a line of clouds clung to the horizon, their edges gleaming scythe-like as they cut into the pure shell of blue sky above them.

Ahead of the beast lay a fortress of hard stone that—having been constructed in the earliest days of the European invasion—radiated an essence of permanence, a place built of power and for power, ringed by rows of freshly painted cannon that spoke in ironic defiance against those who might invade.

The grounds shook with the beast's heavy gait, though.

Bits of mortar between stones crumbled to dust at its approach.

The beast's throaty roar drew fire from the garrison's security force, and then again from ordinary men and women who pulled handguns from belts and purses to defend their ground.

Huge, sweeping blows from the beast's thick arms sent the shooters crashing against fortress walls, or against rows of tour buses idling empty in the lots, or simply cartwheeling across the plaza like so many human tumbleweeds. The people's bones cracked as they fell. The meat of their bodies split to leave bloody pools of scarlet that seeped into pavement. The beast felt anger in the people as they died. It tasted fear, and righteousness, and the stubborn nature of change as these men and women faded, still clutching their weapons as if they contained the freedom they so coveted.

The force of its victory cry threw what tourists remained to the ground.

The beast swung another a bulbous arm, and the row of black-painted cannon that had been pointed so defiantly out at the sea flew through the sky.

Immortal stone crumbled under the beast's pounding.

The beast's ancient strength ripped apart impenetrable walls, the very atoms of which wailed with a blast of grief strong enough to say the stones themselves had been harmed by crimes committed within them.

It leveled barracks.

Fouled manor yards and destroyed cold-floored prison blocks that had once held captive negroes and natives and others the Europeans had seen fit to chain.

The beast destroyed the people here, too, adding their self-deceit into its bulk, feeling the power of the tales they told themselves take hold in the core of its own beginnings.

We've done nothing wrong! they cried as the debris of this shrine to war disappeared into the morass of time.

Nothing!

As coldly, passionlessly, the beast grew taller again.

Wider.

Fouler.

For this was a part of the beast's message, too: *I am grown of your foulness*, it would say if it could, *and your foulness is greater than the sum of its parts.*

As the beast turned back to the ocean, a gray-painted warship appeared on the horizon, its big guns blasting powerful shells to fall at first behind it and then beside, triangulating a position as the beast lumbered into the salty currents.

If the beast were a creature capable of taking notice of such things, it might have reported that the shells fell regardless of whether any humans still here might be alive. And though none *were* alive, the beast might have registered that the power of launching these shells was not in their result, but instead their intent.

The ground concussed, though, and the beast's leg erupted into a shower of mire.

Pain laced the beast.

Ice and fire, freezing and burning throughout its existence.

The beast teetered and fell, its groan of ire a vibration that came from the center of the earth itself. The impact of its crashing to the ocean birthed waves that carried its putrid debris for miles up the shore.

Gasping, the beast gripped the fragile shelf of the earth's crust to pull itself toward the protective waves.

More shells fell, but the beast made the surf, then pulled itself deeper and deeper and deeper still into the water, propelling itself into the currents, and gliding once again into the depths.

The burn of salt stung its wounds, but the memory of dark water gave it comfort.

As it dove, the beast felt the fortress seep through its body: the strength of stone foundation, the firmness of thick walls, the determination of flags that once whipped in the strong air currents above. Here, though, amid strength so overwhelming it buoyed the beast's own power, was still the taint of fear.

Fear under the cover of strength.

Fear of defeat.

Of loss.

Of death.

It is that fear that has killed them, the beast would have thought if it could.

As it once again reclaimed the molecules of its matter, the beast dug claws into the silty floor of the seas, breaking coral and crushing the worm-eaten wood of shipwrecks both ancient and modern, gathering refuse into its body as it made for deep water where the propellers of the gray warship turned languid knots, and where the captain of that ship scanned reports of the beast's ominous nearing.

Torpedoes made pressure waves as they sped through the dark green water.

It was a simple thing, however, for the beast to let the torpedoes motor through, to open gaps in its flesh that left them free to concuss in the distance, killing fish and eels and mammals of the sea without even a single consideration.

Below the ship, the beast flexed its rotting muscles of grime and muck to coil against the ocean's bottom and load itself like a spring.

It was larger now, more powerful.

It released its coil and rose from the depths, its arms pushing forward and transmuting to fists of power.

The ship split to halves, metal girders shredding with long metallic shrieks and plates of armored hull crumbling with a chorus of screeching banshees.

Men and machines flew into the air.

Weapons bays exploded into balls of fire so hot they melted iron and incinerated flesh.

The beast grasped both portions of the ship, popping rivets and crushing iron girding. Sheets of titanium crumpled like paper giving plaintive, waterlogged wails heard oceans away. Angry weapons spiraled unfired down into the darkest water to where urchins and eels and sea crustaceans would feed, and where the earth itself would reclaim it all.

The beast drew in the debris and detritus, the ship's crew and its officers.

It absorbed the crew and the officers, sucking them all down into the darkness where, regardless of rank, they heard the call of harpies and sirens rising up from the depths in ways that had filled mariners' nightmares since the time of the first sailings.

The beast breathed a mouthful of water, then, and strode back to the shore, where it turned northward to complete its travels.

Northward, leaving a wake of destruction and fire burning in cities the reverse of Sherman's scouring of the southlands, northward defiling and destroying properties, leaving behind suffering and despair with disregard.

As Jacksonville smoldered, politicians swore safety.

As Savannah's old slave market crumbled, armies mustered.

As Charleston was left in shambles, the people began to understand what the politicians couldn't.

That the beast, once birthed, could not be killed.

Or reasoned with.

Could not be stopped.

Cruise missiles battered the beast. Artillery blew it to shreds. Nuclear explosions pummeled it into great, gooey gobbets. Yet each time, the beast grew back, stronger and taller, each attack purifying the eternal pull of its urgency, each provocation proving its mission was just.

When the Norfolk Navy Yards were left in a crumbling heap of mire, the world finally understood. As the beast made its way further northward toward the capital, the President, the figurehead of all fears and the man these people had chosen to make their own—the man who had at first even denied the very existence of the beast—called for the entire arsenal of the country to be focused upon it.

Every bomb, every plane, every tank, every bullet.

Every shell of war.

Every weapon from the most secret corners of the most secret military labs.

The nation's capital cannot fall, the President said, as he fled the city.

And in this, the country was finally in unison.

Bullets flew. Bombs fell. The beast was beaten back into the depths again, and for a moment the people cheered and hugged at the sight of the capital city standing—its monuments intact, its structure secure.

Even this arsenal of destruction was not enough to stop the beast.

But the beast huddled against its wounds and brought itself together again, growing stronger with each dismemberment, learning more from each pain, remembering its purpose more clearly as it travelled farther northward, knowing there could be, after all, only one ending to this story.

Far to the north, striding through the bay like a malignant colossus, the beast came ashore for the last time.

It waded past the Statue of Liberty and past the ghosts of Ellis Island to make land at Battery Park. It kicked over buildings and crumbled the subways in lower Manhattan. It crossed through the open scar where once two towers had stood, swaying with the maddening mix of heroism, violence, and vengeance that had attached itself so firmly to this ground.

It was this place, perhaps above all, that gave the beast its fullness—this place where damage had been so real and where reaction had been so grave.

The beast roared as it rose from the morass, barnacles clinging to its haunches and ocean weeds trailing behind. Its horrendous sound shook souls across the land as it climbed from the water.

I am here, the beast called as it beat its crud-encrusted chest to send reverberations that were felt by every human alive. *Your time is over.*

There is a god, after all, a streak of divinity that runs throughout all creation, though perhaps not the god to which is prayed.

The beast took the last of its steps northward, then.

It twisted itself into a whirling cyclone that crumbled buildings to limestone grit, ravaged East Village and tore down Greenwich Square. It watched the Empire State Building topple and savored the electric snap of power that gathered within it as it stepped through Chelsea, through Hell's Kitchen, and through Midtown. It obliterated the Essex House, destroyed the Plaza. Hunter's College was demolished in a single blow, Saks and the Lincoln Center fell with two more. The beast ravaged Central Park. Blasted away Subways and pizza bars, Dunkin Donuts and fashion centers. It tore down Carnegie Hall, wailing as it raged, screaming with its devastation until finally it came to the place it knew it had been beckoned to find: a skyscraper, tall, smooth, and glassy with a gilded name on its front and back, reeking of putrid excess even though it was in this place where the world was nothing but putrid and excessive.

The smell was primordial now, a raw mix of ozone and swamp refuse that covered the exhaust of ancient souls rising up from the grounds of a Manhattan that had once been bought for trinkets and booze.

The beast rose a final, deafening cry.

It was not like us, after all. It could not change.

To force the beast, at this point, to gain a sense of humanity and perhaps then even to spare the world, would be, at best, mere authorial meddling.

So, standing before this final tall tower, glassy and golden in the setting sun as ruins stretched to the horizon, the beast did not change.

Instead, it felt simple joy in the growing that came with its gluttony. The beast took all its fear and all its retribution, all the horrible hatred and desolate despair that had birthed it, and pressed it all into a single, concentrated disgust as it flowed its massive body through doorways and into the lobby,

Through the offices,

And into the hallways,

The staircases and elevator shafts,

Pushing upward to suffocate the space,

Filling the building with its oily plastic repugnance,

Scenting it with the scour of old blood, filling it with the fear

That had created such hatred as led to the fall.

When it was finished, the beast was spent,

Its travels complete.

Its teeth,

Eyes,

And rancid tongue filled the penthouse

That loomed over the barren wasteland around it,

Its body a solid husk, a tower

That would stand

Forever.

About the Author

Ron Collins has contributed stories to many premier science fiction and fantasy publications, including *Analog*, *Asimov's*, and several issues of the Fiction River series. He is the award-winning author of *Stealing the Sun*, a series of space-based SF books, and the fantasy serial, *Saga of the God-Touched Mage*, which sat at the top of Amazon's Dark Fantasy best seller lists for several months. His work has garnered a *Writers of the Future* prize, and a CompuServe HOMer award. His short story "The White Game" was nominated for the Short Mystery Fiction Society's 2016 Derringer Award.

Find out more about Ron at:

typosphere.com

Goblin Road Trip

Jamie Ferguson

Bean hated road trips.

He used to love them. Driving along a road in the sunshine, the window cracked open just enough to feel the wind in his hair, but not enough to drown out the sound of his stereo. For a goblin who'd spent most of his life in caverns deep underground, road trips were a wonderful adventure.

Or at least he'd enjoyed them until *this* trip.

"I forgot to pack my toothbrush," his cousin Heinrich said, and took a big bite of the candy cane he held in one large, sticky hand.

Bean's fingers tightened on the steering wheel of his little sedan. Storm clouds filled the sky, they were barely out of the Pittsburgh city limits, and he was *not* going back to his cousin's apartment to pick up anything else. They'd already gone back three times: the first time to get Heinrich's down pillow, then to get a grocery bag filled with snacks, and finally to get his favorite pair of sneakers. Why Heinrich wasn't actually wearing the sneakers was unclear. For some reason he'd insisted on wearing a pair of fuzzy, red-and-green striped slippers with silver bells sewn on the tops instead. It was the end of June, not Christmas.

They'd left a little before ten a.m., two hours later than planned, since Heinrich had been asleep when Bean arrived to pick him up, then insisted on making pancakes before starting off. This might not have been such a bad thing—Bean loved pancakes— except Heinrich turned out to be an appallingly bad cook. Now they were finally on the road, and had removed the illusions they wore to hide their true selves from the humans they lived among.

"We can stop and buy you a new toothbrush," Bean said. Tiny droplets of rain began to patter on the windshield, and he flipped on the wipers.

"But what if I can't find the same brand?" Heinrich asked. He poked at his teeth with a charcoal-gray fingernail. "Dental hygiene is important. I don't want to risk getting a cavity or gum disease or something."

"It's not like you're going to be gone for months," Bean said. "It's a two-day drive from here to Denver. We'll be back home by Saturday. You can deal with a different brand of toothbrush for a week."

"Fine," Heinrich said, pressing his big nose up against the passenger window. He'd already left nose smears all over the glass.

Bean gritted his teeth and tried not to think about how dirty his car was going to be by the end of the trip. He really shouldn't have agreed to go at all. His master's thesis was due in a month and he hadn't even started writing it, plus once he graduated with his mechanical engineering degree—assuming he passed his verbal exams, which loomed ominously on the horizon—he'd have to find a real job. His scholarship only covered his rent through the end of August, and even if he went from part- to full-time at the grocery store, he'd barely be able to make ends meet. He had plenty of problems of his own to deal with.

But Heinrich didn't have a car, in spite of the fact that he had lived aboveground his whole life. He didn't even know how to drive at all. While he was brilliant in some ways—he was the only person Bean knew of outside the university whose job was being a mathematician—he seemed completely unable to maneuver the world of transportation. He'd gotten lost every time he'd travelled anywhere on his own. Last fall Heinrich had ended up in Miami, even though Bean had watched him board a train headed to Seattle. So Bean couldn't turn down Heinrich's request for help, and now he was stuck helping Heinrich in getting his great-grandmother's wedding ring out a storage unit in Colorado, so Heinrich could propose to his girlfriend, Laura.

Laura had broken up with Heinrich last month, saying she was tired of waiting for him to propose. Then she'd moved back to Colorado and hadn't responded to any of his many, many calls or messages since. So it remained to be seen whether or not the ring was really worth the trip.

Bean didn't have a girlfriend of his own. He was a long, long way from even thinking about matrimony. It had been hard to figure out human dating norms when he'd started college—at first everything seemed to involve a phone app, which was really confusing. That was not how it had been in the caverns. And even after he'd gotten up the nerve to ask girls out in person, there was always the question of his goblinhood. Was it right to go out on a date with a human woman while wearing his illusion?

He had to wear the illusion; otherwise, he'd risk humanity finding out that goblins were real, and thereby put his people in jeopardy. And human physical norms were quite a bit different from goblin norms. Anyone looking at him would see a short, squat, muscular young man with peach-brown skin and a larger than normal nose and ears, but wouldn't be able to see through his disguise to see the bluish-gray color his skin actually was. Nor would they realize just how big his nose and ears really were by human standards. Dating someone under false pretenses felt unethical.

Heinrich didn't have to worry about ethical dilemmas. His girlfriend—ex-girlfriend, now—was half elf and half human, and she knew all about Heinrich's goblin nature because they'd met at her sister's wedding.

"Are we there yet?" Heinrich asked. He giggled and took a swig of ginger ale.

Bean gritted his teeth and glanced at the odometer. Only about fourteen hundred miles to go. Fortunately there wasn't much traffic. At the moment.

Heinrich rummaged in one of the many bags he'd jammed around himself, then looked out the front window just as they passed an exit. He let out an ear-splitting shriek and grabbed Bean's arm with both hands.

"What now?" Bean asked, trying to focus on the road.

"You have to pull over!"

"We're on the highway. I can pull over at the next exit."

"No, you have to pull over now!" Heinrich squeezed Bean's right bicep so hard his grasp felt like a tourniquet.

"For the love of… Fine, let me go," Bean said, as he slowed the car and pulled over to the side lane. He turned on the hazards, brought the car to a stop, and stared at his cousin, who still held Bean's arm in a rather sticky death grip. Heinrich's gaze remained fixed on something ahead of them. His candy cane now rested on his bare, hairy left thigh. "Heinrich. We've stopped. The car isn't moving. Would you please let go of my arm?"

"Okay," Heinrich said in a small voice, his gaze still locked on whatever it was he was looking at. His bluish-gray skin had taken on an odd pallor, and his dark eyes were opened so wide that his thick, bushy eyebrows almost reached his hairline. He released Bean's arm and continued to stare out the window.

Bean peered in the direction his cousin was looking. All he could see were cars driving past them, a few warehouses on the side of the highway, and an overpass. The wiper blades scraped against the windshield with that scraping, rubbery sound they make when there's hardly any water to wipe off. Bean switched them off and took a deep breath.

"What's wrong?" he asked.

"*That*," Heinrich said, pointing straight ahead of them. "We can't go under *that*."

"Under what? The overpass?"

Heinrich nodded. Some of the tiny bits of candy that clung to one corner of his mouth fell off and landed in between the passenger seat and the console.

"Seriously?" Bean rolled his eyes, trying not to wonder whether he'd be able to vacuum up the candy after their trip, assuming it hadn't melted and oozed into the fuzzy fabric. At least it smelled like mint. He resolved to sneak the package of chili pepper and ranch potato chips out of Heinrich's bag and toss it into the garbage at the next rest stop. If they managed to stay on the road long enough to make it to a rest stop. "Come on, Heinrich. We're driving from Pennsylvania to Colorado. You can't expect us to avoid overpasses."

Heinrich shook his head. "We can't go under them. At *all*."

"Why?"

Heinrich shrugged. "I don't know. I just don't like them."

He picked his candy cane up from where it rested on his leg. He removed a piece of hair from the candy, then jammed it back in his mouth.

"Too bad," Bean said. He put his turn signal on and started the engine.

"No!" Heinrich wailed. He threw what was left of his candy cane onto the dashboard and grabbed Bean's arm again. "No, no, *no*! I'm too afraid! Please! We *can't* go under them!"

"Okay, okay," Bean said. He sighed and looked over his shoulder. The last on-ramp was maybe five hundred feet behind them. He took a deep breath and began to back up the car. "Can you go over underpasses?"

"Of course," Heinrich said, rolling his eyes. He grinned and fiddled with his phone. "Thanks, Bean. I'm going to send another note to Laura and tell her how much I love her. I don't think she's blocked my number."

"You're welcome," Bean muttered. "But you're going to have to deal with getting a new toothbrush."

What had started off as a two-day road trip to Denver turned into a six-day journey zig-zagging across the country on back and side roads. Bean tried to keep an eye out for overpasses, but quickly realized that backing up a highway on-ramp was not an ideal solution. He tried asking his cousin to navigate, and discovered that Heinrich not only had a terrible sense of direction, but he also seemed completely unable to read maps. Bean ended up plotting and re-plotting their course on his phone every time they stopped at a rest stop or gas station. Heinrich contributed by supplying an endless stream of conversation, which ranged from pointing out whenever the mileage on the road signs didn't match, to talking about how wonderful Laura was, to talking about candy.

"Have you started looking for a job?" Heinrich asked as he ripped open a new pack of bubble gum.

They were on a two-lane road somewhere in the middle of Kansas. It was late in the afternoon, and the weather was overcast and drizzling, as it had been for most of the trip. For a summer road trip, there hadn't been very much sunshine.

"Not yet," Bean said. "I've been too busy working on my thesis."

"Aren't you done with that yet?"

"I haven't started writing it," Bean said.

"Wow, talk about waiting until the last minute." Heinrich said, and popped his gum.

"I was going to start it this week, but obviously I'm doing something else instead," Bean said, trying not to lose his temper. The original plan hadn't seemed that onerous, but, thanks to Heinrich's inexplicable terror of overpasses, the trip was taking three times as long. The month he'd thought he had to write his thesis was going to be more like two and a half weeks. Yes, he had procrastinated…but if he'd known about this trip, he would have started his thesis earlier.

Bean gritted his teeth as he watched the rain change to pebble-sized hail.

"You'll get it done," Heinrich said, slapping him on the shoulder so hard that Bean jerked the steering wheel and swerved into the next lane. Fortunately they seemed to be the only car on the road at all. "Besides, this is an adventure. We're on a quest for love!"

"*You* are," Bean said. "I'm on a quest to get back home and write my thesis."

And find a job.

And then…

What?

What was the point of all of this anyway? Sure, he couldn't have studied mechanical engineering at the goblin universities down in the caverns. Civil engineering, yes, but the idea of designing tunnels, or bridges, or coming up with new approaches to water infrastructure, was completely uninteresting to him— whereas he found turbines fascinating. His goal was to be a wind energy engineer and design turbines or rotor blades, something along those lines. Maybe he'd even invent a whole new system to harness wind energy in a way no one else had ever thought of!

But in order to follow his dream, he had to stay on the surface and live among humans. And that meant he had to wear his illusion unless he was alone at home, or in a private place with one of his few goblin friends and relatives. He and Heinrich had dropped their illusions once they'd gotten into the car, but they put them back on every time they stopped for gas or snacks, or checked into a motel at night. Sure, maybe eventually Bean would meet a girl at an event like the wedding where Heinrich had met Laura, but since he only went to events like that every few years, it seemed unlikely.

The choice was clear. Move back home and find romance, or stay here and follow his dream of being a wind engineer. Alone.

Bean set his jaw and stared at the long, straight, empty stretch of road in front of them. Hail pattered on the hood of his car, the sound oddly soothing.

"Wow, it really is an adventure," Heinrich said. "Huh."

"What are you talking about?" Bean asked. He shot a glance at Heinrich, who stared out the passenger window, idly munching on a piece of licorice.

"That," Heinrich said, gesturing vaguely to their right. "It's pretty cool."

"What is?" Bean looked past Heinrich out the window, but could only see dark, greenish clouds and fields of what he thought might be hay.

"Did I ever tell you about the four-dimensional model I put together last year?" Heinrich asked. "You know, the one where I simulated perturbation of the temperature inversion?"

"I have no idea what you're talking about," Bean said.

"Huh," Heinrich said again. He stared out the window for a moment, then ripped the top off a box of malted milk balls. "You like wind, so I'm sure you know tornadoes create a wind-tunnel effect under overpasses."

"Yeah, I knew that," Bean said. What a weird comment to make, especially coming from someone terrified of overpasses. Why would—

Bean's breath caught.

They were driving through Kansas, it was hailing, the sky had an eerie green tinge, and his cousin who had a bizarre fear of overpasses had just mentioned overpasses and *tornadoes.*

Bean bit his lip, scrunched down in his seat, and looked through the windshield on the passenger's side to see the unmistakable funnel shape of a tornado on the north side of the highway in front of them. A small cloud of dust and debris swirled where the tip of the funnel met the ground. Bean slammed his foot on the brake so hard they were both flung forward and stopped by their seat belts. The car shuddered to a stop.

"Isn't it cool?" Heinrich asked. "I just sent Laura a picture."

Bean looked over his shoulder to make sure no other cars were headed toward them. Other than the thin layer of hail that carpeted it, the road was empty. He spun the car around as quickly as he could.

"What are you doing?" Heinrich asked. "We're pointing the wrong way."

"Escaping," Bean said, and floored the gas. The car fishtailed on the slick pavement, and he pulled his foot off the pedal.

"No, I mean this is the *wrong way.*" Heinrich jabbed a thumb to Bean's left. "There's another one over there, and it's heading right toward the highway."

Bean bit his lip and glanced out his window. Sure enough, there was a *second* tornado. He slammed his foot on the brake and they skidded to a stop.

"Now what?"

What were you supposed to do when there was a tornado—much less *two* tornadoes? Hide in a basement or storm cellar or something—not sit in a car waiting to be sucked up by the winds, or have a cow or tractor or something thrown on top of you.

"Hold on," Heinrich said. He stared at the tornado in front of them for a moment, then at the one behind them.

"Hold on how?"

Heinrich chuckled. "I get it now. Turn the car around, pull off on that dirt road that parallels the highway, and then take a right."

"You want me to drive into the tornado?"

Heinrich rolled his eyes. "Of course not. I want you to drive *past* it. It's not moving toward us."

Bean turned the car around and stared out the window. The hail stopped and turned to light rain. "It sure looks like it's moving toward us."

Heinrich shook his head. "Watch it for a few seconds and compare it to that gray barn over there. See how the tornado looks like it's moving to our left, toward the barn?"

Bean swallowed. "Yeah," he said.

"That means it's not moving toward us, although I certainly wouldn't want to be in that barn."

"Okay," Bean said.

"But it would be a good idea if you started to drive, because the other tornado *is* moving toward us."

Bean turned his head and looked back. The sky was dark and scary, and the second tornado was larger than it had been before…it was definitely moving toward them. He put his foot on the gas and drove off the road over the gravel shoulder, across the grassy area, and onto the dirt road that paralleled the highway. He headed west, driving as fast as he could without losing control on the hard, washboard surface of the ridged gravel, then turned right at the corner and drove north on the dirt road. The only sounds were of the wind outside the car, the rain splattering on the windshield, and the crunching sounds of Heinrich eating the bag of chili pepper and ranch potato chips that Bean had meant to throw out. The air smelled like jalapeños, sour cream, and unwashed goblin.

"You might want to stop now," Heinrich said.

"What?"

"The car. You might want to stop it. The road dead-ends up there."

Bean blinked and slowed the car, pulling it to a stop. The sky to the east was still dark, but the sun peeked through the clouds to the west. And, more importantly, there were no tornadoes in sight.

"We made it!" Bean said.

"Go, us!" Heinrich said. He held up one gray hand; Bean slapped it, and they grinned at each other.

"Thanks for keeping your cool back there," Bean said. He took a deep breath, then grabbed the bottle of warm ginger ale from the cup holder in the console and took a deep swig.

Heinrich shrugged. "It wasn't that hard. Last year I put together a lot of tornado simulations, so I knew I just needed to figure out where those two were going."

"You said earlier that underpasses are bad to be when there's a tornado. Is that why you're afraid of them?"

"Nah," Heinrich said. "I've been afraid of them since I was a kid. No idea why. They totally freak me out."

"On the way back, how about if we go through Nebraska instead of Kansas?"

Heinrich chuckled. "There could be tornadoes there too, you know."

"Is anywhere safe? South Dakota? Canada?"

"Tornadoes can happen anywhere," Heinrich said. "They're more likely where it's flat. But you're never safe."

"How about if we look for a less flat stretch of road?"

Heinrich raised both eyebrows. They looked like giant fuzzy caterpillars framing his eyes. "A less flat stretch with *no overpasses.*"

"Deal," Bean said. "Now let's get to Colorado and get your ring."

They arrived at Denver late that night, checked into a hotel, and went straight to bed. Bean normally had to drag Heinrich out of bed in the morning so they could get an early start, but, after the excitement of escaping from a tornado, even he felt like sleeping in. Besides, they were *finally* at their destination. All they had to do today was drive to the storage unit, pick up the box with Heinrich's great-grandmother's ring, then drive Heinrich to wherever his estranged girlfriend was, and see if she'd accept his proposal. Whether she did or not, they'd be back on the road in the morning, and, in another five or six days, Bean could finally get to work writing his thesis.

They put their illusions on, had a leisurely late breakfast of hash browns, feta, tomato, and artichoke omelets with a side of gluten-free toast, then headed back to the car. Bean placed the empty drink containers into a nearby recycling bin, brushed the crumbs off his seat, and tried to remove a piece of what looked like it might be marshmallow from a corner of the dashboard. Finally he gave up and made a mental note to try again later in the day, when it was warmer and the marshmallow, or whatever it was, had softened. He climbed into the car, pulled the door shut, and buckled his seat belt.

"Okay, where's the storage locker?" Bean asked.

"What do you mean?"

"The storage locker. Or storage unit. Wherever the box with the ring is."

"Oh. Right." Heinrich furrowed his brow. "Hmmm."

Bean took a deep breath. "You remember where it is, right?"

"Um. Yeah." Heinrich screwed his eyes shut for a minute, and then opened them and grinned. "It's by a tree!"

"A tree."

"Yes! A big cottonwood." Heinrich beamed. "Laura likes cottonwood trees, that's why I remember that. Hold on, I'm going to send her another note."

He pulled out his phone and began tapping.

"What is wrong with you?" Bean asked. "I can't find the storage unit if the only reference point is that it's *by a tree*. Do you remember the name of the place?"

"Just a sec," Heinrich said. He pressed a button, then looked up from his phone. "It had the word 'green' in the name. It was almost two years ago, you know. You can't expect me to recall every single detail."

Bean sighed, pulled out his own phone, and looked at the map.

"There are three self-storage companies in the Denver area that have the word 'green' in the name. Are you *sure* you're remembering that part correctly?"

Heinrich nodded. "Positive."

"Okay, we'll check all three if we have to. But I'm heading home tomorrow, whether we find it or not."

"We'll find it," Heinrich said. "I'm going to tell Laura I'll be at her favorite park in Boulder around six. Hopefully she won't figure out I'm going to propose."

"Has she replied to any of your messages?" Bean asked.

"No, but I'm not worried," Heinrich said. "This is true love. It's going to work out."

Bean started the motor and headed toward the nearest storage facility. At least there were only three places to check.

Assuming Heinrich hadn't mixed up his colors.

Of course, none of the three turned out to be the right one.

"Is this place even in Denver?" Bean asked. They sat in the car in front of Green Tree Storage, which Heinrich had declared was not the right place even though the lettering on the sign was green *and* a cottonwood stood next to the office. There weren't any clouds in the sky to block the afternoon sun, the air conditioning didn't seem to be working very well, and they were down to their last ginger ale.

"Huh. Good question," Heinrich said. He pulled the ginger ale out of the cooler, popped it open, and took a big swig. "Maybe? If not, it was near Denver. Or pretty close. I don't really remember."

Bean's hands tightened into fists as he tried to resist the urge to throttle his cousin. "I was going to drink that. You drank the last three."

"We can share," Heinrich said. He let out a belch and then held the bottle out to Bean.

They might be cousins, but some things shouldn't be shared.

"I'll get one when we stop for gas. We're almost out." Again.

At least the car was still running. "Are you really, really sure it has the word 'green' in the name?"

Heinrich nodded.

Bean pulled out his phone again and widened the search. There were potential options in Greeley, Boulder, and Castle Rock. Heinrich used to work at some government agency in Boulder, so that seemed like the best option. Besides, Heinrich was meeting Laura in Boulder at six p.m., and it was almost four. They had just over two hours to drive to Boulder, find the storage unit, get the ring, and head to the park to see if she showed up or not.

"The one in Boulder is named Green Bean Storage. Does that sound right?"

"I don't know," Heinrich said. "I'm really bad with names. I'd have to see it."

"Here," Bean said, and held up his phone. "Does that look right?"

Heinrich shrugged.

"Fine. Let's check it out," Bean muttered.

It took about forty-five minutes to get to Green Bean Storage. As they pulled into the street Bean's heart lifted. The sign on the building had green lettering, and there were two giant cottonwood trees next to the parking lot. This had to be the place.

"What do you think?" he asked.

Heinrich nodded. "Yep, this is it! I remember parking by that tree. Well, I remember Laura parking by that tree, since she drove me here."

Bean parked the car. They got out and went into the office. Heinrich pulled out his rather rumpled passport and showed it to the man behind the desk, who directed him to Unit 77 inside the climate-controlled building. At least they hadn't had to rely on Heinrich to remember *that*.

They walked down a hallway with rows of green garage doors on either side. Bean's sneakers made small scuffing sounds on the concrete. Any sound Heinrich's soles might be making was drowned out by the tinkling of the tiny bells sewn into the tops of his slippers. They reached Unit 77 and stopped. Heinrich stood there and stared at the combination lock on the door.

"Well, open it," Bean said finally.

"I can't," Heinrich said.

"Don't tell me you forgot the code," Bean said. "Seriously. Don't."

"I forgot the code," Heinrich said in a small voice.

Bean took a deep breath and clenched his hands into fists.

"You can remember it," he said, willing his voice to sound calm and soothing even though he wanted to grab his cousin by the shoulders and shake him until his big ears rang. "Maybe it's the code you use for your phone?"

Heinrich shook his head. "No, that's easy. It's just a bunch of 2s because I like the number 2. Laura made me set this one to something harder to remember. And it is harder, because I don't remember it."

"How have you made it this far in life?" Bean asked. "You can't read a map. You don't drive a car. You get lost at the drop of a hat. You leave your great-grandmother's wedding ring in a stor-age unit, and then forget which city you put it in. What's the matter with you?"

A tear trickled down Heinrich's cheek. "I'm sorry. I've taken all kinds of classes to improve my memory. I try to use mnemonics. Like whenever I forget your name, I remember you like things neat and tidy, so I repeat 'Bean is clean' to myself for a while. When I put my things in the storage locker, I remembered Green... Well, I can't remember the name of this place, but it's green and there's a cottonwood tree, and trees have green leaves. I just don't remember things like you do."

"You actually forget my name?" Bean shook his head. "You've known me for your entire life. Seriously?"

"I forget *everything*," Heinrich said. He hung his head. "The reason Laura left is because I kept forgetting to propose to her. I knew she wanted to get married before she turned thirty, and then I forgot what month it was, and I missed her birthday. I even put a reminder on my phone, but I forgot to tell it to notify me.

"I remember math formulas, and things that have patterns. Like with the tornado—I could see the pattern it made, so I knew where it was going. I forget everything else. Everything. And now I won't get the ring and Laura won't marry me and I love her and *I don't know what to do!*"

Heinrich's illusion wobbled, and then was gone. Bean looked around to see where the nearest security camera was, positioned himself between it and his cousin, and put his arm around Heinrich.

"I'm here," he said. "I'll help you figure out the code. It's a numeric code, so it's kind of math, right? That means you actually remember it."

"But I *don't!*" Heinrich said. A tear trickled down one grayish-green cheek.

"Sure you do," Bean said. "Laura helped you figure out the code, and she knows you, so it's something easy for you to remember. You just have to stop and think. There are five numbers on the lock. What numbers might you associate with Laura?"

"I don't know," Heinrich said. "I mean, maybe...her birthday?"

Bean nodded. "That's great. When is her birthday?"

"I can't remember. That's why she left me. I love her, Bean!"

"It's in your phone," Bean said, hoping he was right.

Heinrich pulled out his phone, unlocked it with his big, gray thumb, and opened his calendar. "May 3rd," he said.

"That's great. What's another important date for the two of you? The day you met? The day you first, uh, went to dinner, or something?"

"Christmas," Heinrich said. "Laura and I both love Christmas."

"So that's 5, 3, 12, and 25." Bean took a deep breath. "What else? Your birthday?"

Heinrich shook his head. "No. I remember now. It's things I love. Laura, Christmas, and the number 2."

Heinrich grabbed the lock with his hairy hands and entered 5-3-2-12-25.

The lock slid open. Heinrich reached down and pulled the garage door open. The storage unit contained a fuzzy purple sofa, a floor lamp, and a stack of neatly labelled cardboard boxes lined up on one wall. They walked in and looked at the boxes. Heinrich pulled the one labeled "family treasures" off the top of one stack and set it on the floor. He crouched down next to it, ripped off the tape, and opened the flaps. He rummaged around inside and pulled out a small wooden chest. He lifted the lid. A ring of white gold, with a diamond set in between two bright blue sapphires, lay on a bed of black velvet.

"This is it," Heinrich whispered. "I'm really going to marry Laura."

"You've still got to propose to her," Bean said.

"Yes!" Heinrich leapt up. "We have to get to the park! Let's go, or I'll be late!"

"I'll get you there on time," Bean said. "But first you'd better put your illusion back on."

—

It took a while to find a parking spot near Chautauqua Park in Boulder. Finally, Bean parked on a side street, and he and Heinrich walked the few blocks over to the park. Heinrich made a beeline up one of the dirt trails.

"Are you sure you know where you're going?" Bean asked as he tried to keep up with his cousin. The summer sun was bright and hot, they were hiking uphill, and of course he wasn't used to being a mile above sea level.

"Yes," Heinrich said. "Laura and I used to picnic at a spot near one of the Flatirons."

"What's a Flatiron?"

"See how the mountains look like big, flat pieces of rock turned sideways? Kind of like an old-fashioned iron? That's why they're called Flatirons. Those ones up there are the big ones; there are little ones all around this area."

"Yeah, I guess so," Bean said.

Heinrich paused to look at a tall pine tree, then headed off the path and into the forest. Bean trailed behind. They wove through the trees for a while.

Then Heinrich stopped so suddenly Bean almost ran into him.

"She's here," Heinrich whispered.

On the side of the trail ahead of them, Laura stood next to a boulder almost as tall as she was. She wore a white T-shirt, bright pink shorts, and held a small pack in one hand. Her auburn hair was pulled back in a ponytail revealing her long, narrow ears—part of her elf heritage. Unlike pointed goblin ears, they were not too out of the ordinary for humans, so she didn't have to wear an illusion. She looked at Heinrich and smiled.

Heinrich stood as still as if he'd been frozen.

Laura's smile wobbled a bit.

"Go on," Bean said, giving Heinrich a gentle shove. "Go ask her!"

Heinrich took a deep breath, and then dropped his illusion.

"What are you doing?" Bean whispered. His head whipped around, but they were far enough from the trailhead that no one else was in sight.

"I'm asking her to marry me as me," Heinrich said. "Me, the forgetful goblin, who loves Laura with all his heart."

He walked over to Laura, bent down on one gray, hairy knee, and fumbled in his pocket. Bean gritted his teeth, hoping Heinrich hadn't forgotten the ring in the car, but then relaxed when Heinrich pulled out the ring and held it up. A beam of sunlight glinted on the diamond.

Laura squealed and grabbed Heinrich's hands, pulling him to his feet, then gave him a big kiss.

Bean smiled and turned away. He wandered through the trees, pine needles crunching underneath his feet. He was probably getting lost, but how hard could it be to find the trail again?

Finally he sat down on a small rock that stood next to three gray-and-black boulders. One of the boulders had a long white streak running through it. He stared up at the mountains through the pines. This close up, the mountains didn't look nearly as flat as they had from further out. The sun was still high in the sky. The summer solstice must be just about to happen, or maybe had already happened. The whole week had been so long and crazy he couldn't remember what day it was. Was today the twentieth, or the twenty-second?

He saw movement out of the corner of his eye and froze. He was in a forest. With wild animals. What if it was a bear? Or a mountain lion? Or something worse?

He stood up and spun around to see a barefooted young woman tiptoeing away from him, just past the two boulders. She wore a blue sundress with a pattern of pink flowers. A streak of white ran through her coal-black hair. One hand held a pair of white sandals, and the other a matching handbag.

"What are you doing?" he asked.

She turned around to face him, her hazel eyes narrowed. Bean had never seen a woman look both annoyed and charming at the same time. "What do you mean? I'm just walking through the woods. It's not a crime."

"I'm sorry," he said. "I don't mean to be a jerk. But you scared the bejeezus out of me. Where did you come from?"

She waved a hand in the air. "Over there. I gotta go."

"Wait a minute," he said. There were *two* boulders in the little clearing…but there had been three. Hadn't there?

Even if he'd miscounted, which he was sure he hadn't, the one with the white streak was missing.

The woman couldn't possibly be a rock.

And yet…the rock was missing.

He was a goblin. Who was he to say a rock couldn't turn into a person? What kind of creature would that make her, anyway?

"You're a troll!" he said. He'd never met a troll personally, since they tended to live in rocky areas, or, for some reason he'd never been quite clear about, under bridges.

"What?" She wrinkled her nose and took a step backward. Her toenails had been painted the same shade of blue as her dress. "I don't know what you're talking about. I've got to go. I'm meeting my friends for happy hour."

"It's okay, I'm not human either," he said. Her eyes widened. Great. That sounded really weird. "I mean, I'm a goblin."

She raised an eyebrow and tilted her head. The movement made a lock of white hair fall in front of her face. She brushed it back behind one ear.

"You don't look like a goblin," she said.

"Here. I'll show you," he said, and dropped his illusion.

The woman's eyes widened and her mouth formed a perfect pink *O*.

Bean's heart thumped. What had he done? The cardinal rule of living among humans, a rule to never, *ever* be broken, was to stay cloaked in illusion whenever there was any chance a human might see. What if he was wrong? What if she wasn't a troll?

She chuckled. "I guess you are a goblin after all."

At least she wasn't running from him in terror. He took a deep breath.

"Sorry," he said. "I spent the last week driving my cousin out here from Pittsburgh so he could propose to his girlfriend. It was an epic trip. I'm not sure I'm thinking straight anymore."

"It took you a week to drive from Pittsburgh? Seriously?"

"He's…well…it's a long story."

They stared at each other for a moment. Bean's heart thumped so loud she must surely be able to hear it across the little clearing.

"What's your name, Mr. Goblin from Pittsburgh?" she asked. Her smile was so bright it made him want to smile as well. "I'm Alana."

"Bean," he said.

"Are you going to be in town for long?"

He shook his head. "I have to head back tomorrow. My master's thesis is due in a few weeks."

Her smile diminished.

"But I think I might come back after I graduate," he said, realizing as the words came out that he did in fact want to come back.

"I've never been to Colorado before. I like it. The mountains, the trees, the rocks..."

He swallowed as he realized how silly he sounded.

"If you do..." she began, and then blinked. "I mean, it sounds weird, since I just met you and all. But if you come back, maybe we could meet up for a ginger ale or something. If that's your thing. I really like ginger ale. I make my own, actually."

"I *love* ginger ale," Bean said. "That's my absolute favorite thing to drink."

Alana grinned. "Then it's a date."

"Should I look for you here?" he asked, gesturing toward the spot where the third rock had been. "Are those boulders...um..."

"No, I was just taking a nap," she said. "And those rocks are just rocks. Stop by the Flowering Tortoise and ask for me. It's the jewelry shop I work at."

"I will," he said.

"I've got to run or I'll be late," Alana said. "I'll see you in a few months, Bean."

"I'm looking forward to the ginger ale," he said.

"Me too," she said. She gave him a little wave, then trotted through the trees. He watched until she was out of sight, then looked up at the mountain through the pines. He hadn't thought about looking for a job out west, but why not? He'd lived in Pennsylvania ever since he'd left the caverns, but there was no reason he had to stay there. Plus he'd seen some big windmills when they'd been driving around today. There were a lot of them. Surely there were plenty of jobs here for a wind engineer, even one straight out of college.

And, once he got here, he had a date with the most beautiful troll in the world.

Now he just had to figure out how to tell Heinrich he was moving. And figure out where to live while he looked for a job.

He headed back the way he'd come. Or at least he thought he'd come that way. The trees and rocks kind of looked the same after a while. Well, except for the one rock.

"Hey, Bean!"

Bean turned to see Heinrich and Laura walking hand in hand through the trees. They both glowed with happiness.

"Congratulations," he said.

"Thanks," Laura and Heinrich said at the same time. They exchanged a glance.

"Uh, Bean..." Heinrich said. "I have something to tell you."

"Okay," Bean said.

"I'm going to move back to Colorado," Heinrich said. "I'm sorry. I know you love it back in Pittsburgh. And I'll have to move my stuff, and figure out what to do about a job, and all that. But I love Laura, and Laura loves Colorado, so I love Colorado too! Plus I'd love it anyway. But I love it more because of Laura."

Heinrich planted a big, sloppy kiss on Laura's cheek. "What I'm trying to say is, I'm sorry, Bean. I'm not going back with you tomorrow."

Bean blinked.

"Wow, okay. I guess that means I can drive on the interstate, then," he said.

"I'll take care of getting Heinrich's things moved," Laura said. She patted Heinrich on the shoulder. "It...well...it will just go more smoothly if I do it."

"Understood," Bean said. "So...I'm actually going to move out here myself. After I graduate in August."

"Oh!" Heinrich said. "You can stay with us when you get here! Tonight, too."

Laura nodded.

Bean said, "Uh, okay. Yeah, that would be great. Thanks."

They heard voices and realized they were close to the trail. Bean and Heinrich put their illusions back on. They reached the trail and paused to let some hikers pass.

"What made you decide to move out here?" Laura asked.

"I've got a date with a rock," Bean said, and grinned.

A rock who'd seen his real self, his goblin self, and who wanted to make him homemade ginger ale.

He was looking forward to the road trip back to Colorado in a few months.

Bean *loved* road trips.

About the Author

Jamie focuses on getting into the minds and hearts of her characters, whether she's writing about a saloon girl in theAmerican West, a man who discovers the barista he's in love with is a naiad, or a ghost who haunts the house she was killed in—even though that house no longer exists. Jamie lives in Colorado, and spends her free time in a futile quest to wear out her two border collies since she hasn't given in and gotten them their own herd of sheep.

Find out more about Jamie at:

jamieferguson.com

The Squatchers

Jason Dias

Tim shut off the engine. "We're here." A country motel stretched to either side of the car, all dark clapboard and little windows full of stained blinds. The sign proclaimed it as *The Clairmont Motor Hotel*. The last of the evening sun reflected off the motel's window glass at eye-level, then sank into the dark brown siding. Birdsong trilled from the nearby woods, and a tanker truck kicked up dirt along the access road.

Dorothy sighed. "At last. I need to pee like…"

"TMI!" called Dave and Sandy from the back.

Tim said, "Maybe you can check us in, and me and Dave will unload the camera gear."

"Fine." Dorothy slid down from the van and trotted towards the office.

Tim jumped down, too, and walked around to the back doors. Sandy and Dave had already gone out the side of the van. Tim grabbed the nearest cases, both containing cameras with stands. Dave, looming over him, reached for the heaviest bit of luggage, a giant box of audio gear, batteries and leads.

"Glad you're here," Tim said. "It would take two of us to carry that thing otherwise."

"Happy to help," Dave replied, setting the crate down. "This is a squatchy-looking place."

Dorothy came back with keys. "We have eight and nine. Over here." She led the way.

Sandy said, "Why not just leave all this crap in the van? Not like we can't see it from the rooms."

Tim spat on the ground. "That would be a rookie mistake. We lost all our gear in Kansas City back in 'thirteen."

Sandy had only joined the crew at the last stop—recruited from her persistent YouTube comments, which had led to a dialogue. Blonde, photogenic, with square eyebrows and a square chin, she'd make a great addition to the series. Even her naïveté would play well with the fan base.

"Really?" she said. "People are unbelievable."

Dave had already set the audio crate inside the room. He went wordlessly back for more crates.

"That is a big man," Sandy said. "He doesn't look so huge on the screen."

"He's six-five," Tim said. "Try not to harp on it, though. He's kinda sensitive about it. Don't know why. I assume he got a lot of crap about it in high school or something. I'm only five-five myself, so it's really hard to minimize the difference on camera."

Sandy stepped towards the van, leading Tim along. "That's why you never stand close together, or Dave sits down in the shot. Right?"

"That, and a few other tricks."

Dave passed them with another huge crate in hand.

Tim grabbed the last of the luggage. "But it's no big deal. People come in all shapes and sizes. He always gets good shots."

"How long have you been together?"

"About eight years. We started the YouTube show about four years ago."

Dorothy leaned in the doorway of one of the rooms. Dorothy was like a big sister. Taller, just starting to go gray at the temples, eminently pragmatic.

"Boys in eight, girls in nine?" Dorothy suggested. "Nine has a slightly bigger bathroom."

"Fine," Tim said. "Meet for dinner?"

Dave, from the doorway to room eight, snorted. "Dinner is going to be peanut butter and jelly. Again. I haven't seen a restaurant or a diner or even a coffee shop for thirty miles."

Sandy went into her room, muttering, "Nobody told me the squatching lifestyle could be so glamorous."

Tim laughed under his breath, joining Dave in the cool shade of their room. The place smelled vaguely of formaldehyde and Pine-Sol. So many hotels over the years, so many indifferently-cleaned sheets and grimy showers. Hunting sasquatch meant cabins near the woods, mom-and-pop hotel-motels, sometimes camping. The website and YouTube channel paid for it all, and it was only summers, but Tim found himself suddenly tiring of the whole affair.

"What's wrong?" Dave asked. He'd sprawled over the bed furthest from the door, lost in the crazy comforter pattern, feet dangling over the end. "You look like all the wind just went out of you."

"I guess it did for a minute." Tim sat on the edge of the other bed, glaring at his tote bag. "Eight years of squatching, Dave. And what have we got to show for it? No prints, no hairs, no photos. Just a bunch of stories, ever less credible, that only imply Bigfoot exists because of some clever editing. I'm tired."

"Cheer up. We get to be together. See the back corners of America. And we're celebrities. Well, of a sort. Remember those girls in Memphis?"

"Don't remind me. Might as well unpack."

"Tomorrow's clothes? Your toothbrush? Just relax, Tim. The girls will come over in a few minutes. Then we'll eat sandwiches, complain about the accommodations, take a little nap, and maybe get some night shots. I think the moon is going to look nice over the office building. And we're way out in the sticks, man. Could be we'll get some spooky noises tonight."

"I don't know how you can stay enthusiastic about this. I envy your optimism."

Dave smiled again. An ugly guy with a giant honking nose, lips like rubber bands, eyes like marbles set in wormholes, the grin did nothing to beautify him. It showed grayish teeth that seemed too small and too numerous. "I don't know, Tim. Just relax. I have a good feeling about this one."

Tim sighed, kicked off his shoes, and lay back on the bed. "I'm sorry, Dave. Don't mean to be a downer." He shut his eyes for a second. Taking a long, slow breath, he smelled his own feet, the detergent smell of the comforter, a hint of mold somewhere.

When he opened his eyes again, startled awake by the sound of his own snoring, the room had surrendered to darkness, and Tim found himself alone.

Well, shit. I missed dinner.

Sleep tempted him. When he'd said he was tired, he meant soul-tired, not sleepy, but he must've been sleepier than he thought.

May as well see if they saved me a sandwich.

He stripped off his socks, tossed them into a corner, and padded next door barefoot. The door was shut; usually, if Dave was in Dorothy's room, they left the door open. Part accountability, part open welcome. Tim shrugged and knocked.

"Come in."

He did. Dorothy and Sandy each sat on a bed. "Am I interrupting a tête-à-tête? I thought you were coming over to eat."

Sandy waved him towards a chair against the far wall. Dorothy said, "We came over. Nobody answered. Assumed you'd crashed out. You've been looking used-up lately."

"I'll be sure to tell my cosmetologist." A joke; Dorothy did everyone's make-up when it was needed. "Hey, where's Dave? You seen him?"

"No," Sandy said. "Figured he was napping, too."

"Huh. He's probably out getting some night shots he was talking about. You guys eat? I'll go back to my room and get the peanut butter."

Dorothy made a face, but Tim took it for token resistance.

Back in his room, Tim flipped on a light and rummaged through bags and crates until he came up with the carboard box containing their humble groceries. The economy-sized jar of peanut butter had rolled into the loaf of bread, smooshing it somewhat. He stood the jar on end, made sure the paper plates, napkins, and knives were where they were supposed to be, and lifted the whole box to take it next door.

Then he stopped and surveyed the boxes, crates and bags once more.

He mentally tallied all the video cameras. One for each team member, one back-up, and a high-def camera for special sequences. All three of Dave's still cameras. Tim tapped the cases to make sure they weren't empty. Nope; present.

Huh.

Wherever Dave had gone, well, he was a big boy. He could take care of himself.

Tim went back to number nine with the box of food. "Here we are, ladies. Room service luxury."

Dorothy took over, as she usually did. The big sister act. She knew how to not leave crumbs, not smear peanut butter on the comforters, put in the right amount of jelly so it wouldn't squirt out the sides. "This what you expected when you signed on, Sandy?"

Sandy laughed. "Tim tried to explain it to me. I guess I was so starstruck and flattered that it didn't really register. Put the blame on me, though. And really, this is all right. It's more than that. It's great. Not the dream, but even better than the dream."

See if you still think that seven years from now, Tim thought. He covered up his uncharitable musing by stuffing a peanut butter sandwich in his face.

"Save me any?"

"Dave!" The word hardly sounded intelligible through the mouthful of food, but Tim found he meant the enthusiasm. Grape soda washed down the bite as he stood. "Where'd you go, man?"

"Just getting a feel for the place. Restless."

Dorothy said, "Get in here. I made you four. Big man's gotta eat."

Dave smiled and found an unoccupied section of bed to sit on, after carefully getting permission. "Across the county road and a creek are some big woods. I walked out there just far enough to start getting scared of getting lost, then found a nice little clearing. All sorts of night noises. Gonna be a good show."

"I can't wait to start," Sandy said. "It's already dark. Let's eat fast and get out there."

Their enthusiasm started to rub off on Tim. He popped the last bite of sandwich into his mouth and chugged the soda. "I'll start prepping camera gear. How do you guys want to set this one up? The old 'Sally Ride'? Or do you want to do 'Night Calls' this time?"

"I like 'Night Calls,'" Dave said.

Sandy raised an eyebrow.

Dave said, "'Night Calls' is when we go looking for vocalizations. Episode Twenty-Two, for example."

"Bozeman?"

"That's the one." He grinned that ugly, endearing grin. "I go out with the sound kit and try to provoke a response by doing squatch calls. You stand in the parking lot taking night-sight shots of the woods. But you hear the provocation calls. They sound different through the woods than when I record them on-site. With a little echo off those hills back there, it could even sound like call-and-response."

Sandy looked a little crestfallen. "Oh."

Tim put a hand briefly on her shoulder. "Come on. I explained all this. It's a show. Entertainment. Gives people hope that the world is bigger than them, that there's still mystery and wonder. Like a magic show."

"Except the magician knows how all the tricks are done," Sandy said, standing. "Well, let's get to it. You're right. I knew what I was signing on for. Come on. It'll be fun."

"Boys versus girls?" Tim said.

"Sure," Dorothy replied. To Sandy, she said, "That means you and me stay here, and the boys run off into the woods. Don't worry, we'll do the night-stalking thing tomorrow night. Plus a bunch of interviews with sketchy witnesses."

Dave laughed. "Remember that meth addict in the trailer in Vicksburg?"

Tim said, "Don't remind me. Hey, I'm gonna grab a jacket, and we'll head out."

Appropriately clothed and equipped, they tromped down a gravel path through clouds of their own breath. A half-moon guided the way to the road. Dave sloshed across the little creek down the embankment and Tim followed, easily stepping into Dave's much larger footprints.

"You've been a little down lately, Tim," Dave said over one shoulder.

"Yeah. Guess I have."

"You were a little rough with Sandy. I bet she got the impression you're not a believer anymore."

"Maybe." Tim couldn't breathe and talk both, making him more reticent than he felt. "Could be...you're right...old buddy."

They waded into the trees, underbrush grabbing at ankles and shins, low branches assailing faces in the dark. Tim let Dave get ahead a few paces. He was tired of getting whacked with every branch the bigger man pushed back, then released.

Dave called, "Can you see it up ahead? Where the hill sticks up from the trees. If we stop just short of that, we'll get the echo we want."

Dave had a way of knowing these things, which Tim really admired. "Sounds good. If I don't...pass out."

"Come on, man. You can do it. It's good for you. Nice woodsy walk in the moonlight!"

Said the tall guy to the short guy. Tim didn't even have the breath left to complain aloud.

At last, the trees thinned into a clearing. Tim grabbed a seat on a fallen tree trunk, certain that if there had been enough light to see by, he'd have seen his own life flashing before his eyes. Sweat tickled his back; he tossed the jacket on the ground.

Dave seemed ready to work. The camera light illuminated his long face as he held it at arm's length, pointed at himself. His other hand clicked the CB radio to send. "In position here. Dorothy, are you reading? What's happening at base camp?"

Dorothy came right back with: "We thought we saw something in the woods. Turned out to be a deer, but it was pretty scary."

Standard-issue ploy, Tim thought. *I wish we didn't have to build fake drama like this.*

Dave said, "That does sound scary. We know this area is very squatchy. A lot of local reports in the last three years, and that hair they found where one rubbed up against a cabin. We're going to interview the cabin owner tomorrow."

Tim sighed, hoping Dave's mike hadn't picked up on the sound. Obviously the hair had only been a black bear hair, and the expensive DNA test would say exactly that. Although it might be possible to spin it otherwise, with some care.

Dave said, "I'm going to try out a new call tonight. Not one reported locally, but from the Catskill mountains. Ready, Dorothy?"

"Go," she said.

Dave cried out, a sound like a baboon fucking a rabid dog.

Tim covered his ears, not sure whether to laugh or cry. But, at the same time, it stirred something in his memory. Something old.

After a minute, Dorothy came back on cue. "Did you hear that, Dave? Tim? It sounded almost like a reply."

"I didn't get it," Tim said, finally forcing himself to get his head in the game. "Maybe these hills blocked it. What did you hear?"

Sandy's turn, finally. "We heard Dave's call, then one almost just like it. Hey, do it again. If we hear it twice, we'll know it was not our imagination."

That played out, and then they had their tape for the night. Dave smiled and offered Tim a hand up. "Ready for the hike back?"

"Not just yet, old buddy. I was just thinking. I want to do something special tonight."

"You know you're not my type."

"Shut up." But Tim laughed as he said it. He put his camera safely on the ground next to the branch he'd been sitting on. "Point that thing at me. The *camera*, dummy. Okay. Three, two, one…

"This is Tim Youngblood reporting for Squatch Team One.

We're out here in the woods again, maybe closer than we've ever been to making contact. We're going to wait here a little while and see if anything else happens. But while we're waiting, I wanted to share something.

"This spot, it looks almost exactly like the place I first saw Sasquatch. The thing that got me into this. It's not a lifestyle. It's sure not a hobby. I live for this. It's a calling, a passion, because of that first time. 'I know what I saw.' People say that all the time, and I get it. Because I know what I saw.

"It was nine years ago in a forest just like this one. My dad's passed on since. It was the last time we went camping together. We were coming back to our site from fishing. It was late. I had a big old catfish and he had a couple little trouts and we were happy as hell. Talking about building a campfire and cooking up our dinner, feeling like pioneers in eighteen ninety.

"Then we heard something. A roar like an animal, a human cry of distress. We dropped our catch and burst into a clearing just like this one, rifles out, ready to shoot. What I saw then...

"I told the story before, in Episode One, but this place is so much like that one, it's been on my mind tonight.

"Well, there it was. A bigfoot. Bigger than old Dave here and twice as ugly, long brown hair all over, long old fingers. It had some backwoods-camper's cooler in one hand and a surprised look on its face. In front of the bigfoot was this guy, a camper, who had a rifle pointed its way, a flashlight in its eyes.

"Now, I don't know for sure that the camper was about to shoot the bigfoot, but I couldn't let it happen, no way. Without a thought in my head, I dove for the rifle, pushed the barrel aside. A shot went off. Whether it happened because I tackled the rifle or because he was already pulling the trigger, hell, I just don't know."

Dave brought the camera a step closer to get Tim's bemused, wondering expression. "You said before that you were sure you saved the squatch's life."

"I'm not sure anymore. But who could take the chance with a clear conscience? Anyway, Ole Squatchy boogied on up outta there. It turned out the camper was just relieved to get away with his life. He made me promise to never tell anyone his name, wouldn't even tell me, so I couldn't find him later. You all know what people think of us when we tell our stories, right?

"The next morning, I couldn't find any signs of the bigfoot, or ever after. We've had stories and clues, the odd hair that turns out to be nothing, a few prints here and there that aren't definitive. But I know what I saw. Tonight, it feels closer than ever."

Dave shut off the camera. "That was good, Timmy. I almost believed you still believe."

Sandy's voice creaked over the radio. "Wow. That was great. That's the spirit that hooked me on the show to begin with."

Tim sighed. "I *do* still believe, Dave. Sandy. I really—"

A noise. Tapping, clicking… A rock lay at his feet.

"What was that?" Tim asked. "Did you just kick that my way?"

But he hadn't seen Dave move.

"Holy shit," Dave whispered into his CB. "A rock just landed in our camp. Just like the Cascade incident."

"Shh."

Another rock flew into the clearing from the west, the mountain side. And another. One bounced off Dave's back.

The camera lights went out.

Tim flipped the switch on his hand-held camera back and forth, getting nothing. He tried the radio, the *send* switch making no noise, no static greeting him. The moment of panic gave way to sheer terror.

Then they came out of the trees. Three of them. Two of them even bigger than Dave, a small one the same size. Hairy, malodorous, confidently striding in the dark. They rumbled, voices like rocks falling into distant chasms.

Dave rumbled back.

Tim backed away, dropping his radio into the dirt, and tripped over his camera. The light came on while he fell onto his backside and sprawled in the musky leaves and rich soil.

One of the big ones embraced Dave, who shook hands with the other, then hugged the smaller one.

"What...?"

Dave turned to face him. "That day, Tim. It was me you saved."

"I need to sit down."

"You are sitting down."

Tim looked around. Dave wasn't wrong; he'd dropped to his perch on the log. "I can't... This is incredible." Joy smeared his face into a goofy grin, and terror tripped his heart. "But I don't know what you're saying."

"I'm saying that I'm the sasquatch you've been looking for. Of course, we don't call ourselves that. We call ourselves..." He made a noise like a cow falling noisily downstairs.

"But you aren't hairy."

"Humans invented shaving razors, Tim. Why do you think I take so long in the bathroom?"

Tim rubbed his chin. "Can I..."

"Touch us? How many times have you bumped into me or hive-fived me or... Ah, go ahead. Touch that long brown Chewbacca hair."

Ecstatic, Tim jumped up. He reached towards the biggest sasquatch slowly, touched its forearm. "Wow. You're really real. Aren't you? Not three friends in Wookie suits or something?"

Dave said, "Real, Timmy. After you saved my life, I came looking for you. I've been protecting you ever since, in big ways and small. I owe you a life. Well, that, and you're kinda cute, like a kitten or a baby owl or crocodile in mating season."

Tim sat back on his log, not sure what to do now. He felt the goofy smile on his face, innocent joy and pure satisfaction battling delightfully in his core. "I don't know about all of that, Dave. Just… This is amazing. Words…"

The sasquatches stood around like travelers at a bus stop. Like it was no big deal. Dave let him revel in the experience a moment more. But then he hit Tim with a serious look. "Hey. You have a choice to make now, buddy."

"I do?"

"Yeah. I've been watching you get run down, Tim. Get tired of searching and not finding, or looking and not seeing. When that happens, a few of us come together to ask you what you want to do. One of us alone can make cameras unfocus and mikes fuzz up. But we can turn electronics off if we're together."

"Damnit, that explains—"

Dave chortled. "Yep. We can also wipe memories, too. That first time you saw me, I was in a hurry to get away from the rifle. And by myself. So I didn't erase yours. That time. But you have seen us before. You just chose to forget us."

"Why would I do that? This is the best day of my ever-loving life!"

"The choice is like this, Tim. If you remember, you have to keep it secret forever. We'll put a curse on you so nobody believes what you say."

"*That's* why everyone we talk to is so freakin' hokey!"

"Right. But if you choose to forget, I'll stay with you, and you will keep on squatching. Run your YouTube show, stay friends with Dorothy, raise up Sandy into the trade. I'll still be your friend."

The sasquatches shambled around to encircle him. He should have felt threatened, but was so high on elation he hardly noticed. "I have so many questions."

"I've answered them all before, and you've chosen to forget."

"If you say so. God, it's like my whole life makes sense right now. I can't imagine wanting to forget all this, even if I were the only one to know, forever. Man."

"You don't have to choose now," Dave said. "Here. Let's all sit down and hang out for a while. Chuck, tell him about that time you thought you saw a werewolf, but it turned out to just be a feral pig stuck in a fence."

"Chuck?"

Dave gestured at the smaller of his friends.

"Hi, I'm Chuck."

"You talk, too? Wow!"

Chuck said, "I'll try not to be insulted by that. Sasquatches have spoken English on this continent for four hundred years and other languages for thirty thousand. So, there was this werewolf..."

An hour later, surrounded by squatches, delighting in their stories, Tim snapped his head at a sound from just beyond the clearing.

"Uh oh," Dave said.

"Time to choose," said the largest sasquatch, who'd introduced herself as Philomena at some point.

"Hurry," said Chuck.

Tim stood, shaking his head. "What's happening? Choose? Hurry? Oh, the girls came looking when the radios went dark. Damn. I don't..."

Dave took him by the shoulders. "Time to choose, Tim."

"I, uh… I…"

"Tim? Dave?" Dorothy's concerned voice echoed into the clearing. "You guys out here? Oh, there you are. What have you been doing? I was worried about you."

Sandy was right behind her. "I didn't know I'd be traipsing through the woods at night looking for you, Tim."

Tim turned in a slow circle, feeling totally disoriented. "How did I get here?"

Dave said, "He heard a noise and went to investigate. We got separated in the dark." He leaned toward Dorothy, lowering his voice. "But I think he saw something."

Dorothy took Tim's face in her hands. "Tim? Are you okay? Did you hit your head?"

"I don't…"

Sandy went for his camera. It lay on the ground, its light beaming into the underbrush. She cued up the last recording. "It's dark. But I see… figures? Three of them? They're blurry, but they aren't bears. Not people, either. Here, how high is this branch? That's six feet, and this figure here is well over that height. Tim, you did it! You got Bigfoot on film!"

"I did?"

They crowded around the camera, watching the footage over and over again, a ten-second loop of three creatures walking off into the darkness. Dave clapped Tim on the back. "Congratulations. This will keep people coming to the YouTube site for another three years. We can double our subscribers."

Tim looked around at his friends. Dorothy, his oldest friend in the world, his big sister since the Nineties. Dave, who'd stumped around countless woods with him, always with encouraging words and endless patience. And his new friend and perhaps protégé.

"Guys," he said. "I'm so glad you're here with me. I want to do this forever. This is the best night of my life."

"The footage is great," Sandy said. "I never thought we'd be so lucky so fast."

"It's not tonight. It's all the nights. This… It isn't proof. I want to keep looking, find the sasquatches one more time. But I want to do it with all of you."

"Are you all right?" Dorothy asked again, this time feeling his forehead. "What happened out here tonight?"

"I don't know. But it was amazing."

"We should head back to the motel," Dave said. "I'm starving, and we have those witnesses to track down tomorrow. Are you up for it all, Tim?"

Tim stood, surprised to find himself smiling. "Up for it? Of course I'm up for it. Eight years of squatching, Dave, and look what we've got to show for it! Sixty thousand YouTube followers, all these friendships with eccentric people, nights in the outdoors, and all these years together. And finally a video I don't have to edit to help myself keep the faith. If I ever look like quitting again, promise me you'll bop me upside the head and remind me what it's all about."

Dave smiled. "Of course I will."

About the Author

Jason Dias is a neurodivergent existential psychologist living, loving and working in Colorado Springs. He uses horror, science fiction and fantasy to reveal the inner worlds of diverse characters, and to think through hard philosophic problems. These days, he teaches psychology at a community college and keeps largely to himself.

Find out more about Jason at:

jasondiasauthor.com

The Plague Comet

DeAnna Knippling

Mack and I had been caught out in small-town Barstow, California, when the plague comet hit in '57 and everything went to hell. Although it didn't feel like it at the time, we got off easy. If it had hit a day or two earlier, we would have been in L.A. or Hollywood. In fact, two days before that, Mack had dragged me to a live taping of *The Frank Sinatra Show* at the El Capitan, while we were waiting for the go-ahead.

So it could have been worse.

But fortunately by the time the first waves of the plague rays hit, we were in good old Barstow, in this tin-sided train-car-style diner—five customers out front, plus the two waitresses. It was slow and the shift had just changed, so I'm guessing it was about three o'clock in the afternoon. It had been a long night and I still had sand in my hair and down my silk socks. My suit was torn, although I had changed into a clean shirt. I needed a shower and a White Russian. Then about sixteen hours of sleep. I wasn't going to get any of it—not until we made it to Vegas. But at least I had a cup of coffee in front of me, trying to be grateful for the fact that it could have gone worse. A *lot* worse.

Those jobs never go quite like you think they will, but me and Mack, we're good at adapting. Except for that time. Mack seemed to be stiff about the whole situation, like either he recognized the guy or he had something on his mind. I had promised myself that, after we had everything wrapped up, I'd ask him what was up.

But I was hungry. So instead I promised myself I'd ask him after we ate.

I was tapping my fingers on the red-and-white tablecloth and straining my neck to see if my food was coming, a couple of chops with sweet potatoes and apple sauce. Even a green salad would have been welcome at that moment.

The other three customers were all at the counter, one guy in a white button-up with the sleeves rolled up and a suit jacket and fedora on the seat next to him, and two blue-collar guys with dirty blue jeans at the other end.

We heard a crack like a sonic boom and a flash of light.

That's it, I thought. *The Russkies bombed us.* It was '57 so of course everybody had Reds on the brain.

Then the guy in the button-up started shaking, bent over his plate of steak and tomatoes and spitting out white foam. He half-choked and half-moaned.

"You all right, Mister?" said the red-headed waitress who had just come on shift.

He turned his head to look at her, took a wet-sounding breath, and started howling. Then he reached for her. She stepped back out of the way, reaching behind her to pick up a bread knife and putting it between them, eyes almost mad with panic. The cook came out to see what was going on. He was a big bald guy with a greasy white t-shirt, eyebrows like fuzzy caterpillars.

"What's going on?" he shouted, acting like he owned the place.

The guy in the button-up turned toward him like a hawk. In about a second the guy jumped over the counter and attacked the cook, biting and tearing at him. The guy whipped his head back and forth like a terrier killing a rat. Every so often he would stop to spit out a chunk of flesh. Meanwhile the cook was screaming and trying to push him off.

I dumped coffee all over the table at our booth as I started to get up and draw my revolver from the holster under my suitcoat.

Mack stepped on my foot and I sat slowly back down again. He shook his head and pointed outside. I glanced out the window and saw a lemon-yellow Bel Air convertible swerving crazily, then crash into a light pole. The woman driver, wearing a print dress with white gloves and a square purse on one wrist, got out and staggered down the street, howling at the top of her lungs and holding something in one gloved hand that left a trail of blood.

The redhead had climbed over the counter to get away from the cook and the guy in the button-up. The other two customers—both blue-collar men, sitting at the counter—were trying to pull the guy away from the cook, but the guy seemed to have superhuman strength.

One of the waitresses, a blonde we later found out was called Candy, tore off a handful of tinfoil and wrapped it around her head in a hat, sobbing and saying that it was a Communist mind control plot and we better watch out for the mind rays. The other waitress, who turned out to be called Ruby, leaned over the counter and literally pulled the blonde across to the other side, to safety. I wouldn't have guessed she'd had it in her.

Mack jerked his head toward the back. I put on my hat and we both eased out of the booth. The guy in the white shirt had bitten both the two blue-collar guys but hadn't killed them, although one of the blue-collar guys' eyes were rolling up in his head. The cook was starting to stand up. He looked like he'd been through the meat grinder. He spat out a mouthful of white foam, cracked his neck, and looked at us.

We grabbed the waitresses and ducked through the door to the back. Luckily it had a bolt. Mack shot it before I could even think to look.

It wasn't much of a bolt, though, and it quickly groaned and started to twist on the screws holding it in place. It was the kind of door that swung both ways. That bolt wasn't going to last.

I pointed toward the back door. "That way?"

"Nah. The walk-in."

The place had an extension built out back for extra storage, including a walk-in fridge. Mack turned up the fan and turned off the refrigeration with two slaps as I threw the door open. We piled inside and closed the door behind us. The girls, dressed in their pink diner uniforms complete with name tags, immediately started to shiver.

"Won't we get locked inside?" Candy asked. Too late, the latch had already caught.

"I can kick it open later," Mack told her.

"But what if you can't? What if they can open the door?"

You know how it goes, in a stressful situation like that. You put any four people together in a tight spot and one of them will break. That time, the person was Candy, a fact that was obvious even before we shut ourselves inside. There wasn't room to turn around and she was trying to pace, that tinfoil hat still on her head.

"What if they get in here?" Candy asked, maybe a hundred times. "They're going to kill us! How can you know they're not going to break in here and kill us?" You'd have thought she was looking forward to it.

We listened to screaming and banging and scratching at the door. But nobody opened it.

Then the noise faded.

"What's happening?" Candy asked.

"Nobody else to kill," I said. "Musta gone outside."

"We have to stop them!"

"Once I kick that door open, it ain't gonna latch back up again, sweetheart," Mack said.

"We have to get out of here before the Communists get us!"

About two hours had passed by then, and we were all getting tired of being stuck in that little walk-in fridge. The girls were shivering, wrapped up in our jackets. And even with the fan running continually, it was starting to stink—fish and liver and four people's fear.

"Candy," said Ruby testily, "if you don't shut your yap, I'm going to paste you one on the mouth." Ruby was a redhead but not the natural kind, with eyebrows drawn in with a pencil and lips as red as a seal of approval. Not my type.

"You wouldn't!"

The two of them got in a fight with each other, pushing each other against the shelves and making the plastic tubs rattle.

"Knock it off," Mack said.

Suddenly, without warning, the tinfoil hat came off.

Candy screamed. "My hat!"

"Stop being so crazy!" Ruby shouted. "You're fine!"

But Candy wasn't fine. Her eyes rolled back in her head and she started shaking. Mack and I gave each other a look. This couldn't be good. Candy started drooling.

You would have thought Ruby would have panicked and screamed. But, cool as a cucumber, she kicked Candy's feet out from under her and lowered her down to the floor against the door, one fist bunched up in the pink cotton dress her friend was wearing. Then she picked up the tinfoil hat and crushed it back onto Candy's head.

It didn't help. The shaking got worse.

Ruby said, "Sorry, kid," then looked her hands. Then she looked at Mack. The bread knife had ended up on a rack next to him. "Hey, Mister," she said. "Hand me that knife."

Mack said, "You don't want to get blood all over in a place like this. Let me do it."

Ruby edged away from Candy, who was starting to get a wild look in her eyes. The plague rays hit some people like the world's fastest case of rabies. They can't swallow, get real aggressive, suffer confusion and muscle spasms. It burns itself out in a couple of days—that is, if it doesn't spread.

Mack waited until Ruby had scooted behind him and was out of the way, then put his weight into the swing of his foot and gave Candy a sort of sideways kick on the side of her forehead.

The trick is in keeping the toes of your foot up, so that the force rotates the head on the neck instead of smashing into the guy's face. Your heel catches on the guy's nose if you're lucky, which makes for a quick snap of the neck. Technique worked like a charm on poor little Candy.

There was no mistaking the sound, if you've ever heard it.

Ruby said "Poor kid," then burst into tears.

Mack and I waited a couple of minutes to make sure Candy wasn't going to get up. Then we cleared a shelf and hefted her body onto it to get it out of the way. Mack checked the door—still latched—and I drew my revolver.

Mack did this thing he does for luck, not quite crossing himself. A little circle-and-slash thing in the air.

"Hey, Mister—" said Ruby softly, then shut herself up.

Mack glanced at her, then listened at the door. After a couple of minutes, he kicked the door up high, where the latch would be holding the door shut on the outside. It took a couple of kicks but the door was soon open. He stepped out of my way and I checked the back of the house, then the front. The cook was on the floor behind the counter, torn to bits.

"Clear," I said. "Take the cash?"

"Leave it."

It's never a good sign when your partner says to leave the cash behind. It means he's worried about the cops maybe being on your tail.

Fifteen minutes later we had filled every jug in the diner full of water and shoved them into the back seat of the '53 Plymouth Belvedere we were driving. Luckily we'd already emptied the trunk. We managed to fill up the tank at a station without too much fuss, and had stuffed the trunk with spare cans of gas. You don't want to run out of either gas or water on the way to Vegas. It's all desert. I mean, you're driving next to Death Valley. It doesn't get much more desert than that.

Ruby had taken a couple of minutes to cry, but by the time Mack asked her if she wanted to ride with us she was together enough to heft her big fat purse, which she had grabbed on the way out of the diner, over one shoulder.

"I'm ready," she said.

And then I noticed something on her wrist. A tattoo, of a cross with a keyhole and a star in the center. It was covered with scars. Mack saw it too. And shuddered.

Barstow was the kind of place where all roads met. You had your pick of the new Interstate 15; the new Interstate 40 (old Route 66); Route 26; Route 466; and several other back roads. If you ever needed to dump a body in the desert and make a quick getaway, there were worse places: easy access from Los Angeles and

Hollywood, a straight shot to Vegas, and a whole lotta nuthin' to the north and south.

The plague comet had struck out in the Pacific, which was probably better than it hitting land. But it was still hard enough to set off what felt like a hundred earthquakes an hour. When you live on the West Coast, you're always waiting for the big one, the one that will shake you all the way into the ocean. Well, add to that the plague radiation sweeping in with the breeze and rain from the ocean, and you got yourself a whole lot of trouble.

It was just as well that we were headed away from it.

"So what takes you to Las Vegas, Joe?" Ruby wanted to know. After all that, and I had finally introduced myself. That's what happens, when events go by too fast. Ruby was leaning over the back of the seat with her head in her hands, a couple of flakes of dried blood along one temple. She'd put on a pair of white gloves I'd had found in the glove box, and refreshed her lipstick.

"Family," I said. "We're both from the East Coast, but I don't think we're going to make it all the way back there. But I got a sister who lives in Vegas."

I didn't. But she didn't need to know that.

"And you, Mack?"

"Me and Joe work together," he said. "And I ain't go nowhere else to go."

"What about you?" I asked. "You got anyone in Vegas?"

"No," she said shortly. "I was in Hollywood for a while, but that didn't work out."

These girls would come from Minnesota and Ohio, looking for work as actresses, and find themselves stuck in dead-end jobs with no money and more bills than they had ever had in their lives. Either they split or they ended up working for some john on the street. Ruby making it to Barstow meant that she was smarter than most: but not lucky enough to get back home.

"Where you from, originally?"

"Indiana," she said. "I tried to phone from the station, but it was only a busy signal."

"Figures," I said.

"What do you think happened?" she asked.

"I dunno," I said. "Aliens."

I expected to get a laugh out of them, but nobody was in the mood for jokes. I turned on the radio. Most of the stations had gone dead. I scrolled the AM band until we hit a Civil Defense signal.

This is an emergency. A comet has landed in the Pacific Ocean. High risk of earthquakes and tidal waves along the entire West Coast. The comet strike coincides with a strange disease that appears to act like rabies. If you suspect someone is infected, do not attempt to treat them or contact them in any way. Move to safety away from the infected. Civil Defense forces are organizing. Stay in your homes and be safe! Fill all containers with fresh water and eat spoilable foods first, in case of power outage. If you come in contact with saliva of the infected, wash area with alcohol immediately. If signs of rabies appear, YOU ARE INFECTED. Confusion, violent aggression, and severe thirst will soon follow. Put yourself in a place where you cannot attack others! This is an emergency. A comet has landed in the Pacific Ocean—

Mack leaned forward and turned the radio off.

"So that's our answer," I said. "We got hit by a comet."

"A plague comet," Ruby said. "Or else you're right and it's an alien attack."

"Do you think so?" I asked.

"No," she said, quickly. "There's a whole universe out there. It's probably just some dumb coincidence, that's all. A bad case of rabies. Nothin' to do with us."

At first we made good time. There was hardly anybody on the road. Then nobody at all. It was only a hundred and fifty miles to Las Vegas. Three hours of good driving and luck—and Mack had the good driving part covered.

The sky was crystal blue, not so much changing color as growing deeper and deeper in hue. The edges of the horizon were deep purple to the east, and gold and red to the west. It was wide and flat with the Sierra Nevadas dotted along the horizon. A few of the stars had come out. Soon the Milky Way would be a streak across the sky, the stars sharp and clear. It was the kind of magic the universe threw at you, that made you both feel small and insignificant, and grateful at the same time.

Mack hated that part of the desert. He'd never stop. Maybe for gas, but we had to be running pretty close to empty even for that. All three of us were peering through the dirty front windshield, looking for signs of life. But there was nothing. The only radio stations were the Civil Defense stations, still broadcasting that same message.

"See any lights?" I asked.

"No," said Mac.

"And why aren't we getting any stations?" I asked. "There's a station in Baker, isn't there?"

Ruby said, "Mack's right. Someone else should have had the same idea you guys had, to go to Vegas. Where is everyone?"

She chewed off a fingernail.

"Maybe they're hiding from the infected," I said. "Maybe they're actually doing what they're supposed to do, like on the radio."

Mack growled, "Don't get your hopes up, Joe."

I made a fist and punched my leg. Mack kept driving.

"Are we going to keep driving straight through to Vegas?" I asked.

He nodded, his face glowing green in the faint dashboard lights.

I wasn't a good guy. Mack wasn't either. We had both come to terms with that. But Mack saw the world as being darker than I did. The whole world, nothing but darkness. He treated life like a temporary escape from Hell. Me, I was a bad guy so I wouldn't be a worse one. I thought of the world in terms of light and dark, with me belonging in the shadows—but only just barely. I tried to stay as close to the edge as I could stand, like a vampire from a movie backing away from the harsh morning light, then surging closer at sunset. That there were people out there who stood in the daylight, that I was sure of.

So where were they?

Under my breath, I said, "I gotta feeling that something else is going on. Even worse than what it looks like."

Mack grunted. I don't know how he always hears me, but he does.

We were just outside Baker, a small town that was the gateway to Death Valley. Twilight had settled over us like soft, incessant sand blowing off the desert. We were buried in darkness before we knew it. Ruby told Mack in no uncertain terms that she had to "stretch her legs." Mack gritted his teeth and pulled over, then turned off the car to check the engine, his face blank. Ruby excused herself for a discreet errand; I told her to watch out for snakes, scorpions, and fleas. I think she was most worried about the last of those.

I stared up into the Milky Way for a few minutes, wondering where the comet had come from. Aliens? An accident of fate?

Why had it driven some people mad and not others? How did the stuff spread so fast?

What more was in store for us?

Mack slammed the hood of the car, said, "Looking good," and walked toward me. I came back to earth, turning around in a circle to see if there were any other lights around us.

Ahead and to the south I could see a faint glow. "What's over there?" I asked.

Mack said, his jaw clicking from how stiffly he said it: "That health spa run by that wacko."

I vaguely remembered it: a religious quack from out east had set up a "hot springs" spa out in the desert in '44. He had pulled a bunch of homeless men from Skid Row to do his dirty work for him. He built a church and a hotel and put in a bunch of shallow mineral baths. Sharp, but a loner. I remembered thinking that the place wouldn't last.

"It's still there?"

"Yeah," said Mack.

"What's it even called?"

Ruby came back up onto the road. "Where are we?" she asked in a quiet voice.

Mack said, "We're near the Zephyr Health Compound."

"Oh," she said. "Well, I'm done. Let's get out of here."

A look went between them. I couldn't see it. It was dark and the headlights were turned off to save juice. But I could feel it.

The silence hung on for almost a minute.

I decided not to let the matter drop. Whatever the hell was going on out here, I was going to find out. "*That's* the name of the place," I said, snapping my fingers to break the tension. "Zephyr. 'The Last Word in Health.' You used to hear the ads on the radio all the time, years ago. Now you don't. And it's still there? Who was running it? A guy named Parker, right? Supposed to be at an oasis out in the desert?"

"Maxwell Hayes Parker," said Mack. "But let's don't get bogged down with a bunch of health nuts. Better to just drive through."

He was right. And that would have been exactly what we would have done. Except for what happened next.

The sound came from the north, half a sound, barely a sound, just the scrabble of paws shifting the sand and pebbles.

I have good hearing. Mack has better.

"Something's coming," Ruby said.

"Get in the car," Mack told her.

The car door slammed and a window started scraping as Ruby started rolling it up, crank by crank. We had had all the windows down.

I saw four points of movement in the dark. Mack and I drew our pieces and got set. It was too dark to see what was coming, but not too dark to aim. I tracked the movement for a half-second, then anticipated my target, waiting for range.

Mack fired first. I kept the flash of his piece behind me and fired next. My target fell. I didn't know about Mack's. The others were on us in a second, a rush of air and a heavy thump in the darkness that knocked me onto the still-warm macadam. I felt my shirt tear from teeth across my arm as I protected my throat. It didn't break skin, though. I rolled back up onto my feet.

Behind me I heard an animal growl. I didn't look. I had something in front of me to deal with.

In the dark and moonless night, I wasn't sure what it was. It was too big to be one of those Mexican wolves, and too small to be a bear. A dull gray piece of metal caught some starlight, moving with the creature.

I tracked it and fired. It howled and I just about jumped out of my skin.

"Mack," I said, "I think these things—"

His piece went off three times. *Bam bam bam.* The last one was muffled and followed by a thump.

I turned. Mack was on the ground, a dark, loose shape on top of him. A second creature was trying to get past its dead brethren. The corpse was all that was protecting Mack from the creature.

I picked off the live one with a bullet to the skull, then heaved the dead one off Mack.

He was covered with blood and saliva all over his face. He had to wipe it out of his eyes. I stripped off my jacket and handed it to him, then jogged back to the car.

Ruby rolled a window down. "Is it okay?"

"Turn on the engine. I need the lights. But stay in the car."

I gave the trunk a thump with my hip and it popped open. That was the one thing we'd noticed about that car, that the trunk would pop open if you hit it just right, a fact that had been more than an inconvenience earlier but was useful now. I pulled out one of the cans of gas and soaked my shirt in gasoline, then carried it back to Mack.

"We should have brought some whiskey," he said.

"Have some gas instead," I announced. Carefully, he cleaned his face and neck with the shirt. While he was doing that, I dug a clean undershirt out of my bag in the back seat and soaked it with water. He wiped his eyes with it. We couldn't do much more than that but wait. I checked my arm. It was fine.

I walked over to the bodies. In the blazing headlights arrowing down the road, I could see what they were, although I didn't really understand it. Two males and one female lay on the macadam.

They had been twisted. Mutated. Their limbs were stretched out and ended in paws. The thumb had receded up and out of the way for running, but looked like it could fold around a little, not as flexible as a normal human's hand, but better than nothing. The faces were elongated, the bodies covered in fur.

They wore tags in their ears, tin balls that had been punched in like a woman's stud earring, so small that I couldn't read the tiny lettering on them. Two of them also had dog tags around their necks. I took those off and pocketed them.

"Joe," Mack called, and I turned back to him.

He was pointing to the south, where the faint glow at the horizon flashed three times.

"That's gotta be Zephyr," I said, thinking but not quite realizing what I was thinking.

"The last word in health," Mack said softly.

After we lingered out on the road long enough for all of us to agree that Mack wasn't going to turn into some kind of monster, I argued that we should go out to Zephyr and see what was going on. It wasn't a good argument. Basically, I had a hunch that Zephyr had something to do with part of Mack's past that he never would talk about. Parts, plural. I told them we needed to make sure that nobody out at the compound was being attacked by these monsters and we might be their only chance.

Good guy stuff.

My suggestion was met with suspiciously little resistance.

Ironically, as soon as we had turned off onto Zephyr Road, I started arguing against it.

"What if that place is full of those monsters?" I asked. "What if everyone there has been killed or infected? You'd think that anyone who could be taken in by a quack like Parker would be vulnerable to the rays of the plague comet. They've all got to be infected out there, if anyone's left."

We were down to three of us, and I felt like I was starting to crack. I hadn't broken yet, but I could hear the plinks and tings inside my head. I was a windshield hit by a rock on the roadway. The dog tags, which had black rubber silencers around the edges, didn't have the usual names, service numbers, blood types, or religious preferences. I read them against the dashboard lights. One was *MAX* and the other was *ABBY*, with AF and AA prefix codes on the service numbers. Regular enlisted Air Force, one male, one female.

I tried asking more questions.

Neither of them responded.

Mack's lack of response didn't surprise me. I was used to it. But Ruby's did.

I had been starting to think more and more that Ruby was pretty, but she wasn't movie-star pretty. And that she hadn't really arrived in Barstow on the way out of Hollywood, but from the other direction.

And what did that tattoo on her wrist, the wrist covered with scars, mean?

Nothing good.

We drove slowly and with the lights out along that straight and solitary road, which quickly turned from macadam to gravel. Slowly the road bent around a big hill. A salt flat spread out on the other side of the road, shimmering white in the light of the stars. You could see a few dark, parallel streaks here and there where someone had landed a plane on it. We kept driving.

Rows of palm trees appeared out of nowhere, green streetlights sprinkled among them. I saw the sparkle of water under some of the trees, the kind of still, shimmering water that drinks up your eyes. Also under the trees I could see bits and pieces of a Spanish-style hacienda, pale adobe buildings. It was like something out of the Arabian Nights, a djinn's oasis.

Long before we reached the edge of the lights, Mack stopped the car and turned off the engine.

"It's probably too late," he said.

"For what?"

"We've probably been spotted. But we hadta been spotted out on the highway. When we fired at those monsters."

Mack's words redefined the compound from fairy tale to military complex. A hundred different vantages over the road popped into view. I had to stop thinking like a sap. I reloaded my revolver and shoved a box of ammunition in my jacket pocket.

"We're here, Mack," I said. "I want some answers. Or at least tell me what you want to do. I'll ask questions later. Or never."

"Kill them," he said.

"All of them?"

Ruby, her head leaning between the seats, shuddered.

"Not if they're chained up," Mack said.

I looked at Ruby.

"I don't know nothing," she said stubbornly.

"You okay with this plan?"

"The guy in white," she said, belying her previous statement, "he goes down. No matter what he says to you. No matter what he makes you think. He goes down."

Mack nodded.

"The guy in white," I said. "Got it. Make sure you back me up, that's all."

I put the revolver back in its holster under my arm, then opened the door and got out. I started walking up the road toward the compound. I kept my hands spread out and away from my body.

Some moments, all the things you don't know that you know fall down, one after the other, like some kid's chain of dominoes. My shoes crunched on the packed gravel. The dog tags made a hushed whisper in my pocket as the chains slithered around. I thought about that tattoo, about the darkness that Mack carried in him. Maybe he hadn't put it there himself. I watched for movement and saw only the palm leaves moving gently, catching the compound lights.

I waited for a rifle shot—or the sound of paws on desert sand and rock.

A dog barking.

Anything.

Instead I heard the hum of an airplane out in the dark. I turned to look over my shoulder and didn't spot it—I had been looking too intently toward the moth-swarmed, hideously bright mercury-vapor lights of the compound and spoiled my night vision—but it was getting louder. It was going to land on that salt flat, I just knew it.

A figure stepped from behind one of the buildings.

A woman, dark-haired in an Italian cut, in a black silk cocktail dress covered with rhinestones and spangles. It was a dress to make you think of the Milky Way, with three-quarters sleeves. The woman wore silk stockings and black pumps, and was carrying a cigarette. She looked too perfect to be real. That was my impression of her. She was as perfect as a movie projection. Faintly, I heard the clink of silver against glass, a man's low murmur, a woman's laugh.

"Why, hello," she said, as if she had just stepped out of a Manhattan apartment. "What are you doing here?"

"It's an emergency," I said, grasping at straws.

"What happened?"

"We need a doctor. Friend of mine got bit by what might have been a rabid dog or coyote."

"Oh, no," she said, putting one hand up theatrically to her mouth.

"Do you folks have a telephone?"

She laughed, a false and tinkling sound. "All the way out here? No, but we do have a shortwave radio. We might be able to reach someone in Baker, which is a little town just to the west of here. And a much more powerful transmitter, but I *don't* think you want to try contacting anyone from beyond the stars!"

She laughed again, this time far more amused with herself.

I said, "There's been a tragedy, ma'am. I don't know if any of you have been listening to the AM band radio, but a comet crashed down in the Pacific a few hours ago, and everything's been a little strange since then. We haven't seen anyone out on the roads at all since then."

"Oh, we haven't heard anything," she said. "All shut up here and amusing ourselves at the last good cocktail party at the end of the world."

She had a dark spot on her wrist, but I couldn't tell if it was the same tattoo that Ruby had. The light was coming from behind the woman.

"Do you have a doctor, ma'am?"

She laughed again. "Now, that is a complicated story. We have a healer, but I don't think you want him to treat a rabies bite! But you don't have time for that whole story. If you want help, then you should drive to Baker."

"But we're here now," I said. I smelled some kind of cover-up rolling off her the way a Las Vegas hooker smells of cheap perfume.

"Don't be silly. We have no course of rabies shots here. You'll have to keep driving. Now—" she gave a little wave with her hand: *shoo!*— "please don't delay. If your friend really has been bitten, he needs help immediately. I'm sorry, but we have to deal with a lot of people who wish to bring trouble out here, and if you don't remove yourself…"

She drifted into silence, looking over my shoulder.

Caught in the lights of the compound were Mack and Ruby, standing frozen on either side of the car. They looked like ghosts. The lights had washed all the color out of their skin.

"Hello, James," she purred. "I didn't realize it was you."

With the burr of the plane getting so loud it was hard to hear if he made an answer.

"Did one of the watchdogs give you a little nibble? You should have told your friend here that it wasn't anything to worry about. Are you coming back? We miss you, James."

And then she turned to Ruby, called her *Molly* and said something I won't repeat, but that turned my stomach. Something about locking her up again and letting some of the men have her.

Her words seemed to affect both of them equally.

Me, I couldn't see whatever the particular horror was. Something still hadn't clicked. I wasn't sure what hold these people had over either of them. It had to have been in their heads. I couldn't see it. But whatever it was, was what must have given Mack his dark view on life, blacker than sin: despair, shadows, ugliness, and death, if not worse. And what did I really know about Ruby, anyway? But she looked at least as terrified as he did.

Mack had saved my ass too many times to count. If this was his weak spot—then I'd just be grateful to have the chance to pay him back a time or two, that was all.

My feet crunched on the gravel as I walked toward her. The pale, pretty woman in the night-spangled cocktail dress blinked at me several times, then stepped backward and made that same circle-and-slash gesture that Mack makes for luck. I expected her to stumble, but she didn't. I kept walking toward her.

"Don't come any closer," she said. "Don't! Stop him, James!"

I reached her and grabbed her arm. "Do you have a *doctor* or not, lady?" I asked. "It's not a hard question." I twisted her arm and looked at the spot on her wrist.

Cross. Keyhole. Star in the middle.

I looked around the side of the building. A party was in full swing by a long, tiled pool. Everyone was dressed to the nines, diamond cufflinks and boutonnieres, hair oil and fine cologne, highball glasses with ice and slices of lime.

A group of people strolled toward us, saw Doris struggling with me. "Doris, what is it?" "Who is that?" "Is it one of those dreadful government men again? Tell him that we're not a kennel!" More laughter.

"We are very spiritual people," said one woman, also in a cocktail dress, to her companion. "I don't like that Mr. Springer's tonics are being used like this. It's disgusting."

The shoe dropped.

I knew Mack had been here before. So had Ruby. Mack had *belonged* here. Ruby had been, or had been intended to be, used for breeding experiments. These people weren't health nuts. Or even religious nuts. They were creating mutants. And talking to the stars.

Somehow, I didn't know how, they were behind all *this*.

I made a lightning-fast guess, and decided to see if I could use it to jerk someone's chain.

"Haven't you been listening to the radio?" I asked. "They've been using your tonic on people. *Giving* it to them. For free."

"On purpose?" said a shocked voice. "Who?"

"The government," I said. "You know. The guys in the plane."

The woman with the Milky Way dress had stopped struggling to get out of my grip. She was looking at me with large, violet eyes. The kind of eyes that drink you up. She looked angry. Shocked. Outraged. Appalled.

At me? Maybe. But her eyes kept darting toward the desert.

Her chain...had been jerked. And not just hers. The rest of the party-goers all seemed to be baring their teeth. Not smiling.

Baring their teeth.

The engines on the plane cut out, and everyone turned in that direction. Nobody could see the plane. We were all on the wrong side of the building.

I said, "I bet they're coming for some more. You know the government. They can put pressure on a man like you wouldn't believe."

As silent as breath, the people in evening clothes disappeared.

I didn't expect what I'd said to be anything more than a distraction. But they *believed* me. God help anyone passing out immortality, or whatever they had.

They didn't vanish. They weren't ghosts. They turned and moved past me, the only sounds those of falling cloth and footfalls on adobe and gravel. Maybe the swish of a tail or two.

Gone.

Cocktail dresses and dark suits, upended shoes and silk stockings that seemed half alive, caught in the last exhalation of a breeze. That was all they left behind.

And...one last man, who had just stepped out of one of the buildings.

He had an ordinary, suburban kind of face. He had a big bald spot, a big gut, and wore a pair of white slacks and a white, short-sleeved button-up shirt with the belt up too high. I hadn't noticed him until the others had left.

The man in white.

He walked up to me at the edge of the building and saw Mack and Ruby standing there. For a second he was flummoxed. Then recognition spread over his face. "Hello, my friends," he said. "James, my hunter. And my dear, sweet Molly. Such a co-incidence that you're here together—fate truly has brought you back to me, for I don't believe you'd ever met at our campus." He sighed. "You've both disappointed me so much, in your own ways. You've hurt me. But you find me with open arms, ready to welcome you back."

He spread his arms wide, as if he really expected them to run up to him and embrace him.

They were both shivering, frozen, deer in the headlights.

"You must be Parker himself," I said. "If I were you, I'd get out of here before your guests come back."

"They won't hurt me," he said confidently. He reminded me a little of Hemingway: solid, a little weathered. A face that tried to keep itself straight, open, and friendly, but couldn't help looking a little odd. It was hard to put a finger on what was wrong with his face. Or at least what wasn't quite right.

"You're wrong about the government being involved," he said, eyes twinkling with the lie. "I have friends in *much* higher plac-es. In a moment, my friends here will return. They will be *very* angry with you."

"*Am* I wrong?" I asked. "Because a couple of those dogs that you sent after us had dog tags. Sounds kind of official to me."

And then Mack and Ruby were gone. I could feel them leave. For a second Parker didn't notice.

And then he did.

"Tell me," he said, one side of his smile twitching, "why you came here. What made you think you had the right to do this to us? We are good, upstanding people who spend most of our time on good causes. What makes you think you have the right to invade us like this? To judge us?"

"You're monsters," I said.

"And your friends are not? But we use our monstrosity for good."

"The good of killing people?"

"The good of culling the weak."

I heard a howl rise up from within the compound, then the sound of metal being twisted and bent until it snapped. It's a musical sound.

"You're a good talker," I said, "but what you have to understand here is that I've worked for better."

He smiled. It wasn't a bad smile, but it made my skin creep. "You work for *me*, son. You're the ones that your boss loaned to me for the job in Hollywood. I didn't recognize the names—but of course James changed his when he left. What a coincidence. 'Mack.' I should have suspected it was a false name. You must be 'Joe.'"

It made me sick, knowing that this guy had used me. But he still couldn't get to me the way he got to the others.

Here was a man who had stood in the light. Not a *good* man. But a man who could easily stand in the desert sun without getting burned. A man to give strange tonics to his guests and tell them it was spiritual. A man who needed to be reminded that his health spa was not a "kennel" for secret Air Force bases. A man who turned people into monsters, and told monsters that they were the best sort of people.

So much for the light.

In the distance, I heard a scream. From the plane, no doubt.

"I am," I said. "But that's not all I am."

"Oh?"

I didn't tell him my life story. I'm not stupid.

I just went to work.

I left the man in white where the sun would hit him first thing in the morning, on top of a roof and out of sight. I did it quiet, without a bullet. I didn't have any silver ones, and I didn't want to risk the stories being true. When I was done, I wiped my shoes on a welcome mat and went through the rest of the place, looking for anyone left.

I found the kennels.

They were open.

Another scream echoed across the desert. I decided it must have been the copilot thinking that he could run.

Or maybe the ones in the kennels, discovering freedom. And their teeth. I wished them luck.

I waited ten minutes, leaning against the side of the car and cleaning under my fingernails with a penknife. I still needed a shower. I picked up the clothes on either side of the car and tossed them in the back seat among the jugs of water.

Then I got in the car and started driving for Las Vegas.

I picked up Mack and Ruby around the California-Nevada border. I didn't ask any questions, just stopped in the middle of the road to let them in. They got dressed quietly, in the dark.

Nobody followed us.

The next day the aliens invaded. It would be nice to say that we'd saved the world from a bunch of aliens, rich people, and religious health nuts. But it's never just one person who stops something like that. One person can't even turn the tide, most of the time.

It isn't fair. One person can open a door that a million people can't shut.

And yet. There was the satisfaction of having killed the man in white. The sweet victory of seeing those empty kennels and knowing their prisoners were free. The self-knowledge that even a guy who lived in the shadows could still help draw the line between right and wrong, once in a while at least.

And the hope that someone who lived in darkness as profound as Mack's could find his way back from it. He looked at me like I was some kind of hero to him. I wasn't. All I had done was the thing he could have done himself, if the man in white hadn't screwed with his head.

Ruby started talking and didn't stop until dawn. It was ugly. Her words were a crusty bandage that had to be soaked off so that the skin underneath could heal.

Mack listened to her, eyes wide. Whatever he had gone through, it hadn't been *that*.

The Rocky Mountains are tricky. But if you keep driving, you can make it all the way to Colorado, to somebody's abandoned cabin stocked for nuclear war, and a future full of trouble. Not a great place to be.

But better than Hollywood.

What I'm saying is, it could have been worse.

About the Author

DeAnna Knippling is always tempted to lie on her bios. Her favorite musician is Tom Waits, and her favorite author is Lewis Carroll. Her favorite monster is zombies. Her life goal is to remake her house in the image of the House on the Rock, or at least Ripley's Believe It Or Not. You should buy her books. She promises that she'll use the money wisely on bookshelves and secret doors. She lives in Colorado and is the author of the A Fairy's Tale horror series which starts with *By Dawn's Bloody Light*, and other books like *The Clockwork Alice*, *A Murder of Crows: Seventeen Tales of Monsters & the Macabre*, and more.

Find out more about DeAnna at:
wonderlandpress.com

Alexander's Gate
From the Secret Chronicles of Roland Eckstein

Sharon Kae Reamer

Epigraph 1:

"All the monster-species derive from the first murderer, Cain… elves and demon-corpses, and the giants, who fought against God for a long time."
~Anonymous author of *Beowulf*

Epigraph 2:

"A black elf, a giant, and a dragon go into a bar…"
~Grendel

Mid-morning traffic on the A3 south was heavy, and this wasn't even the first jam where the lines of cars and trucks merely crawled along. Everyone wanted to get to Frankfurt today. Summer vacation had started less than a week ago.

Roland and his companions were not headed to Frankfurt. Their eventual destination was still somewhat nebulous, but was somewhere between their current location and the Caspian Sea. First they would head to Ancona, Italy, though, taking an overnight ferry, then driving through Turkey, with an overnight stop near Istanbul.

And then.

That was the end of the story, as planned. Put an "X" on the map somewhere east of Turkey and north of Iran, and proceed.

They were searching for Alexander's Gate.

An entirely mythical place. According to many, among them most prominently Sir John Mandeville, Alexander's Gate contained mythical beings—monsters all—and also, by the by, the lost tribes of Israel.

But not all the monsters were behind this mythical gate. Some of them were sitting more or less comfortably in Roland Eckstein's van.

The thoroughly remodeled Transporter van was his trusty (and somewhat rusty) vehicle, which he had used in his career as the undertaker of his former village. The van was a decent shade of dark gray and had opaque windows—absolutely necessary, given the appearance of his current passengers.

Monsters, at least the ones he was chauffeuring, were not like his (former) regular customers. For one thing, they weren't dead. Although he wasn't sure whether they could be considered alive in the traditional sense, either.

Roland still had trouble getting used to the idea that he was no longer an undertaker. Nowadays, since giving up the family business, he endeavored to talk to the dead, hear their stories, and piece together parts of the past, the history of his own village and others nearby—all gone now thanks to brown coal—and their people. He was especially sought out by the very old folks before they passed on. Most of the time he was successful in speaking to them before they did.

When forced to talk to them—his former customers—*after* they passed on, it was harder to hold their attention.

The recently deceased, preoccupied with being newly dead, did not want to spend time thinking about a life past. Roland could well understand that. He had lots of experience with the newly dead, talking them down from a state of afterlife panic, but he more enjoyed talking to those still on this side of the last divide.

"We have to make a stop to pick up Medusa," Andvari said.

There was a pause, punctuated by a non-monster-like giggle and an exaggerated monster-like growl. Roland glanced in his rearview mirror, but only the top of Andvari's head, seated facing away from him in the back, was to be seen.

"I'm not sure I heard you right," Roland said.

"We have to make a stop to pick up Medusa. She's in Lesbos. It's on the way," Andvari repeated, still not turning around.

"On the way?" Roland gripped the steering wheel. "It's not 'on the way' in any sense of the phrase. We'll have to schedule an extra ferry to Lesbos just to pick up the…head."

"I'm on it," Jo said, "looking at ferries now."

"Not in a hurry, are we?" Andvari's voice was bigger than he was.

He had told Roland, when they first met as he was climbing into the Transporter this morning, that he was a black elf or dwarf. Not a human dwarf, but the supernatural Germanic version, complete with a secret hole in the ground in the heart of west Germany, deep in the Elsbach Forest. Andvari was not technically a monster, but he self-identified as such. The ancient dwarf claimed he could change into a pike, which, although a carnivorous fish, did not to Roland's mind contribute significantly to monster status.

But to each his own.

Andvari had also claimed that, in addition to a history of ensconcing women in his subterranean palace, a certain portion of his anatomy more than qualified him to be a monster.

"Too much information," Marshall had crowed.

Jo had snickered.

The Elsbach Forest bordered Perchta, Roland's village Former village. The mining company had destroyed it just a few months ago, relocating the entire village population to Neu Perchta. Elsbach Forest had also been scheduled to be demolished, in the never-ending excavation of brown coal necessary to sate Germany's appetite for energy. However, eco-protesters had successfully halted the excavation in a startling, last-minute occupation of the ancient forest, which had garnered a lot of bad publicity for the mining company.

But, ultimately, it was only a matter of time. The forest, like Roland's former village, was doomed.

The dwarf claimed that he'd built his lavish palace in the early Middle Ages after his waterfall dried up. There was something ancient, even noble about him. It would be a shame if his castle and grounds were raked up by coal-grubbing monsters—his words, not Roland's—but there wasn't much Andvari could do about it. The European Monster Party did not exist. For good reasons.

Roland glanced in the mirror again. He was trying to get used to looking at the monsters. It was taking a while.

Marshall and Jo, the only other humans on the trip, were already doing their jobs, which were to take care of any technical problems that involved navigation, attend to monster comforts, and just generally have Roland's back. Being teenagers, they had no such qualms about interfacing with the non-human passengers. They, together with their smartphones, were conferring with the monsters who sat across from them, and, using Andvari as their spokesdwarf, were contacting Medusa.

Roland was stuck trying to imagine how a head could manipulate a smart phone.

"She don't take up much room," Andvari was saying. "Just a head. And some snakes."

"Snakes?" Roland said.

"You know. Them what's on her head. They don't bite unless you provoke them."

Roland coughed. "Who else do we have on the trip? I wasn't officially introduced to anyone else before we left."

During the predawn hours when they'd piled into the van, Roland had been too occupied with loading up to pay much attention to the passengers. Truth be told, he hadn't wanted to pay any attention to them. He was still shaken up about the whole idea of driving across Europe with a van full of monsters. Even though he'd been persuaded to accept the mission, it didn't mean he was doing it without misgivings.

Strong ones.

"Him what's in the middle seat is named Grendel," Andvari informed Roland. "He's living wit' me. Guarding me gold. It's what his mother done too, you know. Family tradition. I told him he might as well come along for the ride. If they're going to dig it all up, it's on their head if they take the gold. By way of it being cursed."

Grendel, not a small creature, sat squeezed between a giant, who had to slouch way down to fit in the seat, and a clay monster. The giant announced his name was Hrungnir. He also told Roland that the clay man, also of giant size but not as big as Hrungnir, possessed a heart of stone and went by the name Mokkerkalfe. Mokkerkalfe must be the source of the funky saturated earth smell, Roland decided. Hrungnir carried a normal odor of sweat. And Grendel smelled like the grave, a smell that Roland knew all too well. But it had never bothered him before now.

Grendel shimmered like a banked fire, his skin scaly and shadowy dark all over with glowing edges. And deep-set fiery eyes. They were brown. Or gold. Or red. Definitely red. Was that a gold crown embedded *in* his head? It seemed tarnished or maybe it was just the reflected flames that shone in the metal. But reflected from what?

"Wait. What?" Marshall asked, setting aside his phone. "Are you *the* Grendel?"

Grendel gave a defiant jerk of his head that could be construed as a nod. The more Roland looked, the more he felt sweat forming, then trickling down his neck. He kept his hands tight on the steering wheel and shifted in his seat, glad he'd redecorated the interior, courtesy of some of Andvari's gold. It made everything more comfortable. But hadn't Andvari just said his gold was cursed? Did that make Roland's van cursed now, too?

With three monsters and a shapeshifting dwarf-pike, it was going to be a very long ride. Now with the extra trip to Lesbos, the long ride just got longer.

They'd all been sitting for several hours, as Roland had pushed hard once they left the Alps and hit the Po River valley. Standing outside the van while waiting to get onto the ferry at the Italian port of Ancona, Roland discussed strategy with Marshall and Jo. The ferry terminal parking lot was filling up with cars. Their ship was scheduled to leave in about two hours; Roland had wanted to get there early. The ferry terminal had the same dingy smell as the other ports he'd visited: Calais, Lisbon, Hamburg. It stank of diesel and dead fish.

Jo was Roland's cousin, his name short for Johannes, a proper German name. But everyone called him Jo and always had.

Marshall was, as Jo put it, "his pigmented ABF" (*Allerbester Freund Forever*). Marshall had an eternally absent Nigerian father, a German mother, and a bevy of half-siblings from different fathers, none of whom were German. Marshall, with his handsome face, creamy brown skin, two meters' height (not including his Afro), was already attracting ardent female admirers. Jo was an unwitting beneficiary of this popularity, but neither of them seemed too interested in women yet, except as friends. They would face their last year at gymnasium once school started up in the fall. It was a crucial year, during which they'd take their exams, the *Abitur*; the results would determine places at the Uni and their prospects for the next few years. No time for girlfriends in the near future. So when the opportunity arose to transport a few monsters on a journey of epic proportions, Roland didn't hesitate to ask if they wanted to join him. Compared to *Abitur*, it would be a simple endeavor.

They didn't hesitate in accepting. The half-truths Jo and Marshall told their respective parents varied. "Road trip" was common to both stories. Monsters didn't occur in either.

"Crazy. They all have German passports, except Grendel," Marshall said. "We breezed right through passport control on the Swiss-German border."

At first, Roland had wanted to hide the monsters in the van. He had brought along a couple of coffins as potential stowaway freight. But giant-sized monsters were something he hadn't anticipated. Fortunately, the monsters had assured him passports wouldn't be a problem. Andvari even had a handicapped document. Who knew that shapeshifting dwarves were considered handicapped?

"And Grendel? Didn't even need a passport," Jo said in a quiet voice. "The Swiss passport control officer in Basel? He asked

Grendel to get out of the car, but then...it was like he just disappeared."

Roland blew out a breath. "What?"

"You were busy showing the other Swiss guy the back of the van," Marshall said. "Grendel went with the guy to his booth. Then Grendel came back, but the passport guy didn't."

"He ate him?" Jo asked, his voice cracking. He was at least a year late for a changing voice, but Roland loved that his cousin still had one foot in childhood.

Marshall shrugged and spoke in a stage whisper, "He is carnivorous. The real Grendel is reported to be cannibalistic, but...he's not human...so that's not correct, is it?"

"Right. We don't know if he's really *the* Grendel," Jo said in an excited hush of words. "He could just be *a* Grendel."

Roland did not want to hear that one of his passengers had eaten a passport control officer.

"He didn't eat nobody."

Marshall and Jo lowered their gazes.

Andvari had approached them so silently, they hadn't heard him come up, "I made him swear not to."

"Well, that's a relief, then," Roland said, not bothering to keep the sarcasm out of his voice. "Would you mind telling me then what he did with the passport control officer? Is there an Interpol alert out now for my van?"

Andvari laughed and rubbed the stubble decorating his chin. "He brung on his stealth magic to slip away. The officer lickety-split forgot he'd even been there."

"Stealth magic. That's so cool," Marshall said. "I just wish he didn't hate all of us."

Andvari said, "Grendel's no different than the rest of us."

"You all hate us?" Jo asked.

Andvari shrugged. "Maybe not Mokkerkalfe. With a heart of stone, he's not got enough heart to hate. Not yet, anyway. Goes with the territory of being a monster. Hating humans."

Car engines revved to life around them.

"But of all humans, Grendel hates the Danes the worst. Let's hope there aren't any on the ferry."

"Can he smell them?" Jo asked.

"Possible," Andvari said. "I've not quizzed him about it."

"Time to go," Roland said, not eager to continue this conversation.

The cars began jockeying into position to line up for the ferry. He had parked farther out, away from the other cars, and was now glad of it, even though they would not be anywhere near the front of the queue for driving onto the ferry.

"Last on, first off," Jo said, sighing.

That suited Roland just fine.

Roland convinced Grendel to hide out in the back of the van, stuffing himself into one of two coffins that Roland was glad he had brought along (along with his still-active undertaker's license, to ward off awkward questions). It was a handy storage facility for things that weren't quite dead. And also not quite alive. Then they all piled back into the van, and Roland lined up near the end of the queue to drive on board the ferry. Roland breathed easier in anticipation of the brief respite he would be spared having to look at Grendel. The other monsters weren't quite so fearsome, even if they were bigger.

Once on board, Jo, Marshall, Roland and Andvari would join the rest of the passengers on the ship, leaving their cars. Roland and Andvari would share one cabin, Jo and Marshall another. The giants and Grendel would be staying in the van. Roland decided to let Andvari handle the explanations to the Monsters Who Would Remain for why that was. As if that explanation was anything but obvious. But it was only overnight. In a few hours they would reach the port city of Patras, Greece. Then he'd drive them to Athens, where he would have to endure yet another ferry ride to the Greek island of Lesbos to collect Medusa the Head, and then continue on to Turkey. Lesbos was indeed *mostly* on the way. Turkey was close to Lesbos. Nearly within spitting distance.

After fifteen hours of solid driving, Roland could hardly wait until his head touched a clean (but probably not fluffy enough) pillow. And until he'd had at least one Mythos beer, possibly three, to pave the way to sleepland.

Jo and Marshall were already debating the merits of Mythos versus any of the other export beers likely to be available on the ferry, and looking forward to some social interaction. There were other young people on board, most of whom couldn't afford cabins, and would be spending the night wherever they could find a halfway comfortable corner to throw down a sleeping bag. If they slept at all. There seemed to be a definite party atmosphere on board.

Roland couldn't, and wouldn't, deny the boys a chance to have some fun.

Because it wouldn't likely last.

Because who knew what horrors awaited them if and when they found Alexander's Gate? Or what they would do if they didn't. And how many border control agents had to be hoodwinked in between.

Because at the end of things, when all was said and done, they would need to figure out just what the monsters wanted to do.

—

As expected, Andvari was a snorer. He'd fallen asleep two minutes after they'd returned from their rather lackluster dinner of warmed-over goulash and watery potatoes. He'd only drunk two beers, but maybe the drive had been as exhausting to him as to Roland.

Roland wondered if he also snored in his pike form.

That thought was all he needed for his mind to start wandering on other paths. Sleep did not come on slippered feet. Or claws. Or fins. Instead, his thought paths diverged, became curved, and formed tangents. And it all ended up back where they started.

It had only been a few short weeks ago…

Roland's new house in Neu Perchta had been built from the proceeds of the sale of his old house, the duplex where he'd lived alone after his parents died, where he'd grown up, where his parents had lived most of their adult lives and all of their married ones. The mining company had paid generously for the duplex. Seemed like a lot of money for a house they were just going to plow under.

Roland had moved to the outskirts of the new and shiny village, wanting some solitude and a bit of land now that he was no longer in the undertaking business. What business he was in was still something of a mystery to him. But not, apparently, to others. He had a steady stream of visitors, first encouraging him on his decision to take up the role of town chronicler, and then to tell their stories. It seems people really wanted to have someone to listen to their stories.

There were young people, and some very old people. A few in between, but not many. Roland was in between youth and middle age. He'd just turned thirty. Maybe his contemporaries, the people he'd grown up with, felt funny talking to him. Or maybe they weren't sure of their stories yet. Also, he was single—did not have a serious girlfriend, did not even have *any* girlfriend—and that might have posed its own barrier.

His visitors brought family records and journals, old photographs, and recollections. Some of the memories were as faded as the photos. Some people, especially the very old, wore a lingering sadness, an almost visible shadow that accompanied the shared remembrances of a town that no longer was.

It quickly became overwhelming. As an undertaker, Roland had dealt with grief on a daily basis. It was a part of his job to make sure a spirit found its rest. He'd never failed, even though certain spirits required patience. But this was different. He was responsible for the past, which was a spirit that was not easily settled. The shadows of his visitors remained after their owners left his house. The shadows slid across the walls at dusk and deepened the gloom of the evening. Roland was not much of a drinker, but he'd begun taking a shot of *Eversbusch* in the evening to help him to sleep. He'd even begun to fancy the scent of the strong juniper schnapps in the early afternoon, after he'd ushered out his last visitor for the day.

After a couple of months of losing the struggle to pacify his demons, Roland knew he needed help.

Help had come from Elsbach Forest.

Before the mining company came, Elsbach Forest had always been a blend of mystery and peaceful solitude for Roland, juxtaposed right on the edge of Perchta's small graveyard. He'd spent much time there, eating his packed lunch and contemplating its quiet beauty.

Sometimes the restless spirits of the recently deceased would wander there among the stately trees until they could be coaxed by Roland to accept their fate.

That there were other kinds of things living in the forest was not entirely unknown to at least one of Perchta's former residents, his former neighbor, Frau Geisen. Frau Geisen had rented the other half of their family's duplex, and been a deeply irrational woman most all of her eighty-something years. She must have known about the monsters in Elsbach Forest. But she had never told him about them, even though they'd lived next door to each other all his life.

It wasn't that she had been reticent. Oh, no. Frau Geisen told everyone a lot about everything, up to her dying day, which had not been long after the duplex had been sold and she'd had to move to Neu Perchta. She'd not lasted more than a month.

It was as if her spirit deserted her before her body decided to stop living. Her death saddened Roland, even though they'd never been close. He missed her. She had been a presence that was always there, a superstitious force of will he'd always found slightly annoying, even though she was completely harmless. A batty old lady who never stopped reminding people of how to watch out for when the wind turned bad, what was unlucky for a young person's future, and how to avoid catching a curse.

After her death, she'd left all of her books to him: some antique, some weird as all heck.

Frau Geisen had no direct family, being a childless widow. Her books had been delivered to him about a week after she died. He hadn't known what to do with them, but thought they might be useful to him in his new chronicling job—as soon as he figured out how to go about it. The strange thing was that Frau Geisen had made out her will some time ago. She couldn't have known about his sudden change of occupation.

One evening when his desire for another drop of gin threatened him, Roland pulled out one of Frau Geisen's books. Its worn leather cover appeared innocent enough. But it happened to be the one detailing the part-history, part-legend of Perchta's beginnings as a crusader stronghold—hence, its original name, Lordship of Perchta. The legend of Lady Perchta told that she still haunted Elsbach Forest, which had originally been part of the castle grounds.

Lady Perchta did indeed still haunt the forest. The book recounted an anecdote from someone who had met Lady Perchta. But Roland already knew how to do that. He knew because he'd met her there one night. At midnight.

Frau Geisen was the one who had told him how and when to meet the ancient ghost.

Lady Perchta had helped him. By willfully haunting the villagers of Neu Perchta into aiding Roland, she had ensured that he'd been able to fulfill his obligations in exhuming and relocating the former residents of Perchta's graveyard in the ridiculously short time frame given to him.

His promise to her, to tell the stories of those who had passed or were about to pass through the gate between the living and the dead, was what had set his life on its present course.

It was time he sought her out again, to help him figure out what he was supposed to be doing.

Equipped with a *Leberwurst* sandwich on *Schwarzbrot*, a handful of cornichons, and a bottle of water, Roland entered the forest near where the graveyard had been. It was hard to tell if he was in the right place, since everything, including a venerable border oak, had already been plowed under.

The evening had not deepened enough to be scary dark yet—although he'd never had a fear of the dark, which might have been a mistake.

Roland patted his pocket where he'd stuck in a flashlight. He missed the oak, his favorite spot to have lunch. He found another tree, just within the forest entrance, comfortable enough for him to lean against and eat his sandwich and wait for midnight. Maybe he'd just close his eyes for a few minutes. It had been a long day.

When he woke, cold and disoriented, there was a man standing in front of him. A tall, broad-shouldered giant of a man with a gleaming green coat of armor. And an axe held in two strong thick hands. It wasn't the kind of axe used to cut down trees, but had a wicked wide blade of tempered steel. An instrument designed to kill. The heft was such that it would take a man's head off if wielded by someone able enough. The green-clad knight definitely looked the part. Roland stood and clenched his thighs to run.

Next to the man was the ghost of Lady Perchta. He held off, his breathing rapid and uneven. The trees had gone from being merely watchful to closing ranks, hemming him in.

"You are scaring him off, sir," Lady Perchta said to her companion. "Lower your axe."

"Sorry, force of habit." The green knight dropped the weapon to his right side, where it clattered against his armor. His voice was deep and lilting, in broken German, with a heavy British accent.

Roland hadn't been counting on encountering a British ghost. He'd come in search of Lady Perchta, not to be accosted by this behemoth dressed up in medieval metal the color of green neon.

The apparition removed his helmet and set it on the ground beside his axe.

And then, with another simple gesture, he removed his head. It was also green.

The head's fiery red eyes didn't look angry, but they still blazed brightly as they stared out at Roland, the head cradled in the crook of the man's arm.

"Lady Perchta," Roland stammered out. "I've come to ask you—"

She waved his words away with a flick of her hand. An aftermath of shimmery light strobed where her hand had been. It lingered and spread, bathing them in a soft glow. "We have something to discuss with you, Herr Eckstein. It is urgent."

"Urgent…" Roland didn't know what else to say.

The head spoke to him. "I've come seeking asylum in your forest. Lady Perchta has been so kind to grant it to me."

"Asylum." Roland couldn't seem to find any words of his own.

"Them crazies in my own land," the green knight said and stopped. "Those crazies. Sorry. German grammar. I'm up on my Anglo, but the Saxon parts have slipped over the past few centuries. *Those* crazies in my own land are bent on isolating themselves from the rest of Europe. I have no choice."

This was not just any green knight. It was *the* Green Knight. It had to be. That meant not only his armor was green. All of him. Except for those glowing red eyes. Monster eyes.

Roland cleared his throat. "You're escaping Brexit?"

The Green Knight nodded. "'Tis not something I can abide. Even the fools at the Round Table weren't so dense as this lot."

Roland felt a laugh trying to form, but he held it back. The legend of the Green Knight told of a basically friendly (but mysterious) warrior who was nevertheless feared by the other knights of the Round Table. He *did* have an impressive axe, and he knew how to wield it.

Lady Perchta smoothed down her simple, homespun dress, adorned with a starched, white apron. Her legend said that she'd given up her finery later in life to tend to the knights in her care, while being estranged from her noble but faithless husband. "There is room in this forest for many dwellers of a monstrous nature, as you may have guessed."

Roland shook his head, words deserting him again. "Monstrous…"

"Do you mislike monsters? I would have expected better of an aspiring Chronicler," she said, lifting her nose.

"About that," Roland said. "It's why I've come."

She managed to stare down her nose at him even though she was barely came up to Roland's chest, her shimmery white hair floating as ghostly tendrils. "Please do listen. We need your help."

Roland sighed inwardly. He owed her. Roland fought the urge to tug on a lock of his hair, as peasants had done in ancient times. "What can I do?"

"The monsters here need a new home before the forest is destroyed. I need you to help me relocate them. You are very good at accomplishing relocation," she said with a ghost of a smile.

Lady Perchta was one of the most determined ghosts (and the only perpetual one) that Roland had yet to encounter. But she wasn't a monster. Why was she concerning herself with monsters? And what were these monsters she spoke of? Other than the one right in front of him.

"But…why…?" Roland said.

"I think you are forgetting. I am a monster, too," Lady Perchta said, in a perfectly civilized tone.

"I…didn't forget. I just didn't…why do you think you are a monster?"

The Green Knight giggled, an incongruous sound coming from one so big. "You *might* be forgiven for not knowing. But most of us can change our appearance. You are seeing a not-so-frightening visage of the lady. But I can assure you, she has others."

Lady Perchta looked down momentarily, as if embarrassed. The legendary White Lady—*Weisse Frau, Dame Blanche*—had many names. Her folk tales, likely based on something older and forgotten, were not always savory, and had been used to frighten children over a century ago. Roland was quite sure that a female apparition with a grotesquely misshapen foot and who disemboweled naughty children would still put a scare into little ones in this day and age. The Lady Perchta legend, one of many White Lady stories, was unique to his village and a part of its history, but no less terrifying.

Roland refrained from rolling his eyes. "Monster relocation. Okay. Something that I'm sure will be a wonderful addition to my resume. Right up there with exhuming the dead. I'm assuming you'll want me to come equipped with a moving van? My undertaker's van? Do you have a new forest picked out? Preferably one not about to be destroyed by a brown-coal mining company? Of course, the monsters will need to register their new residence at the city hall closest to their new homes. We'll need identification. And an asylum application from Mr. Green Knight here. Wouldn't want to get him deported before he has a chance to settle in, would we?"

Roland's natural tendency, when nervous, to go for the absurd had sprung forth before he could rein it in. A ghostly green knight with an axe had the effect of making him nervous. And Roland had no doubt the Green Knight's axe would have permanent consequences if the axe connected with, say, his neck.

Lady Perchta crossed her arms, her petite features screwed up into a scowl. "There is a legendary home for monsters. This gentle knight has been so courteous to tell me of it. It should be the right place. We just need to pinpoint its present position."

Roland pointed to the Green Knight's axe. "Would you have used that on me if I said no?"

The head smirked. "A man with an axe walks into a bar. Bartender says, 'What'll it be?' 'What have you got,' the man says. Bartender says, 'Anything you want.'"

"Not many of them will go..." Lady Perchta glanced away, but he caught the sadness in her voice and a touch of panic. She added, "I am not planning on leaving. I do not know if I *can* leave. And I don't want to. In the end, it may not be many who decide to go."

What did a ghost have to be afraid of?

The Green Knight glanced around as if the forest itself might disappear in front of him. "If you are staying then I am, too. Oi've just left my homeland and have no will left now to find another one. It...the world...already feels fainter."

He was right, the world they knew *would* disappear. Sooner rather than later.

Roland sighed.

On the ferry, Roland woke to the sight of deep blue water and a light blue horizon outside their porthole window. Andvari was staring out of it with a wistful expression. Did he miss being in the water? Was he aching to swim in his fish form? He had slept in his clothes, a cloth bag draped over one shoulder, a bag that he never seemed to remove. His features were bold and—Roland couldn't help but think—*chiseled*. As if the centuries themselves had etched the lines on his face.

Andvari turned to regard him. "You look knackered."

Roland ran a hair through his hair, which had decided to stand up in all directions. His pajamas felt as rumpled as he did. "Am going to take a shower before breakfast."

"Better hurry. I think we dock presently."

"Coffee. Need buckets of it."

"Aye."

The intercom sounded with a loud gong and a staticky announcement that all passengers should exit their cabins and proceed without delay to their automobiles. Roland and Andvari collected a disheveled and exhausted Jo and Marshall, and they trooped down endless stairs into the bowels of the ferry. Roland's stomach jumped with unease. He hoped against hope that the monsters were still in place, and the ferry bay wasn't littered with dead Danish citizens.

Grendel, Hrungnir and Mokkerkalfe sat in the back of the van, just where he'd left them the evening before. The giants had stripped down to their underwear. Grendel wore extra clothes, the giants' clothes, and had wound a T-shirt into a turban on his head, for what purpose, Roland did not have a clue. A disguise, perhaps? It didn't make him look as comical as it should have. Roland wondered where he'd gotten the T-shirt from. He didn't remember either of the two giants having worn one. Both had been clothed in old-fashioned garments of linen and wool. Grendel looked pleased with himself, if his glowing red eyes were any indication. Green beer bottles, the labels peeled off, littered the floor of the back seat of the van.

Jo and Marshall piled into the van, kicking the bottles. "What's the deal with the clothes?" Jo asked.

"Learned how to play cards," Mokkerkalfe said.

It was the first time Roland had heard him speak. His voice was low and hesitant and not as gravelly as Roland had expected from a man made of clay.

"We lost," Hrungnir said. "Not sure it was all done in a fair manner."

"Whoa," Marshall said. "Poker-party night. Cool. Where'd you get the beer?"

"Beer truck. Very convenient," Hrungnir snorted out. "Mokkerkalfe fetched them for us."

Grendel's red eyes flashed. "All's fair."

"He knows Shakespeare?" Marshall asked.

Grendel laughed, a low scary sound. "War and love, not so different. But I meant the card games, all fair." Then the monster swiveled his glance to Roland. "I didn't eat anyone."

It was the first time Roland had heard the ancient monster speak as well. Grendel's voice sounded deep *and* gravelly. And dark. Just like the grave he might have crawled out of.

Andvari rode shotgun to help with navigation. Roland propped him up on a small wooden crate he found in the back of the van. The dwarf handed the other monsters sandwiches that he'd purloined from the breakfast buffet, which was a nice gesture. Monsters helping monsters. Roland began to hope things would go more smoothly.

Then they got snarled in an endless amount of traffic trying to motor their way free of the city of Patras. The sun in Greece was already relentless, without even a wisp of cloud in the sky, and it wasn't even mid-morning yet. The GPS kept trying to lead them in circles. Andvari was cursing.

Jo and Marshall were busy with smartphones and discussing something with Hrungnir. Roland only heard snatches of their conversation. It seemed they were debating the kinds of monsters they would be encountering at Alexander's Gate. There was talk of headless men with faces in their stomachs, dog-headed men. Snake-like creatures. Cyclops.

Roland stopped listening. He despaired of ever leaving Patras. It was yet another dingy, smelly city, a port of call that reeked of despair and poverty. Finally, they reached the highway. A tall suspension bridge stood out in the distance. It could lead anywhere, Roland thought. To fairyland, or Oz. Or to a gate behind which all the monsters lived.

"There," Andvari said. "Finally. The road to Athens. Is it true all roads lead there?"

"Once upon a time, all roads supposedly led to Rome," Roland said. "But maybe before Rome, it used to be Athens."

Medusa lived in a large but unassuming Greek stucco house with a tiled roof. The roof needed reshingling. The walls needed paint. Roland could well imagine that it might be difficult to arrange those things, for a person without many resources. Including hands and legs. Or even a body. But the house was directly on the beach and had a stunning view over the water.

Then again, who needed new roof tiles?

Roland was surprised when the door opened upon a stunning woman, certainly of Greek descent, with long dark brown hair and warm brown eyes. And a lithe figure. Beautiful, smooth olive skin. She wore capri leggings and a lengthy, sleeveless top. Bare feet. Beautiful, petite feet. Slender graceful arms.

She smiled at him.

Roland was speechless.

She appraised him openly, her smile not lessening. "Hi," she said. "You are not Andvari...?"

Roland shifted and cleared his throat. "I'm Roland Eckstein. Andvari is...just around the corner."

Upon arrival, the dwarf had jumped out of the van and headed for the nearest clump of bushes to take a leak. Roland might have screamed at him, and wanted to, but he had continued on to the house. They had exactly one hour before their booked ferry left. Otherwise, they'd be stuck here overnight.

And Roland liked to be early. *Very* early.

But now, watching the woman in front of him, not too young and definitely not too old—just right—Roland thought "being stuck" might be the wrong description.

Blessed. Lucky. A week would be good. The Lesbos beach just behind the house looked inviting. Jo and Marshall had complained loudly about a deep desire to feel saltwater and sun on their skin. They were on holiday, they said. Their complaints had been a concerted effort. Roland didn't doubt they'd rehearsed it the night before, hatching out their plan to delay the monster road trip for a much-needed pause.

Roland was beginning to agree.

"Would you like a cup of coffee? And I have some Greek pastries. I picked them up this morning. I also have some Peloponnesian wine in the fridge for later. Olives, bread, feta, some wonderful fruity olive oil, locally sourced. You must be hungry after the long drive." The woman gestured into the house, opening the door wider. She spoke English with a delightful accent.

Roland took a step forward, but then remembered his manners. He held out his hand. "I'm Roland Eckstein. The...um...driver."

The woman's smile grew larger, and she shook his hand. "I'm Phose, Medusa's companion."

A sigh escaped before Roland could hold it back. Overnight. Maybe just the once...Andvari had said he wasn't in a hurry...

—

Settled in on the terrace of Medusa's house with strong Greek coffee and ultra-sweet confections arranged on a heavy wrought iron table in front of them, Andvari and Roland watched while Marshall and Jo frolicked in the Aegean Sea, mainly floating about with an occasional mutual splash attack. The sea's salty smell produced a heady feeling of relaxation that Roland didn't exactly try to fight off.

Phose had left to busy herself in the well-equipped modern kitchen. Roland tried not to look too often through the French doors for her return.

He'd taken off his shoes and socks. The rasp of the cream-colored terrace tiles on his feet dissolved some of the exhaustion of the last couple of days that had seeped in through his skin. But at the moment, he felt only a contented sort of tiredness. He could stay here maybe forever. Especially if Phose was nearby.

"Yer've got it bad there," Andvari said. "That was the quickest sting from Cupid's bloody arrow I've seen since all those daft knights were throwing themselves in the Rhine after losing their hearts and then getting jilted."

"Knights," Roland said. "Are you talking about the Rhineland romances? Weren't the stories just made up?"

Andvari laughed. "Good one." He'd already scarfed down most of the small squares of pastry and slurped his coffee. But he did drink it with his pinky extended.

Roland found the cakes—baclava and similar things—a little too sticky, but ate one out of politeness. He'd have eaten more if it would make Phose happy.

"I'm wondering where the giants have gotten to. And Grendel," Roland said.

Andvari waved. "Down the hall in one of the bedrooms. They're in wit' her Majesty."

"Hmm?"

"Medusa. Queen of Lesbos. Or so she fancies herself."

"Oh."

"What are they doing?"

"Gabbing."

"Erm. Andvari?"

The dwarf was stuffing yet another pastry in. He raised eyebrows in response.

The house didn't contain much in the way of furniture. A modestly large flat-screen television hung on the wall. A sofa. And a cushioned rattan chair in one corner. A coffee table in front of the couch. It must all have been for Phose because—

"About this turning to stone thing…"

Andvari held up a finger while he finished chewing, then took another slurp of coffee to wash it down. "Ah. Wonderful. Greek food." He wiped his mouth delicately on a napkin. "Not to worry. Her majesty wears sunglasses. Balenciaga. To go with her Hermes scarves. Woman has expensive tastes. But then she don't need to wear *much*."

"But I thought it was…that looking on her face turned men to stone."

"Nothin' wrong with her face. B'lieve she's had some work done." He gestured, a circle of his index finger around his face. "It's really the eyes. Monster eyes. Wish I had 'em. They're the most powerful things on earth."

Roland took a sip of coffee. "Just *her* eyes, or is it all monster eyes? And what is it, exactly?"

Andvari shrugged. "Depends on the monster. The eyes are the seat of power, and that power is not, whatchacallit, *distributed*

289

evenly. You'd have to ask Medusa—although I don't advise it—about her power." He leaned back in his chair, his legs dangling. "She was a rape victim, Poseidon was the culprit, and then she got slut-shamed by Athena, which was when she became a monster. According to the myths. Reality was prob'ly much different. But I don't doubt for a minute about the rape. The gods were such bastards."

Roland recalled from some of the medieval romances that dwarves also kidnapped women, but was too polite to say so.

Andvari, perhaps following Roland's thoughts, added, "I *did* kidnap my share of women. Wasn't hard, most of them were runaways. I fancy the blonde ones. But I didn't violate them or do them any bodily harm. Treated 'em good, gave them a place to stay. Let things progress on their own. All of them did stay unless some idjit hero showed up to save them. Then they had to pretend they needed rescuing. Didn't want the world to know they were shacked up with a black elf. A few snuck back, trying to find me again."

"Why do you want to go to this place, this land of monsters? Can't you just build a new castle? There's plenty of forests left in Germany," Roland said. "And blondes."

Andvari rubbed his stubble, which had grown so quickly it could already be considered a beard, especially by today's über-cool urban gentlemen standards. "Been askin' myself that very thing. Not sure if I can answer it yet. We'll see. A spread like this here, right on the beach, now this is something special."

"Do you want to…swim?"

"You mean as a pike? It's saltwater, but, yeah, maybe I'll go later. I assume we're here for the day, then?"

Roland glanced at his watch and nodded. The last Mitilini ferry was just leaving. They would have to wait to get a boat tomorrow morning. "We're here until tomorrow, then. I hope everyone enjoys it. Feels like one of those last meals at sundown kind of thing."

"I hear ya on that one," Andvari said.

Roland had had an intense reaction to the monsters at first. They repelled him. But they also fascinated, each in a different way. Maybe Grendel most of all. Even Andvari, who styled himself a monster but had as much, or more, humanity than many humans Roland had met.

But the dwarf also had his not-so-human moments. Although he didn't gush about it, he cared about his fellow monsters, gave them a place to live, stole breakfast for them. This road trip was as much Andvari's doing as Lady Perchta's. Even the Green Knight was under his protection, happily residing in the dwarf's castle. And he'd also given Grendel a home there, even if the monster did have to guard the cursed gold. Did that mean Grendel was a dragon? Wasn't that what dragons did, guard gold? Roland was sorry he hadn't gotten a look at the palace.

So much information to gather.

Why he wanted to know all these things and more was only just becoming clear. If he asked the right questions, this trip could constitute a part of his research, a part of the history he was trying to accumulate. Too bad it would have to remain a secret history. No one would believe him if he tried to publish it as truth. End of career as chronicler. He'd have to take up writing popular fiction instead.

But Marshall and Jo accepted the monsters at face value, so to speak. There must be others who would accept his secret history, if he wrote it. It could be circulated to a particular clientele. Roland felt a passion rising within. These were stories about another kind of people. Monsters. And if they were going behind this mythical gate, there would soon be fewer of them around. Their stories shouldn't be lost.

He wished Frau Geisen hadn't died. She would have been the perfect person to talk about all this when he returned.

After everyone's stomachs began to growl, and some haggling occurred, they reached a consensus: Roland would drive for Greek take-out. Phose would go with him to make the order, at a local restaurant just up the road along the Bay of Kalloni, and they would drop Andvari (literally) into the bay, an unpolluted wetland environment rich with wildlife, and pick him up on the way back.

The plan would give Roland uninterrupted minutes, he hoped many of them, alone with Phose. She sat next to him in the van, close enough that he caught her fragrance. Light and airy, rose-scented, and something innate beneath it that he surmised was her skin. A touch of citrus but light, like lime. Wonderful.

Andvari grumbled in the back seat of the van.

Phose fidgeted in her seat.

The grumbling continued.

"What is it?" Roland asked with a glance in the rear-view window.

"Yer ought to tell him," Andvari said.

Phose gave a bare shake to her head.

"Then I will," he said.

She held up a hand, wagged the fingers. "All right."

A final grumble-grunt.

They drove in silence on the road paralleling the bay, Roland now agitated. Driving cross-continent was easy, mostly uncomplicated, even in heavy traffic and with unpredictable fellow drivers. It was his passengers that made everything difficult.

The spot seemed right to Andvari, who whistled them to a stop.

"Enjoy the sardines," Phose called out, but didn't look around.

Andvari pulled on the sliding door of the van and hopped out. The door slammed closed behind him. Roland's last glimpse of the dwarf before he drove away was the progressive parting of cane grass that marked the dwarf's progress toward the waters of the bay.

He would have liked to watch the transformation into fish form, but Andvari hadn't offered to let him observe. A private thing, then.

The silence continued for a few uncomfortable minutes while they drove. Roland tried to concentrate on the landscape, bare in comparison to Germany's lush but often turbulent—weed-choked might have been a better description—summer growth. Lesbos was full of a diversity of plants. The passed groves of olive trees. Phose *had* said the olive oil was locally sourced. Seemed they must have plenty of it. Wiry shrubs, thirsty-looking trees, also lowland pines, and other scrubland plants dotted the surrounding plains. It was still hot, although the temperature drifted towards a tolerable swelter rather than painfully scorching.

Phose grasped her hands in her lap and looked out the window. Roland didn't know how to talk to her, or even if he should. Andvari's command had thrown a pall over the trip. He had imagined his time with her differently, with pleasant conversation and mutually exchanged smiles. He wondered what her lips tasted like. His stomach rumbled. They hadn't stopped for lunch, as he had expected them to be on a tight schedule. First, pick up the head. Second, drive to the ferry. Third, try to make it to Istanbul for the night, booking a room, hopefully, on the way.

He had yet to even see the famed Medusa. Did she eat dinner? How was that accomplished, and where did the food go? Roland had so many questions, but didn't know where to start.

Phose spoke only to give him directions, which eventually led them to a quaint little tavern of white-painted brick near the town of Kalloni on the northwest side of the bay. He waited on the shaded terrace while she placed their order. She joined him afterwards, with two glasses of chilled white wine in her hands.

"No reason not to enjoy the evening while we wait," she said. Her smile was slight but genuine.

"Fine with me," Roland said, accepting a glass. "Thanks."

They sat at a table for two complete with a checkered table-cloth. The sun had just dipped below the larger hill on the opposite side of the bay.

"The Olympus range," she said and pointed to the peak just visible in the distance. "Not *the* Mount Olympus, but one of many mountains in Greece with that name."

"Oh, that's interesting," Roland said, not trying to hide his sarcasm, his nervousness again driving him to it. He freely admitted to himself that Phose's nearness made him nervous. And now she had a deep dark secret that Andvari had threatened her with.

Phose took a hefty sip of wine. "You're probably wondering what Andvari meant when he told me to tell you."

"Probably."

"It's complicated."

Roland laughed. "Really? More complicated than being a companion to a disembodied head?"

She snorted into her wine. "Wait here." She got up and went back into the restaurant.

Roland chugged what was in his glass. Perhaps not a good idea. But he hadn't seen any police cars on the road coming here.

Phose came back out carrying a carafe of white wine. She poured wine into both glasses, an eyebrow raised that his was already empty. She sat again and pushed her shoulders back. "Okay."

"Okay." He waited for her to take a sip.

"Nice and dry. Drier than the Peloponnesian wines I grew up with."

"You're not from Lesbos."

She shook her head. "I come from a long line of Greeks. Maybe you've heard of us…the *Heracleidae*."

He raised both eyebrows. "Not sure."

"Descendants of Hercules."

"The hero."

"Him."

"It's a long line, then. That was when?"

"The so-called Bronze Age?" She cleared her throat. "My full name is Metamorphoses. Phose is just my nickname." She shrugged. "It comes from Ovid's poems of the same name, but he was a Roman. He in turn took his inspiration from an earlier work from one of my direct ancestors."

"Direct ancestors."

"I'm older than I look."

Roland took a deep sip and refilled his glass. And hers. "Let me guess. You're as old as the so-called Bronze Age."

She nodded and fingered the condensation on her wine glass. "I am, or became, a literal embodiment of the poems. I *am* Metamorphoses.

I represent the poor unfortunate people—let's make things simpler and just call them *Greeks*—who were changed."

"Changed?"

"Transformed."

Roland said, "*Metamorphosed*, like Medusa becoming a monster after being violated by the god of the sea?"

"Like that."

"But you don't look a day over twenty-five. Or twenty-six. At the most."

Phose laughed. "Why, thank you."

Someone inside the restaurant yelled out in Greek.

Phose pushed back her chair to stand. "Oh, our dinner. Can you help me carry it out to the van?"

A blanket of velvety purple darkness had begun to settle across the ocean horizon as they neared Medusa and/or Phose's house. Ronald didn't know the particulars about ownership. He was also still somewhat hazy about what the embodiment of a poem was. But if it ended up looking like Phose, it must have been one heck of a poem. He stifled a laugh. It caught in his throat when they sighted the house in the headlights.

And saw the blinking blue lights of the Greek police in the driveway.

"Uh-oh," Andvari said. He dove out of the van, heading for the bushes. "Got to pee."

Roland sniffed into his cupped hand to sense if he could smell alcohol. He hadn't drunk that much wine at the restaurant, at least, not enough to have earned a visit from the police.

"Let me deal with this," Phose said, and sprang from the van before Roland came to a stop next to the police car, or rather truck, on the driveway. The shiny white and blue-striped pick-up truck was not dissimilar to an American-made one he'd seen one of the newly-rich Neu Perchta villagers cruising around in recently. Roland went inside the house.

Jo and Marshall, as bleary-eyed as if they'd been pulled from their beds, sat close together on the couch in the small living room. There was no sign of Medusa. Or the giants. Or Grendel, for which Roland was über glad. His appetite for the takeout in the van had fled. The room smelled astringent. Something made his nose sting.

Phose, one hand on her hip, the other gesturing, began a discussion with the two brawny policemen who towered over Jo and Marshall.

After a few minutes of back and forth in animated Greek, the police officers consulted with each other. They nodded to Phose, glared at Jo and Marshall, gave Roland the once-over and then left. The front door closed behind them with a solid thunk.

They waited until the truck roared off. Then everyone began talking. Animated German. Animated English. Some Greek cursing from Phose. Arms waving. Yelling over one another in order to be heard. Roland slunk back outside to get the takeout. A peace offering. Andvari popped up by his side.

"Everything *Friede Freude Eierkuchen?*" he asked.

It was a contemporary German phrase meaning Peace and Joy and Cake, usually said sarcastically. Roland thought the sarcasm not out of place.

"Well," Roland said. "Maybe not as good as all that." He handed Andvari one of the Styrofoam crates of food. "But maybe this will help. Are you hungry?"

"I could eat Pegasus," Andvari said.

The general heat of the discussion had lowered some, but not much. Roland headed out to the terrace with the food, as there didn't seem to be enough seating for everyone inside the house. It was a pleasant evening and the lights from a couple of fishing boats twinkled in the near distance.

There was spanakopita, flatbread and feta, wedges of fresh fragrant tomatoes, stuffed zucchini, and pommes frites to go with everything. And of course, a plate of gyros with tzatziki. It all smelled wonderful, overcoming all the other emotions Roland felt surging below the surface. His heart still pounded, but he was finally really hungry.

Roland whistled and called everyone to dinner. They all shuffled out, except the giants and the still-missing Grendel, and took places at the table on the patio.

Roland began quizzing the others while they ate. The food disappeared fast, even without the giants.

"Where are Hrungnir and Mokkerkalfe?" Roland was amused that the ancient Germanic names rolled so easily off his tongue.

"By the water. Fishing for sardines," Jo said, with a mouth full of gyros. He sopped tzatziki up with some bread, then tried to stuff it into his already-full mouth. "We thought it better that they weren't here when we let the police in."

"What did they want?"

The two young men gave each other a look. Jo began to explain: "It seems there was a Danish man on the ferryboat. He was driving the Carlsberg beer truck that our passengers raided that night? But he never drove the truck off the ferry. He's missing. And the police are questioning everyone who was on the boat."

"Wow. They tracked us here? That quick?"

The two nodded.

"They want to search the house and your van," Phose said. "I told them to come back with a warrant. Is there any reason to be afraid?"

"There's a big reason to be afraid," Roland said. "Grendel. Where is he?"

"He ran off," Marshall said. "Or used his special stealth magic. We don't know."

"Then all of a sudden, it smelled funny. Like there was a big stinky animal in the living room," Jo said. "We tried to clean before we let the policemen in."

"They were angry because it took so long to open the door," Marshall said.

"Oh," Roland said.

"We tried to look sleepy, like we'd been napping," Marshall added.

"I gave Grendel one simple *nein*, no-no, uh-uh. Just one," Andvari growled. "*Not. To. Eat. Anyone.*"

"Maybe he didn't," Jo said. "Maybe he just scared the guy off."

"He *said* he didn't eat anyone," Roland said. "Well, the giants would know. They were there."

Phose, attuned to a sound none of the others could hear, headed down the hallway towards the bedrooms.

"What do we do now, Roland?" Jo asked.

Good question. He had joked about Interpol being after them, but that now seemed to be a reality. They were on an island, and to leave it meant going through border control.

"We have to wait and see if they come back with a warrant. In the meantime, let's get rid of all those beer bottles," Roland said. "And..." He remembered the T-shirt that had struck him as out of place, the one that Grendel had used for a hat. Where had he gotten that T-shirt from? Roland groaned. "And look for the shirt, the one Grendel had on his head. We need to get rid of that, too."

Jo and Marshall leapt up at the same time. "We don't want to go to Greek jail," Marshall said.

"You won't," Roland said. "But I might."

It had been inconceivable to Roland that he would even consider covering up a crime—and not just any crime, but *murder*—by getting eaten by an ancient monster. But, if caught, Grendel would not be the one to take the blame. No, the monster would just disappear. Roland would be the fall guy. He was a long way from his peaceful existence digging graves in a west German village.

That he felt relaxed, full, and even happy to be here did not fit in with the way he *should* be feeling. He *should* be paralyzed with fright and remorse.

He was sorry about the Danish man. Very sorry. The man couldn't have known he was locked in the bowels of a ship with a van full of monsters. He was probably just trying to save money by sleeping in his truck. Or guarding his cargo of Danish pilsner. Before they could explore the likelihood of Roland's incarceration, Phose returned.

And she was not alone.

"Darlings! You must excuse me. It has been a dreadful busy week, and I haven't had time to greet our guests." The head of Medusa was wearing sunglasses. She blew air kisses into the night. "Mwah, mwah!"

Medusa spoke English with in a deep, accented voice. How she could have such a deep voice—or any voice at all—Roland wasn't going to worry about that.

Phose placed Medusa's head on a plush red pillow that rested upon a cushioned wicker chair in the corner. Her huge sunglasses had very dark lenses, and the two-toned beige-dark brown frames looked costly. They hid most of her face, and twinkled with rhinestones. Maybe they really were Balenciaga. Medusa's smile was emphasized by deep, red lipstick. Around the base of her neck, she wore a red silk scarf with a pattern of crowns.

And her snakes. *Heilige Krieger*. Tiny, asp-like snakes. They were braided to look like dreadlocks. A few had a platinum sheen and the rest were a dark gray. It was a stunning look, totally unique. The snakes appeared to be resting, but one or two lifted their small reptilian heads to eye the other people in the room from time to time, flicking their tongues.

"Wow," Marshall said.

Andvari was the first to reply. "Hey, Su-su."

She laughed. "Andvari. Finally, we meet in the flesh."

"Right. Love what you've done with the snakes," he said. "Uh, we seem to have hit a snag, a big one. Have you seen Grendel lately?"

She frowned. "He's in one of the bedrooms, snoring like a herd of musk ox."

"Well," Andvari said and scratched his stubble. "He might have ate...I mean eaten...a man on the ferry. The police were here."

"Greek police in my house?" Medusa's frown deepened. "This won't do at all. And you see, darlings, this is the reason I *must* go with you, although I *hate* to leave Lesbos, my adopted home. I have this nice house on the beach—much better than living in a cave, let me tell you—and I can manage my intellectual property, my *legacy* as a world-wide symbol, wonderfully from here:

monitor *all* my licensing deals, consult with the feminists, help people with their logos." She pursed her lips. "But it never stops. One man dies and it's automatically the monster's fault."

"Could have been a mistake. We won't know until we talk to Grendel," Andvari said.

"Hrungnir and Mokkerkalfe could enlighten us as well," Roland said. He had begun to be nervous about their disappearance. Did they hold a grudge against Scandinavians as well? Did it involve eating them?

Medusa said, "Phose, you should wake Grendel. Gently, darling, I don't want to chance you getting eaten, too."

Phose marched off down the hall.

Medusa continued, "Hmm…I may need to make a few phone calls. And we may have to leave sooner than I expected." Her sunglassed head made a sweep of the terrace, locking on each of us individually. "Where *are* those delightful giants?"

"In the water," Jo said while trying to avert his glance from her face.

A chuckle escaped Medusa's expressive mouth. "Darling, don't worry. I haven't turned anyone to stone since the late Iron Age."

"I'm afraid we won't be able to leave until this is cleared up," Roland said. "They tracked down my van from the ship. Sneaking on board one of the ferries doesn't seem to be a viable option, even with Grendel's help."

Medusa regarded him for a short moment. "You are the driver, the one who volunteered for this enterprise?"

Roland nodded.

"Excellent. Phose has spoken fondly of you." She paused as if a thought just occurred to her. "You know, she is mine. I brought her out of that hell-hole of a ruin south of Corinth where she was hiding out. She is the embodiment of—"

"Love," Andvari said, making a sweeping gesture. "The words of the poem are just trappings. Metamorphoses is that secret place in *all* of us. The place that lives beneath the transformations, the hideousness, the distorted—"

Medusa snorted. "Yes, darling. Of course, you're right. She belongs to *all* of us. But right now, I'm the one paying the bills."

Roland bit back an angry response. Phose was a beautiful young woman, even if she was a poem, and she had every right to belong to herself. She didn't belong to anyone. Least of all a diva's head. But he decided to save his ire for later, when they could afford it.

"About leaving," he said. "Maybe we need a different strategy. I think we need to go undercover to get off the island."

Jo and Marshall made dropped-open mouth looks at each other. And then did some sort of secret handshake. Obviously, they weren't bothered by the idea of an illegal subterfuge.

"Well, of course, darling," Medusa said. "My point, exactly. And I know just—"

Phose came back, looking a little breathless. "He's awake," she said, "but not very coherent."

Hrungnir and Mokkerkalfe chose that moment to stumble across the sand to the terrace. The two giants loomed over them, breathing hard. Each carried a string of small fish—sardines— threaded onto a stick.

"We brought dinner," Hrungnir said, his lips spread in a wide grin.

Then he saw the remains of dinner on the table. A momentary anger crossed his features.

Andvari said, "Hrungie, those are some nice fish. We'll be able to eat them on the way. Are you ready to leave?"

Mokkerkalfe's face dropped. He hadn't said much during the journey so far, but now he did. "Want to stay. Here."

Grendel shuffled up to the French doors and stood just inside them, staring at everyone. His eyes seemed even more incandescent in the shadows of the house. In daylight, his form had an insubstantial quality, part shadow, part something else, something manlike. But not quite. As if there were hidden bits. Like a tail, a snout, and whatever else a dragon had. Because Roland was convinced. Grendel was at least half dragon.

And right now he didn't smell good *at all*.

Jo and Marshall stepped away from the house, towards the sand. Roland was tempted to do the same. Medusa's nostrils flared.

"Whoa, Grendel, you need to be cleaned," Andvari said. "Seriously, what have you been eating?"

Grendel heaved a great bellow of a sigh. "Bugs. The waste products come out of my skin. Chickens are better."

Jo made gagging motions to Marshall. Roland didn't blame him.

"Bugs, the other white meat," Marshall whispered.

"You ate bugs," Andvari said, ignoring the boys. "Not the Danish beer man from the boat?"

Grendel looked at Andvari and then at me. "I *said* I didn't eat anyone on the boat."

"And we believed you," Andvari said. "But the police were here. They said the man from the beer truck is missing. He left his truck on the ferry."

The giants laughed. "He got *even more* scared when he saw Mokker and me," Hrungnir said. "He ran off. We thought that meant we could have some beer to drink."

"He ran off?" Roland put his head in his hands. "This doesn't make any sense. Where could he run to? We were on a boat on an *ocean*."

"Saw me first," Grendel said. "The real me. Danes. Killed my mother. Never forget. I told him to go away, but to give me his shirt. As payment. Or I would eat him."

Babble erupted. Laughter.

Roland rapped on the table. "Look. The man is still missing, even if he wasn't eaten. So it doesn't change our situation. Right?"

"Absolutely correct," Medusa said. "So, it's decided. Let's proceed directly to Alexander's Gate."

"You got a plan?" Andvari asked.

"Better than a plan. I know a shortcut," Medusa said.

Roland felt his mind turning and sizzling, like someone flipping a pancake on a hot griddle. "A short-cut? And we're just *now* hearing about it. We could already have been—"

"Medusa wanted to get to know everyone first, before we left," Phose said.

Medusa nodded and her sunglass lenses sparkled. "It was when I was hiding out in my cave. I'd wanted to visit my sisters. You know them, darling?"

"Not personally," Andvari said.

Phose leaned over and whispered in Roland's ear. "The Gorgons." She'd moved to stand next to his chair. He could smell her rose-scented perfume. For a small moment, it made him happy.

"They're very important to me. So I had to figure out a way to slip in between the worlds," Medusa said. "Of course I found one."

"Which worlds?" Roland asked. His curiosity had reared again. There was just so much to learn.

"Our world, and the other one," Medusa said. A few of her snakes stuck their tongues out at him. "Phose? My shield?"

"Are we going in the van?" Marshall asked.

"Oh no, darling, it's not that far. We'll walk. Maybe you should put some sunscreen on that lovely brown skin. Hate to see it get burnt. There's not a square of shade anywhere."

The short-cut from this world to "the other one" was via the walk-in closet in Medusa's room. Or what was cleverly disguised as a closet. In reality, the door led to…somewhere else.

They all entered singly except Jo and Marshall, who went arm in arm, singing a song Roland recognized from an old black-and-white German film about friends. He'd watched *Allerbeste Freunde* many times. It made Roland smile.

Phose had changed into a beige sundress that fitted loosely and fell to her thighs. It didn't emphasize her curves, but didn't hide them either. She wore a floppy straw hat that emphasized her attractiveness. She carried Medusa on a strange contraption that *might* have been a shield at one time and had certainly been a part of some hairy animal before that. Goat, maybe? Now it looked like a ragged, hairy throne. It was round, covered with hide, and with a rim of dark metal chipped in parts. Several rivets were stuck into the hide. A recess in the middle of the shield was a perfect fit for Medusa. When Phose placed Medusa in the recess, she seemed to snuggle down, her snakes waving back and forth before settling again.

A tiny part of him was deeply relieved. Was their journey finally, finally at an end? Roland had expected days more of driving, of not knowing what to expect, of dealing with creative ways to hide monsters from border controls, of…

Adventure.

A larger part of him was deeply *not* relieved. He would be losing his companions and would also lose access to their world, one he wanted to learn more about. And he'd be losing Phose. All he would be left with were the Green Knight and Lady Perchta. At least, until the mining company destroyed Elsbach Forest. Then he'd be alone again. With only gin and lurking shadows to keep him company. He shuddered.

Roland entered the closet portal last. Darkness deepened, and he heard whispering all around him, then cruel laughter. Was someone screaming? Medusa had said to ignore all sounds and just keep going. He smelled something vile. Was that Grendel again? But Phose's rose scent chased that away. She was close by.

He swallowed, his throat constricted. He kept on keeping on.

And emerged to the brightness of day, one even more intense than the Greek sunshine they had left just a few hours ago. The sky was a deep blue, the sun an unforgiving yellow orb. Roland looked up only once and wished he hadn't. His eyes took several seconds before they no longer showed spots floating in front of him.

They continued along on a flat dirt path, wide enough for all of them to walk abreast. The others were scattered ahead of Roland. On either side of the path were impossibly high walls of red sandstone shaded to purple in parts and twinkling with quartz crystal intrusions. The enclosure created the illusion that the sun bore down harder, only on them.

Roland wished he'd brought a hat. Or could borrow Grendel's T-shirt turban. He glanced ahead. Sure enough, the monster was wearing the shirt on his head. His trophy, a symbol of defeating the Danes. Take a man's shirt and half scare him to death. It was an entirely honorable substitute for carnivorous behavior.

Andvari strode onward, seeming unaffected by the glare of the sun, as were the giants as well. Mokkerkalfe stopped every now and then to feel the wall. Its clay was harder than the type the stone-hearted giant was made from. Jo and Marshall stayed close to one another, but had stopped their singing. Phose was just ahead of him, carrying Medusa on her shield—Aegis, it was called, and it had once belonged to Zeus himself. Or so the story went.

The gods were no longer here. Only the monsters remained. They endured, Roland realized. Phose glanced at him, trying to repress a frown.

Roland would miss her. He would miss all of them.

Alexander's Gate lay only a short distance in front of them, more magnificent than the lion gate in Mycenae, of which Roland had seen pictures. This gate was thick and solid, taller than at least three men—six meters or more—and seemed to be of a piece with the surrounding sandstone, as if it were hewed out of the rock. It was made of a dark metal, possibly iron or bronze, and alarming figures had been inscribed within it. Ugly-faced creatures eating each other, eating human arms, fighting. It all looked quite ominous.

Alexander's Gate, through various sources ancient as well as medieval, was rumored to contain any number of enemies the Western world was likely to encounter. While Roland had found mostly anti-Semitic references to Middle-Eastern and Asiatic tribes, some of the tales referenced dog-faced men, men without heads, and other monstrosities that Alexander had managed to enclose within the somewhat supernaturally constructed oiled bronze gates.

If this was really the place, then it was impressive, indeed. On top was a larger-than-life bronze figure riding a horse, the gate's namesake upon his trusty steed.

There was no door, small or large, at the bottom, in the gate. There seemed to be no way for them to go in.

This was the end. My friends.

Roland wanted to shout, "Stop! Let's go back."

Andvari's face screwed up with an emotion that Roland had no trouble deciphering. He was scared. The emotion was fleeting. Andvari pulled himself up, and appeared taller. He could now pass for a short human. He marched back and forth in front of the gate, muttering, scratching his growth of beard, and stopping every now and then to stare at the gate.

"What's he doing?" Marshall asked.

Jo stood next to him, still close. "We don't have to go in there, do we?" Jo asked.

Roland shook his head. "I don't see how anyone is going in there. There's no entrance."

"Maybe a hidden door," Jo said.

"Maybe that's what he's looking for," Marshall said.

Maybe it was. Andvari stopped in the middle of the gate, looking up and then down. Then he smiled and motioned everyone closer. Grendel shuffled over to him. Hrungnir and Mokkerkalfe as well, although they hung back a little. Phose stood next to Andvari, the goatskin shield braced like a tray of hors d'oeuvres against her diaphragm.

Andvari reached into the cloth sack draped over his shoulder, the sack he never removed, and pulled out fragrant herb stems tied in a bunch. He handed the stems around and told everyone to place them on the tongue but not to eat. Roland moved closer to try to see what the flowers were, but he didn't recognize them. The smell was pungent but not overwhelming. They looked like pretty blue weeds.

"What is it?" Jo whispered, next to him.

"Don't know," Roland said.

"Chicory," Marshall said. "My mother uses it as a coffee substitute. Tastes kind of woody. But good. She also lets it grow wild in the garden. A pagan thing. She makes smudge sticks for their meetings."

"So they're eating a coffee analog?" Jo asked.

Roland found it interesting that Marshall's mother was a pagan. She might be one to add to his list for circulating his secret chronicle.

The boys pulled out their smartphones, but, of course, got no signal here in this world. Probably weren't any Google Street-views either.

Next out of Andvari's satchel came a dark blue cloak, which the dwarf draped over his shoulders.

Then he disappeared.

The others followed, including Phose and Medusa.

"Phose?" Roland cried out.

The monsters hadn't even said good-bye. And now they were invisible. Or worse. Gone. Gone forever. Why had he let Phose go? Roland felt a sharp pain, an absence where he thought he had felt something else, a lightness, the beginnings of love. Happiness to just be near her. Andvari had said Phose *was* love. That she belonged to them all.

And now he'd lost her.

They stood there, letting the sun beat on them for a few more minutes, until it became unbearable.

Roland sighed and turned to go. At least he could report mission accomplished to Lady Perchta. And he'd have his memories. Jo and Marshall seemed equally unhappy to have lost their companions so soon. They continued to stare at the gate, expecting something to happen.

But the monsters had vanished.

Roland said, "Come on, *Jungs*. Time to leave. We still have the police to deal with when we're back. But then, hopefully, we can go home." He began shuffling back down the road, his feet leaden and sore, his ankles swollen from the heat. Medusa had said the exit from the closet would look like a patch of darkness from this side. Something that would be out of place in the bright glare of day.

But Marshall and Jo weren't following. He paused.

Jo was jumping up and down. "He's back!"

Grendel had reappeared, emerging from a hole underneath the gate. Next to him was a creature who had presumably dug the hole, a fox. It took one look at Jo and Marshall and ran headlong towards them, intent on running past. They didn't try and stop it. It bounded away from them down the path as if a whole horde of monsters was after it.

Grendel stood, blinking in the sunlight, and then he saw them. He raised a hand in greeting. His T-shirt turban was gone. He took slow steps towards them.

While they waited for him to reach them, Andvari popped up through the hole, no longer wearing his cloak. He ran a hand over his forehead and then grinned. He walked towards them, a spring in his step.

"Might as well wait for the others," Marshall said. "Can't be long now."

Sure enough, the giants—somehow—squeezed out from the hole and joined them.

They waited in silence. Sweat ran in a steady stream down Roland's neck.

But no Medusa.

Or Phose.

Marshall and Jo smeared on more sunscreen. They handed the tube to Roland. He shook his head, wanting to burn off the very skin on his body, erase the memory of his loss. It was ridiculous, and he would pay for it later when his red skin would ache. But it would distract him from a different, deeper kind of ache.

"Let's go," Andvari said. "They're not coming."

Hrungnir gestured, his palm out. "Should we go back? Don't want to leave them in there—"

"Nope. They're not coming."

And then a commotion near the hole. The shield was thrown out, followed by a disgruntled, grime-encrusted head spitting out dirt, her snakes all a-tither. A few seconds later, Phose pushed herself out the hole. She looked around and when she saw Roland, a huge smile broke out.

Metamorphose had come back, and she was looking at him. And smiling.

Roland started forward and lent her an arm. She brushed off her sundress, which was stained and smeared. And then she retrieved her companion, placing Medusa carefully on her shield throne, talking to her as if nothing exciting had happened, as if they were out on a Sunday stroll.

Somewhere, during their escape, Medusa had lost her sunglasses, and, for just a short moment, Roland glanced at those eyes.

He wished he hadn't, and quickly looked away. The ancient gorgon's eyes were brighter, redder, and even angrier than Grendel's eyes. Incandescent lava waiting to boil out. Phose looked around, bent over to retrieve the shades, and quickly snapped them on Medusa's head. Phose tucked the shield under one arm.

"Let's go home, darlings," Medusa said. "And take a nice long nap."

The Danish beer truck driver had been found wandering the ferry parking lot in Patras. He was shirtless and disoriented and had at first been mistaken for a homeless vagrant. The police suspected drug use. He raved about monsters attacking him on the ferry and stealing his clothes.

Roland was content to let everyone else load up the Transporter van with the essentials that Medusa and Phose thought they might need for a longish stay in the heart of west Germany. These "essentials" included large canisters of the local olive oil, scarves, headsets, Medusa's tablet (the snakes were very adept with the touchscreen), and some of Phose's things. Warmer clothing. They locked up the house and put the key in the mail to the caretaker Phose had arranged to look after things until they returned.

No one had wanted to share much about what they'd seen behind Alexander's Gate. But whatever it was, it was enough to put fear into the monsters he called friends. Grendel shook his head when Roland asked him about the adventure, but remained silent about the particulars. He did complain that they'd stolen his shirt, which may have been for Grendel, hater of Danes, the worst price to pay.

Andvari said he greatly looked forward to being back in his underground palace. Medusa planned to organize continued protests against the destruction of Elsbach Forest. Apparently, her global network was not something to be trifled with, and she employed a legion of lawyers besides.

And Phose. She said she looked forward to visiting Roland's home and helping him with his chronicles. While the others slept, he and Phose had sat on the terrace and talked and waited for sunrise to brighten the sky. He'd blurted out his idea about the monster chronicles to her after they returned. Then they'd held hands. And made silly smiles at each other. He didn't care if she was a poem personified. She was kind and beautiful and nice.

That happy memory distracted him. He hadn't noticed Grendel had taken the seat next to him. He held what looked like a cup of coffee in one hand. "Chicory," he said. "Helps my stealth magic."

Roland grunted. He no longer feared Grendel, at least quite so much. And was glad the monster was returning with them. "Are you sad to leave?" Roland asked.

"Leave here? No. In the forests and fens of Germany, there are still wild places."

"Ah."

Grendel put down his cup. "Medusa will meet the green-head. The clanky one."

"The Green Knight," Roland said. "I imagine she will."

Grendel nodded. "They will get along well."

"They might just. Well, I think it's time to hit the road."

They all piled into the Transporter. It was definitely more crowded than on the ride out, with the shield throne housing Medusa taking up a whole seat by itself. Jo and Marshall had decamped to jump seats in the back of the van, shoving the coffins aside to use as footrests. But everyone had just enough room for the homeward journey.

As they pulled out of the drive, Roland cast a longing glance toward the house. They would come back here someday, he was sure of it. It was a good place.

A party mood prevailed. The road trip had been only a partial success, but they had all learned something about home. New homes and old homes. New beginnings and keeping on.

Roland looked in the rearview mirror, and those glowing red eyes stared back at him.

"I have been meaning to ask you, Grendel," Roland said. "Just what kind of…monster are you?"

The ancient being sat back in his seat. "A black elf, a giant and a dragon go into a bar…" Grendel began.

Everyone else stopped talking.

"The bartender asks, 'What'll it be?' The black elf says, 'Something strong, but brewed from a magical herb.' 'Magical herb,' the bartender says and turns, staring at his shelf of liquors. 'What about tequila? Comes from blue agave. It might be magical. Shamans use it.' 'Let's have it,' the black elf says. The giant agrees. The dragon looks around and then says quietly, 'but don't forget the wyrm.'"

Total silence. And then they all broke out in a babble of laughter and chattering and even singing from Jo and Marshall in the back.

Roland smiled. He might just be able to chase back the shadows of the past without the help of that magical elixir called "gin." He had new friends to take to their new home.

And he couldn't wait to tell their story.

About the Author

Now a full-time writer living near Cologne, Sharon Kae Reamer's speculative fiction is inspired by her participation in various archeoseismology projects during her twenty-something years as a senior scientist at the University of Cologne. Locations that include the Praetorium and medieval Jewish settlement in Cologne, ancient Tiryns in Greece, and Greek ruins in Selinunte, Sicily, provide perfect backdrops for creating fantasy stories rich with history and mythology, such as her *Immortal Guardian* and *Schattenreich Mystery* novelette series and her five-book *Schattenreich* novel series.

Her love for mixing and mashing science fiction and fantasy continues unabated. *Night Shepherd*, in the *Schattenreich* universe is a spinoff (one of many) of her soon-to-be-published first novel in *The Sundered Veil* series, a further conception of science fantasy.

Sharon still pursues archeoseismology projects. She also cooks daily (German-English), gardens (chaotically, at best), knits (badly), does needlepoint (rather well) and reads (everything) all the damn time.

And, of course, she has cats.

Find out more about Sharon at:

sharonreamer.com

About Amazing Monster Tales

Monster Road Trip is the second issue in the Amazing Monster Tales anthology series. If you enjoyed this collection, check out Issue 1: *Dawn of the Monsters*! Follow us on Facebook, Twitter, Pinterest, and our website, AmazingMonsterTales.com, to be notified about new releases.

You can never have enough monsters…

About Borogrove Press

Borogrove Press is a partnership between editors DeAnna Knippling, of Wonderland Press, and Jamie Ferguson, of Blackbird Publishing.

Amazing Monster Tales is Borogrove Press's very first project.

Other Collections

Other speculative fiction collections are available through Borogrove Press' cousin, Blackbird Publishing.

As always, this story is dedicated to Lee and Ray,
without whose love none of this would be possible.
DeAnna Knippling

Thanks to Jo (aka Mom) for listening,
and to Jasper for keeping me company.
Jamie Ferguson